Quinn looked at the sprawling view of the ranch below.

"This is very beautiful," she whispered.

"Yes, beautiful," he echoed, and when she glanced at him, he was looking at her.

"I'm glad you brought me here," she murmured. It was a good memory she'd take with her.

She felt a tendril of hair that had come free of her ponytail brush against her cheek. Seth let go of her hand to gently push the hair back behind her ear. "I'm glad you came with me," he said.

As they walked back down the trail, Quinn stayed behind Seth. She'd never forget the wonderful moments on the ridge. She hadn't had too many of those in the past seventeen months, since Michael died. She took a deep breath, part of her wishing they could've stayed longer, then she thought about Seth holding her hand earlier. Maybe it was a good thing they were going back now.

Dear Reader,

When I first had the idea for the story of Seth Reagan, who'd failed at love, and Quinn Lake, who'd found love and tragically lost it, I remembered a quote I'd heard somewhere in the past. It suggested that the wonder of a young heart falling in love for the first time is equaled only by the joy of a broken heart coming to love again.

Her Wyoming Hero is about Seth and Quinn coming into each other's lives when they're both trying to make sense of those lives and give them purpose. Quinn arrives at the ranch in northern Wyoming, never expecting to find that Seth Reagan—a tech wizard who built his own business—is a kind man who just wants to do the right thing for those close to him. Seth finds himself drawn to Quinn but fights it, knowing she isn't over losing her husband. Gradually, unexpectedly, the two find a promise of a home and a love that neither one believed they could have.

I hope you enjoy the journey of Seth and Quinn, how love can bring the most wonderful joy into our lives and the deepest, truest connection with another person we'll ever have.

Mary Anne Wilson

HEARTWARMING

Her Wyoming Hero

—

Mary Anne Wilson

HARLEQUIN
HEARTWARMING

ISBN-13: 978-1-335-17981-4

Her Wyoming Hero

Copyright © 2021 by Mary Anne Wilson

Recycling programs
for this product may
not exist in your area.

This is a work of fiction. Names, characters, places and incidents are either the product of the author's imagination or are used fictitiously. Any resemblance to actual persons, living or dead, businesses, companies, events or locales is entirely coincidental.

This edition published by arrangement with Harlequin Books S.A.

For questions and comments about the quality of this book, please contact us at CustomerService@Harlequin.com.

Harlequin Enterprises ULC
22 Adelaide St. West, 40th Floor
Toronto, Ontario M5H 4E3, Canada
www.Harlequin.com

Printed in U.S.A.

Mary Anne Wilson is a Canadian transplanted to California, where her life changed dramatically. She found her happily-ever-after with her husband, Tom, and their three children. She always loved writing, reading and has a passion for anything Jane Austen. She's had around fifty novels published, been nominated for a RITA® Award, won Reviewers' Choice Awards and received RWA's Career Achievement Award in Romantic Suspense.

Books by Mary Anne Wilson

Harlequin Heartwarming

Eclipse Ridge Ranch

Under a Christmas Moon

The Carsons of Wolf Lake

A Question of Honor
Flying Home
A Father's Stake

Visit the Author Profile page
at Harlequin.com for more titles.

For:
Julie Geisler, Emily Geisler
Amy Levin, Taylor Levin
Kate Wilson and Jodie Gerringer/Wilson

The strong and loving women and girls in my life who have been there when I needed them.

Love you all more than you could ever say you love me!

PROLOGUE

"I SHOULD HAVE called this in," Seth Reagan muttered. Alone in his two-room private living quarters in the S.R. SoffTec corporate tower, he paced back and forth. Seth hated waiting for others to decide what he'd do for the next three or four months. He stopped by the floor-to-ceiling windows and looked down twenty-one stories at rain-drenched Seattle. The storm had passed, but the choppy waters of Puget Sound were almost black.

Seth exhaled and turned away from the gloomy day to glance at his surroundings— the place he'd lived for the past seven years. It was functional, with all-white walls, an exercise room through a door to the left by the sauna and a bathroom. The main space had a long computer center and a large platform bed that faced the views. Only one decoration hung over the bed. It was a framed picture of three teenaged boys with a large rugged-looking man, all four of them grinning into the camera near a horse corral. It had been taken during Seth's last year at the group foster home on a ranch north of Eclipse, Wyoming.

He remembered the day clearly, that moment when James "Sarge" Caine had rounded up Jake Bishop, Ben Arias and Seth by the stables. The man declared that his wife, Maggie, wanted a picture of him and his boys. The boys had been fifteen-year-old strangers when they'd arrived at the ranch, but they were family when they'd each left at eighteen. His family. Seth quickly crossed to the photo and took it off the wall. After he put it in his suitcase, he zipped up the bag, anxious to leave.

When the connecting door to his executive offices opened, Owen Karr, his executive vice president, finally showed up. Seth greeted him with a blunt, "It's about time."

The slender man was forty, seven years older than Seth, and looked more like a CEO than Seth ever had or would. In a gray pin-striped suit and polished oxfords, with his red hair newly styled, Owen was corporate all the way. Seth, on the other hand—wearing jeans, a gray thermal shirt and scuffed leather boots, along with the shadow of a beard—probably looked like he belonged in maintenance.

"I'm here now," Owen said as he motioned Seth to one of two leather chairs by the windows. "Sit and I'll make this quick."

Seth dropped into the chair closest to him and raked his fingers carelessly through his hair, which was in desperate need of a trim. "Okay, what did the board say?"

Owen swiveled his chair to face Seth. "They agreed to your sabbatical with a return set at three months. They also agreed to your request for me to be acting CEO while you're gone."

"Great," Seth said. The priorities that had driven Seth's life as an adult had all been about his company and about protecting anything to do with it. But that had shifted drastically when he'd received a phone call just after Thanksgiving last November. Sarge had taken a fall on the ranch. He hadn't been found until hours later by the only ranch hand who still worked there.

From that moment on, Seth's life had changed. Work had ceased to control his every waking hour. The company he'd founded and grown was strong and could survive without him for as long as Sarge needed him. "Now I'm going home."

Owen nodded. "Got it."

Seth glanced at his wristwatch. Just over an hour before he could make a break for it. "Conrad, my pilot, called ten minutes ago. The storm's over and it's clearing up to the east. So, I'll need the town car in the lower parking garage at one o'clock to get to the airport."

"Got it. There's just one more thing," Owen said, and Seth almost groaned out loud. *Just one more thing* was the magic phrase that usually preceded bad news. Seth braced himself, the way he had years ago when a caseworker came to tell him he was being relocated to another foster facility. Even at five years old, he'd learned quickly to listen, accept it and not fight it. "What?"

"There's a guy waiting in lower-level reception who wants to talk to you about some revolutionary cybersecurity program. The claim is—"

"You do what you want with him," Seth said. "You're the boss."

Owen nodded. "Okay. I will. How's Sarge?"

"When he broke his leg, they said he might have problems walking again, but he's gone from a walker to a cane and gets around pretty well. It's been hard, but he's tough."

"He's a remarkable man," Owen said.

That was an understatement. "When I first came face-to-face with him at the ranch, he was this hard ex-marine, six foot four with big muscles." Seth chuckled softly, remembering that moment. "He stopped me in my tracks and gave me a needed attitude adjustment."

"I can imagine," Owen said.

If Sarge hadn't broken his leg, Seth wondered how long it would've taken for anyone to know he'd been diagnosed with Alzheimer's. He sure hadn't shared that fact. For the past year, Seth had been working on a project to convert the ranch into a summer camp for foster kids. "I want the camp functioning while Sarge is still aware and can understand what we're doing for him and Maggie. Most importantly, I want him to participate in the camp for as long as possible."

Maggie had passed over five years ago, but the camp had been their dream for when they retired from group foster care. Sarge had let everything go when his wife died. But Seth knew he'd still love to see their dream become real. He owed Sarge so much, and establishing the summer camp on the land the man loved was barely a down payment on that debt.

Owen stood. "Okay, you get back there. Do you need me to do anything else before you leave?"

"No, thanks, just go and deal with the guy downstairs who wants to revolutionize our business."

As Seth stood, Owen looked a bit wistful, an expression that was not common with the man. "That ranch sounds like a whole different world."

It had seemed exactly like that to a teenager whom the system had written off. Seth had been beyond lucky that Sarge and Maggie took him in, along with other boys who'd been tagged as irredeemable. "It is a special place, and it's my time to be there. Between Ben, Jake and his wife, Libby, Sarge will have one of us with him all the time to help him remember for as long as possible."

Owen nodded to Seth. "Good luck, and don't worry about anything here."

When Owen was gone, Seth called Julia, Sarge's nurse and caregiver at the ranch.

She answered right away. "Hey, Seth."

"Just letting you know the skies have cleared and I'm going to take off at two o'clock our time. I left the truck at Downer's Landing, so I'll drive myself back."

"Good. Sarge misses you a lot."

He glanced around his living quarters, and all he wanted was to be on the sprawling ranch in Wyoming. "Tell him I miss him, and I'm coming home."

AFTER MORE THAN an hour's wait in the reception area of S.R. SoffTec's corporate headquarters, Quinn Lake had finally been shown up to the twentieth-floor offices of the executive VP, Owen Karr. Since then, she'd been waiting in a conference room, staring at a huge framed poster on the wall. It had white script slashed across a solid black background. *I Turn Coffee into Code.*

One of three doors to the room finally opened at 12:40 p.m. Quinn stood as a red-haired man in a gray suit strode in. He held out his hand to her. "Sorry for the wait. I'm

Owen Karr, and you're Quintin Lake?" His grip was firm.

"Yes, I am," she said, and he motioned her to sit down while he took a chair opposite her at the table.

"First, honestly, I was expecting Quintin to be a man. Sorry for the sexism."

Quinn managed a semblance of a polite smile for him, but she didn't apologize for being a woman determined to impress him with her presentation. "Call me Quinn," she said, ready to give her pitch for Michael's Shield.

Owen cut in immediately. "Ms. Lake, I'm really busy today, so I'll get right to the point." His smile was placating. "We aren't looking to buy, or buy into, any part of work from outside sources. However, if you leave your contact information and the summary of your idea, I'll go over it when I have time. But I can't promise you anything."

She knew it didn't matter if she were a man or woman—he'd come to get rid of her. But she couldn't just walk out without at least trying to change his mind. "Mr. Karr, Michael's Shield is a revolutionary take on corporate cybersecurity. It's the next step toward an almost perfect shutdown of attacks. If you could just see the data, I'm sure you'd be interested in participating when you see how viable it is." Michael had coached her about what to say for the presentation, if she ever got to give one. Beyond that, she didn't understand a whole lot about what her late husband had developed. She wished she did.

"I'm sorry. I told you I might get time later on." He stood, ready to end their meeting. "Best of luck with finding someone who can help you," he said.

She nodded, not even trying to find a smile as she gave him her card and the small packet with the overview of Michael's Shield, then left. If she heard from Owen Karr again, it would be a miracle. Quinn didn't believe in miracles much anymore.

When she stepped into the elevator to head down to the parking garage, she was thankful that the car was already occupied by two women. She wouldn't cry from frustration and disappointment in front of strangers. Instead, she pushed those emotions away as she reached to press the button for the lower-level parking garage. She faced the stainless steel doors as they closed and kept her eyes on

her slightly distorted reflection in the polished metal.

Wearing black pants, a white tailored shirt
and gray blazer, with her blond hair pulled
back in a twist, she looked serious. She was
serious.

Since Michael had died, she'd seriously
been trying to keep a promise she'd made
to him; she would do whatever it took to get
his work in corporate cybersecurity recognized. She wouldn't let Michael's Shield go
away just because Michael had. S.R. Soff-
Tec was her ninth on a list of ten companies
she'd thought might be interested in his work.
It was also her ninth failure.

When one of the two women behind
her spoke with a Southern drawl, it caught
Quinn's attention. "I thought the boss was
back for good, but now he's taken off again."
The boss? Quinn looked beyond her own reflection in the polished door and saw the
lady who was speaking. She was petite, in
jeans and a plain white shirt, with a streak
of bright green in her short brown hair. "I
wish I'd known that before I went up to the
twenty-first floor. I could've had sushi for

lunch. Now it looks like a sandwich out of the machines."

The second woman was tall and thin, all in black from jeans to a turtleneck sweater, with curly gray hair around her pale face. She spoke in a slightly nasal tone. "You'd think someone on his staff would have sent a memo that he's gone."

"Preston, in HR, said he's heading to Wyoming until after the New Year. Owen Karr's stepping in to take over."

A soft chime announced the tenth floor as the elevator came to a smooth stop and the doors slid open. The tall lady slipped past Quinn, and as she stepped into the corridor, she called back over her shoulder, "See you at the meeting," before the doors shut.

As the car continued down, Quinn moved to her right and took a full step back. That brought her almost even with the other woman. The instant she made eye contact, the woman smiled ruefully and drawled, "So, you were meeting with the VP?"

"Excuse me?"

"The twentieth floor is Owen Karr's territory."

"Yes, I met with him, but it turned out to be a waste of time."

"At least you talked to him," the lady drawled. "All we got for our trouble on the twenty-first was a locked office." The woman then answered a question that Quinn didn't get a chance to ask. "Seems the boss has gone off to Wyoming for months, staying on some ranch up there."

Quinn didn't hesitate to pin down who *the boss* the woman had referred to was. "Figures. Owning the company and all, he's loaded, so he's probably heading to Jackson Hole."

The chime sounded for the first floor. "Being a billionaire has its perks," the lady said on a slight chuckle. "But I heard he's going to some small town farther east of there, closer to Cody."

The elevator stopped and the woman stepped toward the opening doors. Quinn was betting on her being enough of a gossip that she wouldn't ignore a direct question if asked. "What town would Mr. Reagan be going to?"

The lady paused, held the door open with her hand and looked back at Quinn. "Eclipse. I guess he lived there as a kid."

Bingo! "Well, I hope you get a decent lunch."

"So do I," the woman said with feeling as she let go of the door and walked away.

By the time the elevator arrived at the parking garage, Quinn had revised her plan of going from Seattle down to Denver where the last company on her list had its headquarters. Now that she knew where Seth Reagan was staying, she couldn't walk away, not before she tried to find him and meet him face-to-face. As she headed over to her old gray VW Beetle, she took out her phone and did a search for Seth Reagan and Eclipse, Wyoming.

It came up with an article from six years ago, and the only pictures attached to it were of the Seattle corporate headquarters called "The Tower." The text chronicled his rags-to-riches story in the powerful tech world. It was about him being orphaned early in life but ending up a wealthy tech giant who dominated the world of cybersecurity development.

Once in her car, she reread one paragraph. *As a fifteen-year-old youth-at-risk, Reagan was assigned to the Eclipse Ridge Ranch, a group foster care facility north of the town of Eclipse, Wyoming. An appropriate starting point for his life at a place known for being one of the best spots to watch both lunar and solar eclipses.* The tie-up line at the bottom of the article read, *He certainly has "eclipsed" other great companies to become a brilliant star in his own right.*

As she started the car, Quinn smiled at the picture of Michael and herself that she kept clipped to the sun visor. They'd been at the beach in Southern California, near the historic Santa Monica Pier. They stood beside their Beetle with the vast Pacific behind them. Tall and tanned with his blond hair windblown, Michael had been grinning into the camera as he held her to his side. They both looked as if they owned the world.

"I'm not giving up," she whispered to the photo, then put Eclipse, Wyoming, into her phone's GPS. The screen flashed and showed her the next stop in her journey was eight hundred and eighty miles to the east. She could be there in two and a half days. She felt better and more focused as she drove up the exit ramp behind a sleek black town car with heavily tinted windows. She followed it out onto the rain-slick Seattle streets.

CHAPTER ONE

IT WAS MIDAFTERNOON on Seth's third day back at the ranch. He was alone in the old red pickup truck that hadn't been new when he'd first arrived at the ranch eighteen years ago. But it was still going, and it had a heater that worked. He was thankful for that as he drove down the county road toward the state highway.

Since his return, every time he'd stepped outside, he'd been reminded how cold it could get in northern Wyoming in October. A fierce wind came and drove frigid air down from the foothills and across the lower valley. That wind was strong right then. He felt it hit the truck suddenly and literally push the vehicle sideways as he reached a blind curve half a mile from the highway entrance. Seth tried to get control but couldn't before another gust hit the truck so hard he lost his hold on the steering wheel for a second and was pushed into the lane for oncoming traffic.

"Stupid!" he yelled at himself, getting a hard grip on the wheel and putting all his strength behind an attempt to move over. He had known the blind curve was there, and he sure knew how much stronger the wind could get. The truck responded for a moment and he started drifting back into his lane. But his heart clenched when an old VW Beetle came out of nowhere heading right toward him. He leaned on the wheel hard, and then the small car was only a gray blur as it passed by him without making contact. His truck hit the gravel and dirt shoulder hard and came to a shuddering stop in a cloud of dust, dried pine needles and dead leaves.

Seth sat back, releasing a harsh breath, his heart hammering. The truck could've flattened the VW if he'd been a moment later going to the right. Relieved, he twisted to look back over his shoulder and knew he might have stopped a head-on impact, but it wasn't over. The pasture fencing was torn and broken on the other side of the pavement. Beyond the damage, a cloud of dirt and churned earth billowed into the wind, swirling crazily upward. He could barely make out the VW bouncing across the rough ground through the haze and it didn't seem to be slowing down at all.

He jumped out and sprinted, leaping to clear the torn fence. He ran after the car as it headed directly toward a stand of old pines. "Stop! Stop!" he screamed as loudly as he could. The car kept going, plowing full speed into the massive trunk of the first tree in its path.

When Seth reached the VW, he was coughing from the dust and exhaust in the turbulent air. The car's front hood was torn and compressed, the engine still running, and he heard a gasping voice coming from inside. "No, no, no, no, no."

Quickly, he bent down to look through the shattered driver's-side window. The only occupant was a woman pressing her forehead to her hands that clutched the top of the steering wheel. Tangled golden blond hair hid her face, and he could barely make out her words. But she was alive and strong enough to keep talking in that unsteady voice. "This can't be happening. It can't." Her shoulders under a gray hoodie trembled. "Not now. Please not now. Please. Please."

Relieved she was conscious, Seth said, "Ma'am?"

There was sudden silence, then the woman slowly sat back to look over at him through the empty window frame. That's when he saw the blood, running down from a ragged gash at her hairline above her left eye. Her face was unnaturally pale, making the bright crimson all the more horrifying.

That was all Seth had to see. Quickly, he pulled his cell out of the pocket of his leather jacket, then punched in 911. "Don't move, please." There was blood everywhere. "I'm calling for help," he said.

She started blinking rapidly, then pressed an unsteady hand over her left eye. When the 911 dispatcher came on the line, Seth quickly gave the details and their location. Their ETA was twelve minutes. He put his phone away, thankful the wind was dying down and the dust was settling. He crouched by the shattered window to get a better look in at the woman.

He thought she'd stopped crying, but he

couldn't be sure. Her whole body seemed to be trembling.

"Help's coming," he said, worried she could go into shock. Thankfully, he'd taken an emergency first-aid course when he'd known he could be alone with Sarge at the ranch and would need to know what to do in a crisis situation. Pressure to stop the blood or at least lessen its flow was the first important step. "We need to get something on that wound."

"Yes, please, yes," she whispered as she swiped at her chin with her free hand. The action only smeared more blood on her face.

He straightened up, grabbed the door handle and pulled. It didn't give at first, then it opened with a screech of metal on metal. Her car was still running, and he knew he needed to keep the heater going for her. With the engine in the back, he didn't think that would be dangerous. He needed a thick pad to put on the wound, but he didn't even have a single bandage in the truck. He had to improvise, and he could only think of one thing that he could repurpose to use on the wound.

"Hold on," he said as he straightened up and quickly took off his leather jacket to toss it onto the roof of the VW. He followed that with his navy thermal. Once he was down to his white T-shirt, he had that off in a second, but realized if he folded it in layers it would be far too big and thick.

He quickly found the side seams and tore up each one, then ripped the neckband off. He tossed everything except the front section of the shirt up by his jacket, then folded and refolded the cotton into a reasonable facsimile of a medical pad. He crouched down to show it to the woman. "We need to get this on your wound. Close your eyes tightly, then try to push your hair out of the way for me."

She scrunched her eyes shut as she fumbled to get her hair back. When it was clear, Seth carefully eased the makeshift pad onto the nasty-looking gash. "You need to hold and apply the pressure yourself so you can gauge how much pain you can tolerate."

She shifted her left hand away from her hair and onto the folded shirt. As she held it in place, he saw a gold band on her ring finger that had been almost hidden by the blood on her hand. She winced, then looked out at him as he slowly stood. He noticed her blue eyes were clear when she looked up at him.

"You…you're going to…to freeze like that," she said in a shaky voice.

He hadn't been aware of the cold until she pointed it out. "Yes, right," he said and quickly reached for his thermal and jacket to put them back on. Then he crouched by her again. "How are you doing?"

"Okay," she said weakly, and he wasn't certain if she was going to cry again or not. He'd never been good at handling a crying woman, especially if he was the reason for her tears. "I just never…you know, I didn't expect this."

"That makes two of us," he said. He'd been afraid with the blow to her head that she might be a bit out of it, but she seemed responsive and aware of what was going on. "Just relax. Help is on its way."

Unexpectedly, she shifted and reached out to him. Her hand was unsteady and blood-stained, but he took it without hesitating. "Help me get out," she said in a faintly breathless voice.

"You're safe in the car, and you need to stay warm." The last thing Seth wanted was for her to stand and pass out or go into shock. "Help will be here soon."

She was holding on to his hand tightly and still shaking. "I need to see my car."

Her vehicle was pretty much totaled, and she didn't need to see that, not yet. "First, we take care of you, then the car."

She pulled on his hand, leveraging herself to turn toward him, slipped her feet out and pressed worn suede boots to the rough ground. "Please, I need to see it."

Before he could argue with her, she was tugging on his hand again, and he finally stood to help ease her to her feet. She was slender, maybe five foot six. Nothing she had on, not even her boots, had avoided being stained by the blood. She slowly glanced to her right, and her hold on him tightened even more. He braced to have her fall into his chest. But with a shuddering sigh, she slowly sank back down onto the car seat and let go of him.

"Just stay put, please," Seth insisted, very uneasy about her paleness and the continued trembling.

Her blue eyes turned up to him, overly bright with the threat of more tears. "Sorry," she whispered, and the tears showed up.

His cell vibrated in his jacket pocket, and he answered it quickly. "Yes?"

"Seth, it's Charlie Hague. We received the dispatch for your accident, and I need to know details."

Seth filled the EMT in on everything as he watched the woman trying to adjust the pad on her wound. Seth answered Charlie's questions as clearly as he could while the woman swiped with the sleeve of her hoodie at the tears on her chin. "Anything else, Charlie?" he asked.

"Is she coherent, her pupils normal?"

He'd noticed her blue eyes first thing. "Yes and yes."

"Okay. We're a unit short, and there's been a major accident near Wolf Bridge. We've been redirected to it. Someone will be sent to you as soon as a unit's freed up. So, just keep her comfortable and make sure pressure stays on the wound. Keep that heater going."

Seth heard someone speaking to Charlie but couldn't understand the conversation. Then Charlie was back on the line. "Got an option for you. Since your truck is operable, how about you drive her to Boone's clinic? I don't see any reason to worry about moving her, and it's a better option than waiting for transport."

He was relieved there was a reasonable alternative to just standing here while the lady bled and cried. "Okay, I can get her to the clinic, but you'll have to contact Boone to fill him in. Also, get Max to send Henry out to pick up her car."

QUINN HEARD THE plans the man was making with someone on his phone—plans for her. Even with blood staining her clothes and the car broken, she wasn't about to drive off with just anyone. She sniffed back tears and opened her eyes. She tried to breathe more easily, to try and forget that horror when the car had been out of her control and headed for the trees. Then the crash. She swallowed hard and tried to not start crying again.

She looked up at the man who must be about six feet tall. Wearing washed jeans, a well-worn leather jacket and Western boots that were definitely not new, he looked like a ranch hand. Unruly dark brown hair framed a strong face shadowed by a couple days of stubble. His hazel eyes never looked away from her.

She knew she was in a horrible spot, but it scared her to think of just going off with a stranger. Maybe just waiting right there was the best idea. "I can wait for them to get here." She wished her voice sounded stronger.

"I understand," he said. "You don't know me, but the guy on the phone is Charlie Hague, an EMT. He's known me since high school. He'll vouch for me."

He took the phone away from his ear and put it on Speaker. "Charlie, you're on Speaker and the lady wants to talk to you to make sure she's not heading off with a serial killer."

"Okay," a male voice said from the phone.

She frowned at the sound of sirens in the background of the call. "No offense, but how do I know who you are?" she asked the man on the other end of the call.

"Ma'am, we can hang up, and you can call 911 and ask to be connected to Unit 15. Would that work for you?"

"I guess, but who is he?"

"He's a good guy, and he'll take you to the clinic in Eclipse. The bonus for you is he's certified in CPR and critical first aid. Now, who are you?"

His description of the ranch hand seemed too good to be true. "I'm Quinn Lake."

"Okay, Quinn, go and let Dr. Boone Williams at the clinic in town take care of you. Right now, Seth can get you there quicker than we can get you back to the ER in Cody."

"Seth?"

"Yes, Seth Reagan—he's perfectly safe."

Quinn stared at the man the EMT had just told her was Seth Reagan. The shock of her car being damaged and the blow to her head had to have done more than make her bleed everywhere. The man right there with her didn't look like a billionaire tech genius and the man she'd come to find. Then he flashed her a crooked smile. "I promise I'm not a serial killer."

She stared at him, trying to reconcile the few pictures she'd found of him online with this reality less than two feet away from her. The photos had shown a man with short hair, a clean-shaven jaw and wearing casual pants and sports shirts. In every photo, he'd been looking away from the camera or down.

She could feel the cold air around her, the throbbing in her head increasing, and her left arm was aching from holding the pad in place. No, this was all real, and apparently Seth Reagan was right there and very real, too.

"So, will you come with me?" he asked, startling her out of her thoughts.

"Oh, yes." Her voice sounded as weak as she felt right then.

Charlie spoke quickly. "Call Boone if you need any help on the way."

"Thanks, Charlie," Seth said, then he spoke to Quinn as he ended the call. "I'll bring my truck over. Don't move."

"Okay," she said, and he took off jogging back toward the road.

When Quinn had arrived in Eclipse in the early afternoon, she'd set out to get information about the Eclipse Ridge Ranch. Luckily, the first person she asked was a man in the general store who was dressed in a garish Western outfit with fringes everywhere. He'd been a talker and glad to tell her how to get out to the ranch, even describing the entrance for her.

She'd planned to come and find it, get the lay of the land, then go back to town, find a room and work out the part of the plan where she'd manage to actually meet Seth Reagan.

It turned out she hadn't needed a plan at all. A bad move on the road in that horrible wind had brought her face-to-face with the man.

The sound of the truck getting closer drew her attention. She saw it coming, dust billowing behind it, then it pulled up alongside her car to stop a few feet from her.

Seth was out quickly, hurrying around to open the truck's passenger door before he came over to her. "We'll take this easy." He held out his hand. "Just lean on me when you get up," he said.

She was thankful for his support as she slowly stood, and she was thankful he eased his arm around her shoulders. That was the only thing that made it possible for her to get across the narrow strip of dirt to the truck. But when she tried to climb up into the cab, her legs felt like jelly.

"I'm sorry, I... I can't," she whispered.

Seth shifted and turned to her, spanned her waist with his hands and lifted her up onto the hard bench seat with surprising ease. The whole situation was oddly surreal. Now she was sitting in an old truck while Seth Reagan reached around her to do up her seat belt. She felt his heat against her right side and inhaled the scent of leather and freshness before he moved back. He'd said something she hadn't caught. "I'm… I'm sorry. What?"

"I have to turn off your car. What do you need out of it?"

She swallowed to try to ease the tightness in her throat. "My backpack and leather purse and the picture on the sun visor."

"Got it," he said and closed her door. Moments later, he was getting in behind the wheel. After he put her bags on the seat between them, he held out her photo. "Here you go."

She stared at it and couldn't bear to touch it with her bloodstained hands. "The small side pocket in my backpack. Could you put it in there?"

He reached for the backpack and slipped the picture safely into the pocket where she kept Michael's small leather box, which she carried with her everywhere. "Thank you," she whispered when he zipped it shut.

He helped her get positioned so her elbow rested on her backpack while her left hand held the bandage in place. "Does that feel okay?" he asked.

The tension in her neck and shoulders

eased right away. "Yes." She looked down at the mess on her clothes. Then she made the mistake of looking over at her car again and immediately wished she hadn't. She was crying before she knew it. The pain of what she'd done to the car that she and Michael had shared their whole marriage was so intense it was unreal, and she could barely catch her breath. "Oh, gosh," she gasped on a sob. "This is horrible."

"It's going to be okay," Seth said in a soothing tone. "I just wish I had some wipes for you." He turned and quickly got out of the truck, and she watched him heading toward her car again. He grabbed something white off the roof of the VW and came back inside.

He handed her the material, and it took her a moment to realize it was what was left of his T-shirt. "Use this to wipe you face or whatever," he said.

She swiped at her face. "I'm sorry, I really am," she whispered unsteadily as she lowered her hand and stared at the rag, now splattered with red. "How can I be bleeding so much?"

"Head wounds are the worst bleeders, and usually not as bad as they look. As for your car, I've always heard that Beetles are fixable as long as there are other Beetles to use for replacement parts. But even if your car's totaled, I'll make sure you get another one. He put the truck in gear, made a wide turn and headed back to the road. He drove slowly over the uneven ground.

"I can't get another car," Quinn said, trying not to cry.

"Don't worry. I'll pay for it. I knew about the blind curve and the wind, and I was on the wrong side of the road. My fault completely."

She didn't remember a blind curve, just the old truck coming at her. She couldn't think straight. "I was... I was driving, and this truck was there." It was like a nightmare she'd had, but it was real. "I think I was driving the wrong way or something." She tried to focus, to remember, but she couldn't.

"No, you weren't, but let's talk about this after we get you to the clinic."

Quinn knew she should just keep quiet until she understood everything and could think straight, but she had to ask something. "That man, Henry, he's not going to forget about my car, will he?"

Seth eased the truck over the shoulder and onto the pavement. "No, he won't forget, but for now we'll focus on making sure you're okay."

She closed her eyes and rubbed the rag over her chin again. All she'd wanted was to find Seth and talk to him. Worse even than the accident was the obvious fact that she had no control over anything that was happening right now. After she was cleaned up and the wound was fixed, maybe she could think straight and figure out what to do next.

Seth startled her when he spoke after a few miles of silence. "I know you're upset. But, believe me, you're going to be okay."

All she really knew about herself right then was she didn't want any more loss in her life, not even the loss of the car. She opened her eyes just as Seth glanced at her before he quickly looked back to the road ahead. She knew she had to look awful, but she realized she hadn't even thought of him being injured. "Did you get hurt?"

"No, I didn't."

"Oh, thank goodness," she said on a sigh of real relief. "I'm sorry I never even asked."

A horn sounded and a large white pickup truck, with a green sheriff logo on its door and a light bar on the roof, drove up beside them. A uniformed man behind the wheel pointed ahead, then he proceeded to speed up and cut in front of them. "The sheriff sent an escort," Seth said.

If it had been possible for Quinn to laugh at that moment, she might have. A police escort. As far as she could see, the road ahead was totally empty of other cars.

As Seth sped up to keep pace with the large truck, he asked, "Mind if I ask you a few questions?"

"No," she said.

"First, how can your family be contacted. They need to know about the accident."

As he spoke, the air in the cab became thinner, and Quinn shivered as the tears threatened to come back. She hated having no control, not even over crying. "Is it cold in here?" she asked, partly to deflect his question and partly because she felt a deep chill all of a sudden.

He reached to turn the heater up a notch. "Is that better?"

"Yes," she said and closed her eyes. If Michael were still alive, she would've called him before she'd even gotten out of the car. But she couldn't do that, and she didn't want her parents or sisters to know because they'd only worry. She was on her own, the way she'd been for the past seventeen months. She couldn't think about Michael, not now, not after everything that had happened. It just hurt too much.

But Seth wasn't sidetracked. "An emergency number would be a good idea."

"I'll give one to the doctor," she said.

He let that go and asked a second question. "Why didn't you stop or steer away before you hit the tree?"

Did he seriously think she'd crashed on purpose? "I tried to stop, but the brakes didn't work and the steering wheel froze. I couldn't move it."

"There's probably damage underneath your car from the fencing you ran through or the rocks you went over."

"I guess," she said. "I was going to downshift, but the transmission's touchy…" Then she'd hit the tree and downshifting hadn't been her worry.

Another horn blared as a black-and-white tow truck zoomed past them, going in the opposite direction. "That's Henry Lodge, the best car doctor in the state," Seth said.

"Is he really expensive?" She had to ask, because her available money was skimpy, and her insurance was even skimpier.

"Whatever it takes, repairs or another car, I'll cover it."

She wouldn't argue about him paying since he seemed to feel he was responsible, but she had to make one thing clear. "I don't want another car. I just want her back." It annoyed her that her voice broke as she added, "She's special."

"You're sure it's a she?" Seth asked with a touch of skepticism in his tone.

Quinn spoke without thinking, "Yes, she is. We actually considered painting her pink for one hot second." She exhaled, wishing she hadn't said that and given him any further reason to think she'd been knocked senseless. "I know how bad she looks, but I don't want some stranger totaling her."

He spoke slowly, obviously trying to make sure she stayed calm. "Henry won't do a thing until he talks to you, and he's never met a car he couldn't do something with."

She knew that was as much as she could ask for right then. "Okay, I just want her back like she was before." She added the only explanation that he might understand. "She's a 1962 VW Beetle with custom factory extras and…other…other special things." She didn't include the top reason she was special—Michael had been driving her when they first met, and she'd been theirs until seventeen months ago. Even now, when she was at home and missed Michael, she'd go driving just to be in that car. It was her comfort.

"If that's the case, I'll have it restored for you."

She figured, with money being no obstacle for him, he would have it gold-plated if she agreed to it and stayed calm. But she didn't want some strangely new/old car. "Thank you, but no." She was relieved her voice was stronger now. "I just want the brakes and steering working, and her looking like she did."

Quinn didn't miss his sigh of relief to finally get a direct response from her. "If that's what you want, working okay is fine by me, along with whatever else it takes to get it to look like it did."

"Thank you," she said. "She was good the way she was. I just wish I hadn't hit that fence."

"I told you, it's all my fault." She heard him take a breath. "Things do happen."

They certainly did. She'd found Seth Reagan and her car had crashed. A blessing and a curse. Maybe the price she'd have to pay for meeting this man would be losing the car she'd had with Michael… She couldn't think about that now. No matter what, she wouldn't have a car for days, if not a week or two.

She was stranded in a strange town with no car and little money. She couldn't think straight enough to tell Seth why she'd been on that road, let alone convince him to take Michael's work and get it out on the market. She didn't want to even think about trying and having him reject it out of hand. If that happened right now, she'd have no hope at all.

CHAPTER TWO

SETH TRIED TO concentrate on his driving, still not totally convinced that Quinn Lake wasn't going to slip into shock. Maybe that was why she was so sure her car was a female. He'd almost laughed at her anthropomorphizing of the old VW. But he could tell she was serious, so he'd take it seriously for now. He'd make sure she got her car fixed to look old but running well. He owed her a lot more than that for forcing her off the road, but he'd settle for making sure she got the best medical attention available and her car back the way she wanted it to be.

He glanced over at her before turning back to the road ahead of them. His stomach clenched at the blood starting to seep through the white of the bandage. Her hand holding the rag was shaking, and he felt uneasy. "Do you know where you are?" Seth asked.

He could sense her looking at him. "In an old Ford F-150 pickup truck."

He was impressed she knew that. "Right, but where are we going?"

"Oh, I get it. You were taught in that course you took to make sure someone with a head injury isn't losing it, then I told you about my car. Okay, I'll play along. I'm somewhere outside of Eclipse, Wyoming, going to see a doctor named Boone with a man who claims he's not a serial killer." He heard her take a breath. "I should also explain I was attacked by an alien that looked like a towering pine tree, and my car is hopefully safe with a man named Henry."

Just like that, things shifted to where he felt a smile twitch at the corners of his mouth. "Devious people, those aliens," he murmured.

"They are. I know who I am, too. Quintin Lake. I was named after my mother's great-great-grandfather, Josiah Quintin Hanover. My family has a tradition of naming their kids after long gone relatives. I'm the second of three daughters and received Quintin, not Josiah or Hanover. I consider myself lucky."

"I don't know. Hanover could be changed to Hannah, and Josiah could be Josie."

"My sisters answer to Hannah and Josie, and I answer to Quinn spelled with two *n*'s. Sometimes Quinny, but I hate that. I'm twenty-seven years old, and I live in Pasadena, California. Is that enough for you to not worry about my head?"

Quinn seemed to be totally in control of her faculties, despite the female car and the alien trees. He also thought it was a pretty good sign that she'd retained a sense of humor. "Yes, that's enough."

Right then the deputy ahead of them put on his siren. Quinn gasped, "Why did he do that?

"He's clearing the traffic."

"This town must be really small if one car is considered traffic."

That single vehicle pulled over to let them pass, and Seth couldn't stop a chuckle. "Valid point," he said as they finally made the transition onto Clayton Drive, the main street in Eclipse. As if reason had finally taken hold of the deputy, the siren cut off abruptly.

Seth drove south through the old town that had certainly changed since he'd left fifteen years ago for college. Parts of it were still there but shared equal space with the newer establishments dedicated to eclipse watching and anything and everything needed for the dude ranch experience, both popular activities in the area. Raised wooden walkways fronted the businesses, a holdover from the past to avoid snakes and mud.

Another holdover was a huge barnlike building coming into view on the left. Garret's General Store looked just about like it had the first time Sarge had taken Seth there to buy him a lined denim jacket.

The deputy kept going south on Clayton Drive, but Seth turned left on Wiley Way just before the general store. They passed a couple of small businesses before he turned into a paved parking lot in front of a sprawling wood-shingled house. A sign above the entrance announced Eclipse Medical Clinic: 24/7 Urgent Care. A car and a couple of trucks were already parked there.

Seth came to a stop in a space designated for emergency parking only. "Hold on. I'll be right there," he said and hurried out and around to open the door for Quinn.

"I have her ride," someone called from the porch.

He turned and saw Millie Greenway,

Boone's nurse and receptionist, pushing a wheelchair down the access ramp in front. The middle-aged woman was wearing green scrubs, and she quickly aligned the wheelchair with the open passenger door of the truck. "Oh, honey," Millie said as she looked in at Quinn. "Let's get you inside."

Quinn seemed to hesitate, then grimaced as she tried to turn toward Millie and still keep the pad on her wound. The nurse moved in front of Seth and eased Quinn around on the seat to face her. She reached in her pocket and took out latex gloves, snapped them on, then said, "Here, let me get that." Seth watched her carefully peel the now blood-soaked cloth away from Quinn's forehead.

He looked away when the gash was exposed, then Millie was speaking to him. "Seth, you're going to have to lift her out of there. I don't want her trying to stand just yet."

He turned back to the two women, and thankfully it looked as if the gash was barely bleeding now. But Quinn's face was smeared with dark streaks and a lock of hair was stuck to her temple. When he said, "I'll get her," Millie moved back to reposition the chair.

Seth put one arm under Quinn's knees and the other behind her back and around her waist. "Okay, here we go," he said and lifted her toward him. For a moment, she was rigid, then she trembled and seemed to collapse into him. As quickly as he could, he turned and eased her down into the wheelchair.

He moved around the chair to push it. "I'll do the ramp," he said to Millie. "You get the door."

Very quickly, they were in the clinic and crossing a waiting room with two people in it. They headed to a door on the back wall to the right. It opened as soon as they approached it, and Daniel Brenner—a doctor who'd joined the clinic a few months ago— was waiting for them. The man was medium height, solidly built, wearing a white lab coat over a yellow T-shirt and jeans. He crouched down by Quinn.

"I'm Doctor Brenner, but please call me Daniel. I've been briefed on your accident."

"Where's Boone?" Seth asked.

"He was called up north. Something about a bad accident near Wolf Bridge." Brenner stood up. "We need to get her into the main examination room."

Millie dropped the used gloves in a container on the wall, then moved behind the wheelchair and pushed it straight ahead. When Seth started to follow them, the doctor waved him off. "Use the restroom to clean up, then go and get some coffee and relax out front." With that, he followed the women as he snapped on his own protective gloves.

An hour and a half later, Seth was the only person in the front reception area. He had just finished his third cup of mediocre coffee when the sheriff, Max Donovan, strode in.

The tall man didn't look much like the law, except for a badge clipped on the breast pocket of his heavy brown jacket. Hair black as night was trimmed short, and his dark eyes were narrowed on Seth as he approached him and reached for a nearby chair. He turned it around to face Seth, then sat down. "You okay?"

"Yeah. I'm good, Max."

"How's the woman doing?"

"I don't know. Brenner's still in with her. It's a simple cut on her head. How long does it take to stitch it and put on a bandage?"

Max sat back with a sigh and undid his jacket, exposing the holster and gun at his hip. "Let Brenner take care of the lady. You tell me what happened."

Seth went over everything he could remember, then ended with, "It was my fault. Totally on me. I know that curve like the back of my hand, and I know how hard the wind gusts. I blew it big-time. No pun intended."

Max shrugged. "I do appreciate confessions, but I'll still have to talk to Ms. Lake to get her side."

"From what I can tell, she doesn't have much, and she's the one who got hurt. I'll take the hit for it. I deserve it."

"If she agrees with you, I'll hit you," the man said with an easy grin.

"Just try it, Max," Seth muttered, but his eyes were on the still-shut door to the back area. Then he glanced past the sheriff to Millie, who had been giving him updates on Quinn every time she came out of the back area. She was sitting at the reception desk on the computer now. "How much longer?"

"Let me go and see," the woman said and hurried off.

He checked his watch. "Maybe I should go and check."

"Stay put," Max said easily. "I went by the

site on my way and got the registration out of the VW before Henry towed it. Quinn G. Lake is from Pasadena, California, and it's registered to both her and a Michael S. Lake."

"Her husband," Seth said, then stood when the side door opened. Millie came out, pushing Quinn in the wheelchair. Thank goodness a clean white bandage was above her left eye, and her blond hair, still matted with dark stains, had been pulled back in a sloppy knot to keep it off her face. She looked even more pale with her face wiped clean. Millie stopped in front of Seth. "Sorry for the wait, but she's all cleaned up and ready to go."

Squatting down by Quinn, he asked, "How are you doing?"

"Fine, good. I got over a dozen stitches on the inside, and I didn't feel a thing, not even when Daniel stitched the outside, too." Her words were coming in a nervous rush. "Daniel is a good doctor, I mean, fantastic. He took very good care of me. Millie, did you ever notice that the two doctors names together make them Daniel Boone?"

Millie smiled. "Many have pointed that out."

"I thought that was pretty cool." Quinn

quickly shifted to another topic and kept talking a mile a minute to Millie. "Did you know that Daniel just bought a ranch south of town or maybe north? I can't remember. He said it was part of a bigger ranch that sounds pretty great, and he's redoing an old house on it and a bunch of buildings. They're making trails for horseback riding, some really cool adventure trails that go up into federal land that they can use. He's getting horses, well, not yet, but he will. Then he said he'll learn how to ride."

"Good for him," Millie said.

"Is he married?" Quinn asked, talking over Millie.

"He's divorced and not dating anyone, that I know of, but I suppose he's at that age where he's thinking about family and settling down."

What Brenner's personal life had to do with anything right then escaped Seth, and it annoyed him to have to listen to it. He cut in to ask Millie, "Did Brenner give her some medication?"

"Yes, something for the pain, and something that calms most patients, but it seems to have had the opposite effect on her. She's been very busy figuring out how the examination rooms need to be redecorated to fit in around here."

Quinn finally looked back at Seth. "I thought there'd be horses and cow things in it, and maybe galaxies up on the ceiling, but it looks like any old exam room anywhere. White, gray, stainless steel. Boring, totally boring, and no character, you know."

Seth looked at Millie with a bit of uneasiness. "Is there a problem with…this?"

"It'll wear off, and then she'll probably sleep a lot."

"Is she okay beyond that?"

"Yes. Dr. Brenner said everything looks good."

He was relieved when he looked back at Quinn, who was smiling now. "I'm okay, really, I am," she said to him, still speaking rapidly. "Daniel washed my face and hands, and he took off my hoodie and shirt, and gave me one of his shirts to wear and his jacket." She looked down at a blue windbreaker she was wearing over a white T-shirt. She frowned suddenly. "I'm real sorry you had to tear your shirt up like that." She looked as if she was going to cry. "I'll buy you another one as soon as I can, I promise."

"No, no, please, it's not important," Seth said as he touched her hand and felt the smooth gold ring on her finger. "Just don't worry about it." He glanced up at Millie. "Did you get an emergency contact number for her?" When Millie nodded, he drew his hand back and stood. "Any special dos and don'ts?"

"She needs to rest."

Seth realized he didn't have any idea where Quinn was staying in town, or even if she'd planned on staying in the area. When he looked back at her, she was staring at her hands clasped tightly in her lap. "Are you staying around here, Quinn?" he asked.

"I… I didn't have a chance to find a place." She looked up at him. "I'll call a cab and find a motel or hotel."

"Honey," Millie began, "the only cabs around here belong to Dan Baxter, and he's kind of shut down since he broke his leg. And from what I hear our hotel, the Clayton Inn, is full for the next week because of overbooking at two of the dude ranches."

Quinn fell silent, and Seth saw her knuckles whitening as she clenched her hands more tightly. "Gabby must have an extra room," Seth said quickly.

Millie shook her head. "Gabby's pretty much closed to have the main B&B's electrical service upgraded."

Max had been standing quietly beside Seth but finally spoke to Quinn. "Ms. Lake, I'm Sheriff Donovan." When she glanced up at him, he said, "Call me Max. I need to get a statement from you about the accident, but there's no rush. Seth has my number, and you can call me when you get settled. We'll arrange a time to talk."

"Okay," Quinn said softly.

Max turned to Seth. "I need to go. Walk me out."

Seth didn't want to, but the sheriff's request seemed more than just a friendly invitation. "Okay."

The two men went outside onto the raised porch, and as the door shut behind them, Max faced Seth. "She won't be able to find a place around here for a while, and she needs to rest and heal. I know you have a lot on you, but you've got space at the ranch, and Julia could keep an eye on her, at least for tonight."

That hadn't occurred to him, but it should have. "That's a good idea."

"See, I come in handy sometimes," Max said and slapped Seth on his shoulder. "I'll be in touch."

As the sheriff headed down to his large white SUV, Seth went back inside and crossed to Quinn. "Okay, there's a place you can stay for tonight, maybe longer. There's plenty of room, and an RN will be there to help you around the clock."

Her reaction was immediate and surprising. "Oh, no, no, not a hospital," she said with what Seth thought sounded like panic in her voice.

"No hospital. I'm talking about the ranch where I live. You're welcome to come back with me for as long as you need to."

QUINN STARED AT Seth in disbelief. "You would do that when you don't even know me?" Why had she said that? She was alone, with limited funds and no car, and she'd be stupid to offer reasons for Seth to withdraw his terrific offer. She also needed to keep in contact with him. "I mean, that's nice of you, really nice, I mean, after everything. It's just…unexpected, you know." It had to be the mention of a hospital that freaked her out. She hated them, and she hated not being able to just keep quiet! "You're a nice man. Really nice. And your offer's really nice. It really is." She knew she needed to stop talking, and thank goodness he cut in on her babbling.

"I *really* thank you for that," he said, that crooked grin on his face. "I mean it. There's space, help and you can stay as long as you need." He paused and his smile grew. "I'm pretty sure you're not a serial killer."

Cautiously, she said, "Okay, thank you. I'd really appreciate that."

"You'll love it out at the ranch," Millie said as she patted Quinn's shoulder. "Julia, the RN, is a real sweetheart."

"Thanks, Millie," she said. "Tell Daniel I'll get his shirt and jacket back to him. I'm sorry about all the blood and mess he had to clean up, and—"

Millie cut her off. "Don't worry about that." To Seth, she said, "If anything doesn't seem right, call us." The nurse took two small pill containers out of the pocket of her scrub top and handed them to him. "For pain and for sleep problems."

Seth pushed them into his jacket pocket. "That's it?"

Millie smiled. "Just keep her calm and watch her. Bring her back in a few days to have the wound checked. That's about it until she can have the stitches taken out." Turning back to Quinn, she said, "Now, let's get you out of here."

Quinn stayed in the wheelchair for the trip to the truck, then Seth stopped by the passenger door and held out his hand to her. "Do you think you can stand?"

She took his offered support and managed to get to her feet. Then he shifted and put his arm around her shoulders, holding her steady as he helped her step up to the cab. "Oh, I need to pay the bill," Quinn said, feeling stupid that she hadn't even thought about it.

"Don't worry about it for now," Millie said. "You'll be back. We can settle then."

"Thank you," she said, and with Seth's help, she got seated into the truck.

A few moments later, Millie waved to them as Seth pulled the truck around to head for the street. Daylight was fading as they turned onto Clayton Drive. Streetlights, fashioned to look like old gas lamps, were starting to light up the main street from one end to the other. Quinn barely glanced at the general store on the corner as they passed it. It seemed like a lifetime ago that she'd gone inside to ask for directions to Eclipse Ridge Ranch. Since then, her whole world had changed.

They drove north and onto the four-lane highway, with Quinn feeling some relief that the pressure for her to act quickly had lessened. She forced herself to keep quiet, worried about saying something wrong if she started to babble again the way she had from the medicine Daniel had given her. Why did she even care what his exam rooms looked like?

Seth finally broke the silence. "How are you holding up?"

She was tired, but her only real complaint was the throbbing behind her eyes. "I'm okay, except Daniel said I can't get the stitches wet, so no showers for three or four days at least." She was speaking fast again and couldn't stop herself. "So, no shampooing my hair, which seems almost criminal to me. But the good news is, I can take a bath. I really want to take a hot bath, just to lie back in hot water and relax."

She bit her lip to try to silence herself and looked ahead, surprised to see they were getting close to the turnoff she'd taken a few hours ago to find the ranch. It seemed too fast to be there already, as if time had sped up. Now, she was almost back to the place the accident had happened. Seth slowed to navigate the turn onto the two-lane road and clicked on his high-beam headlights as dusk settled over the land.

"As soon as we get back, you're more than welcome to take a bath."

"That sounds wonderful," she said on a sigh, and thankfully had no urge to say anything else.

As Quinn looked ahead, she realized there really was a blind curve. She couldn't even remember it from before, just the old truck coming at her out of nowhere. She clasped her hands tightly in her lap and determinedly looked straight ahead, not wanting to see any remnants of the accident. But on the first section of the curve, the lights shot straight toward the torn shoulder and the pile of tangled and broken fencing all stacked off to one side now. More ruts from recent tires showed in the shoulder, then it was all gone as they came out of the curve and the headlights illuminated the straight road ahead.

"Can I ask why you were driving out this way?"

The direct question came without warning and caught her off guard. She thought of vague lies, but she knew that after all Seth had done for her, lying to him was a line she wouldn't cross. She'd thought she'd have time to get her thoughts straight before she told him about Michael's work. But time was up. "I was looking for a place a man in town gave me directions to." Thankfully, that impulse to talk and talk and talk was wearing off as exhaustion crept up on her.

"What place?"

She braced herself, then reluctantly said, "The Eclipse Ridge Ranch."

"Who gave you directions?" he asked, giving her a few more seconds to get ready for impact.

"An older man in the general store."

"Was he dressed in a crazy cowboy outfit?"

Her heart was racing now. Purple and silver Western clothes would certainly qualify at least as odd. "Yes, with a lot of glitter."

"That's Farley Garret, the king of glitter,

and the owner of the store. He sent you out here?"

It was a small town. Of course he'd know the man. "Yes."

Then Seth surprised her. "Oh, that explains everything. I knew you might be coming, just not when."

Quinn thought she'd heard him wrong. There was no way he could have known, no way at all. She hadn't mentioned any name to Farley Garret, only asked about the ranch's location. "You knew?"

"Farley said he'd find someone interested in the housekeeping position at the ranch and send them out for an interview. I just wished he'd called to let us know you were coming today."

He thought she'd been on her way to interview for a job at the ranch? "That's where you live?"

"I sure do. I need someone to do light cleaning and cooking."

She hoped she sounded calmer than she felt as she tried to divert his attention away from herself so she could attempt to make some sense out of what was happening. "Why is a nurse at the ranch?"

"Julia's there to care for the owner, James Caine. It's his fence and field that were ripped up earlier."

The man at the general store had told her the entrance to the Eclipse Ridge Ranch was over three miles from the highway turnoff. Now Seth said she'd messed up his property close to the main highway. Her head was really throbbing. "This is the ranch here?"

"From the time we turned off the highway onto this road, we've been driving along the southern property line. The main entrance is a couple more miles ahead."

"How big is it?" she asked, genuinely curious.

"Six thousand plus acres."

"Mr. Caine owns it all?"

"It's been his for over fifty years."

CHAPTER THREE

"Mr. Caine's a friend?" Quinn asked.

"He's family."

That didn't make any sense. Quinn knew Seth had been orphaned as a small boy and put into the foster care system because he had no family. The name James Caine hadn't been anywhere in the article.

"I almost forgot to tell you that Henry called me at the clinic. He said to come by his place as soon as you feel up to it so he can discuss your car with you."

"Good," she said. Maybe if she had her car back she'd be able to focus and figure out the craziness of the world she'd crashed into. For now, she needed the hot bath and time to think so she could be as coherent as possible when the moment came to explain everything.

"We're almost there," Seth said. There was a glow through the gathering night in the distance that gradually morphed into two separate lights. "See those lamps up there? That's the entrance to the ranch, between the boulders they're bolted to."

Seth slowed and drove onto a sweep of pavement between the massive boulders and stopped at gates shaped by heavy wrought iron frames and wooden inserts. He rolled down his window, put a code into an illuminated security pad on a metal post and the gates started to open immediately. The headlights showed that the pavement kept going on a long sweep of driveway that climbed up from the road. They drove in with nothing but darkness beyond the light beams. Then they crested a rise in the drive, and in the distance she could make out the hulking shape of a massive house with a high center and low wings on either side.

Lights showed in a few windows in the lower part of the house. As they drove closer, the headlights of the truck fell directly on the middle two-story part of what looked like a log structure. A sweeping porch appeared to wrap around the entire building and smoke curled up from a double chimney near the center of the second-story pitched roof.

Seth parked by the stairs to the porch that was lit by lamps on either side of the entry door. He sounded the truck's horn before he got out and came around to open the passenger's side. With her hand in his for support, Quinn managed to step down onto the pavement and stay on her feet.

"Thank goodness, you finally got here," someone called over to them.

Quinn turned. A thirtysomething blond woman, maybe Quinn's height and size—dressed in jeans, a pastel green T-shirt and florescent green running shoes—was hurrying toward the truck. As the woman approached, she spoke to Quinn. "Hi. I'm Julia. I know you're Quinn. Millie called and filled me in after you left the clinic." Julia linked her arm with Quinn's. "Lean on me," she said, and they headed for the porch and slowly climbed the steps.

When Quinn stepped into the wonderful warmth in a two-level foyer, she had an impression of old Western decor and log walls. But Julia quickly guided her across a stone floor to a wide archway and helped her navigate a single step down onto the flagstone flooring of a great room. A fire burned in a huge river stone fireplace that took up a good portion of the rear wall.

"Go with Seth and get comfortable on the couch," Julia said as she motioned to a huge leather sofa on their left. "I'll only be a moment." Julia headed back into the entry and out of sight.

Seth was there, his hand lightly touching the small of Quinn's back. "You need to sit down."

Tiredness was wrapping around her like a cloak, but she managed to weakly sink down on the leather cushions. She saw a pool table across the room. In the other direction, she saw one of the longest dining tables she'd ever seen, and beyond that a step-up kitchen. She'd never felt so tired in her life.

Julia was back, carrying two large pillows. She tossed one onto a massive ottoman that looked like a repurposed watering tub topped with stretched leather. Seth sat down on it, facing her, and took off his jacket, laying it beside him. "Go ahead and stretch out," he said as Julia offered her the second pillow.

Quinn knew if she did that, she probably wouldn't get up anytime soon. Taking the pillow, she hugged it to herself but stayed seated. "Thanks. I'm fine."

Julia sat down beside her. "I hate that blind curve."

"As soon as I can get into town, I'll go and talk to someone in Public Works," Seth said. He sat forward and rested his forearms on his knees. "I'll get it eliminated."

"That's the county's road, Seth, and they'll tie it up for years before they do anything about it."

"Then I'll talk to the local attorney tomorrow. Maybe he can arrange for me to pay with private funds to have it fixed. He knows his way around here. Anyway, beyond the stitches, Brenner says Quinn's okay."

Julia glanced at the bandage, then asked Quinn, "So, how do you really feel?"

"Okay." She hesitated. "Mr. Reagan mentioned I might be able to take a bath when we got here?"

"The guest room in the east wing has a great soaking tub in the adjoining bathroom. You'll love it." Julia studied her for a moment. "Millie said you're from California. So how did a California girl end up on a county road in rural Wyoming?"

Seth cut in before Quinn had to answer. "Farley sent her out to interview for the housekeeper position."

"About that—" Quinn started to say, but Seth stepped in.

"No rush," he said. "We'll talk about the job later."

Later was fine as long as she got to take a bath. Julia patted Quinn's knee. "Come on. I'll show you to your room. I can stay with you for your bath if you need me to."

"Thanks, but I'm not dizzy or anything."

Seth stood and headed for the entry. "I'll get your things from the truck."

A moment later, the front door opened and closed. It didn't open again until Julia and Quinn were slowly stepping up into the foyer to go to the guest room. Seth had her backpack and purse over one shoulder and followed the two women into the east wing hallway. "After your bath, come on out to the great room and get something to eat," Julia said as she stopped by the first door on their left and pushed it open.

Quinn followed her into a large bedroom with a wrought iron bed to the left of the door. It was made up with a periwinkle blue and yellow quilt, a bank of pillows and positioned to face a wide window on the back wall. A braided rug in various shades of blue took the cold edge off the stone floor.

Julia opened a side door and motioned Quinn to follow her into a bathroom almost as large as the bedroom. Across a black-and-white-tiled floor stood a large claw-foot tub against the back wall beside an enclosed shower. "That is an incredible tub," Quinn said as she reached for the support of a double sink vanity just inside the door to her left.

Julia crossed to the tub. "A good friend of Seth's redesigned a lot of the lower level and found this at an estate sale. It was from one of the original cattle baron spreads in the area." The nurse bent over to put a stopper that hung by a chain from the curved faucet into the drain, then turned on the water. "Towels, soap, lotion—help yourself," she said as she motioned to a series of brass shelves by the sinks. "If you need clothes, I think we're about the same size."

"Thank you so much."

"Okay, I'll leave you to enjoy your bath."

"You'll need these," Seth said as he came up behind Quinn to set her medication bottles on the vanity by her. "Your bags are on the bed."

"Thank you," Quinn said and barely stopped a yawn. She hoped her growing weakness came mostly from not eating since the evening before. Or maybe it was the medicine the doctor had given her at the clinic finally doing what it was supposed to do—make her calm and relaxed.

When Seth and Julia left and closed the door, Quinn turned and caught a glimpse of herself in the mirror over the vanity. She looked like the poster child for the old song "A Whiter Shade of Pale." Her skin looked almost as white as the bandage, and the only color in her face came from the dark shadows under her eyes that made them look bruised. She frowned at her tangled and dirty hair Millie had barely managed to contain in a low knot.

It was no wonder Seth kept looking at her as if she were about to crumble. She eased the tie from her hair, carefully managed to gather it higher on her head and wound the tie around the knot again to keep it in place. At least it would keep her hair out of the bath water. She closed the bathroom door, then stripped off her clothes and crossed to get in the tub. She took her time sinking into the lovely warmth of the bath until she was in the water up to her chin. She might not be able to shampoo her hair, but every other part of her loved the sensation of being submerged in warmth and comfort.

She reached with her foot to turn the faucet off, then stayed in the tub until the water grew tepid before she finally got out. She found fresh clothes in her backpack, a blue pullover and jeans, and when she was dressed, she felt immeasurably better physically but still not certain what to do next.

Leaving her bags on the bed along with the doctor's jacket and shirt, she headed barefoot into the hallway and through to the entry. Stopping at the archway to the great room, she found the lights were on, a fire still going in the hearth, but no one was in sight. As she stepped down onto the cool flagstone floor, her stomach rumbled, and she had a thought of going to find a snack or something. But that didn't seem right to her, and she honestly didn't think she had the energy to even search for food.

So she belatedly took Seth's suggestion t

stretch out on the supple leather of the couch. Resting her head on the pillow left there, she sighed as weariness washed over her. She definitely wasn't going to move until she had to.

After several minutes, Quinn heard a sound nearby and slowly opened her eyes to find Seth standing over her. Dressed in an untucked chambray shirt and jeans, he'd combed his damp hair straight back from his face. "Do you want to rest, then eat?" he asked.

As hungry as she felt, she really had no choice. "Rest."

"Okay, I'll be here when you're ready for food."

"Thank you." She closed her eyes slowly.

Moments later, Julia spoke from somewhere above her. "Quinn?"

"Sorry," she mumbled, knowing she should at least open her eyes, but she couldn't make it happen.

When Seth spoke to Julia, Quinn couldn't follow what he was saying and didn't even try. The lure of getting lost in the growing softness around her was far too tempting. As she willingly let go, she had the weirdest thought that this whole day might just be some crazy dream, like the ones she used to have when she'd doze off sitting with Michael in the middle of the night.

Maybe she'd wake up tomorrow in the small house in Pasadena and find out she'd imagined all of this. Maybe it was all an illusion born out of desperation, knowing she'd never be able to keep her promise to Michael.

SETH BARELY SLEPT that night, getting up and down to check on Quinn during the night. Then at dawn, he gave up, showered, dressed in his bedroom upstairs and headed down to the great room. He found Quinn still asleep and he sat quietly on the ottoman. Her left hand with the simple gold band rested by her cheek on the pillow. A husband was out there somewhere, and he wondered why Quinn hadn't said a thing about him coming to be with her. Maybe he was already on his way. He should have asked her before she fell asleep.

She stirred, then settled again, and a fleeting hint of a frown was there before it fled on a soft sigh. He studied her face, the delicate bone structure and the dark lashes against the paleness of her cheeks. There was something appealing about Quinn, but she also seemed very alone. Seth had never been a rescuer, but right then he felt protective, maybe because the accident had been all his fault or maybe because he understood what being alone was all about, even if it was temporary.

He watched as she stirred again and shifted onto her back, then her eyes fluttered and opened. She slowly looked around, saw him and her eyes widened. "I'm sorry I fell asleep," she said just above a whisper.

Seth sat forward, resting his forearms on his thighs. "You needed the rest. It's almost morning."

"Oh, goodness," she said and pushed herself up, her hair loose and tangled around her face.

"How are you feeling?"

She exhaled softly. "I'm okay."

"You never ate last night," he said. "Do you like bacon and eggs?"

She brushed absentmindedly at her unruly hair. "I eat anything."

"Okay. Tell me how you like your eggs, and I'll get breakfast going."

"Over easy, please. But I need to freshen up."

"Go ahead. I'll get the food started," he

said and stood. "Do you need any help? I can call Julia."

"I can manage." He nodded and headed toward the kitchen. "Bell peppers," she called after him.

That stopped him, and he turned. "Excuse me?"

"Bell peppers," Quinn said as she slowly stood. "That's about the only food I don't like, and some people put them in eggs."

"Got it, no bell peppers," he said and went to make breakfast out of the few things he trusted himself to cook.

When he heard Quinn come back into the room not more than ten minutes later, he turned to find her crossing over to the glass doors to the right of the hearth. In a pink sweater and jeans, her hair pulled back off her face in a low twist, she looked as if she felt better.

"That was fast," he called over to her. "How about toast?"

It took a moment before she answered, but she never looked away from the outside world. "Oh, wheat, if you have it." He dropped two slices in the toaster as Quinn added, "I've never seen anything like this."

He crossed over to look past her at dawn spreading its pale colors over the countryside.

He loved this land. "I used to wake at sunrise just to see the day start like this." He couldn't remember ever being up this early in Seattle unless he had a company emergency. But as a teenager, he'd crawl out of bed when it was dark just to ride out to the foothills and sit on the viewing ridge to watch the sun start to push back the darkness.

"Is that deer?" she asked as she pointed to the north.

He saw three animals by a wide swath of old trees that blocked the view to the ranch's original cabin built on higher land. "No, they're pronghorn antelope. They're pretty harmless." When another one came out of the trees and trotted over to stand by the others, their four heads rose in unison to look toward the house.

"They can't see us, can they?" Quinn asked.

"No. But something caught their attention." Then they all turned to look east, and he saw what they had sensed. "Look over where the pasture rises in the shadows of those pines."

Quinn moved closer to the glass to look

where he directed. "Oh, you mean those dogs by the alien trees?"

That brought him an easy smile. "Lodge-pole pines, not alien trees, and those aren't dogs, they're coyotes."

She moved back slightly, as if to put more distance between herself and the animals. "They're after the antelope?"

"They think they are."

"Oh, my gosh, they're going kill them?"

"No, the odds are very low the coyotes could even get close to them. Pronghorn antelope are the second fastest animal around, and no coyote stands a chance catching them on the run."

Right then, the coyotes broke toward their targets, and the antelope became a blur as they darted west to the end of the trees and disappeared to the north. The coyotes slowed, acting confused as they circled randomly around the area. Then they loped off in the direction the antelope had gone.

Quinn whispered, "They're going after them."

"The antelope are probably already near-ing the high country toward the federal lands.

Now, why don't you sit down at the table and relax? Breakfast is almost ready."

Quinn followed his suggestion, and when Seth finally sat across the table from her with the platter of eggs and bacon between them, he avoided looking at her bandage. As she brushed a loose tendril of hair away from her face, he said, "Eat while it's hot."

She helped herself to the food but didn't start eating right away. Instead, she looked across at him. "This place is really so different from anything I've ever seen in person before. It's sort of scary, but kind of fascinating, too."

"It has a way of drawing you in," Seth murmured. It was also the first place he could remember feeling safe. That made such a difference for him as a teenager, taking away the edge of anger he'd had almost constantly while in the system. And along with safety came freedom. He'd embraced that, and his whole life had changed. Now he was back, and he found being anywhere else wasn't even a consideration for him. He was here, now, and no matter why he'd come back, he loved it.

"I don't suppose it's a smart thing to just wander around outside here."

"I wouldn't say that. The antelope will run if they see you, and the coyotes are cowards, cleaning up after the others, mostly. They don't want to meet you any more than you want to meet them." He motioned to her food. "Please, eat."

He watched Quinn taste the eggs, then reach for coffee to take a sip. Unexpectedly, she looked up at him and smiled, a soft expression that came out of nowhere. It caught him off guard to realize how pretty she was. He nearly did a double take, but instead reached for his mug and took a drink.

"I think I'll just stay in the house," she said.

"That's a shame." He put his drink down. "You'll miss a lot if you do."

She shrugged. "I won't be here that long, anyway."

He was taken aback by that, realizing he'd expected her to take the housekeeping job and be around for a while. Maybe after the accident, all she wanted to do was get out of there. He could understand that. "I could show you some of the ranch before you go."

"I appreciate the offer," she said, neither accepting it nor rejecting it, before she reached for a piece of toast. When Quinn finished her meal, she sat back with a sigh. "That was really good. Thank you."

"I have to admit that you've just eaten most of what I can cook."

That smile came again, nudging at him, and he pushed away the errant reaction as he finished off his coffee. He couldn't remember the last time he'd enjoyed breakfast at this table, let alone with a woman whose company, he'd admitted to himself as they ate and spoke, he enjoyed. But if she stayed to work at the ranch, he'd have to push aside any attraction he felt toward her. If she wasn't staying, it was a dead end. Either way, it was moot point because her husband would probably show up soon, or she'd leave to be with him.

IT HAD BEEN so easy to eat and talk with Seth that Quinn had almost forgotten why she was here. Thankfully, her thinking was clearer after the meal. With that clarity came the idea of actually staying on as the housekeeper. It was starting to make sense to her. Seth had offered her a few days at the ranch to heal. Maybe it was also a chance to finally succeed with Michael's Shield. So far, her pitches to tech executives had been rushed by necessity, presented to total strangers and shot down completely. This time, whether she won or lost, she'd know she'd done her best if she could take her time to get to know Seth before she approached him about the cybersecurity software. She'd make sure he was the right man to take it on. Maybe, if she did that first, she'd be able get through the pitch successfully.

Before her husband passed and was still working on the program, she'd had him run through the basics of it so she could understand it better. She'd memorized key information but understanding never came. Instead, she'd learned to quote what he'd told her with the passion she had to see her promise through. Even so, none of the other execs had let her get more than partway into her presentation. By staying to do housekeeping for Seth, she might be able to stretch a short stay into enough time to get to know him and to get her car back. When the VW was fixed, she'd have options about leaving if Seth rejected Michael's work. She'd have the ability

to go to Denver, where the last firm on her
list was.

She stood, picked up her dishes and headed
to the kitchen. She heard Seth's chair scrape
on the flagstone floor, then he came up beside her by the deep double sinks set into a
large granite-topped island that overlooked
the great room. "I feel better after eating," she
said as she swept the few scraps into the dis-
posal sink. Quietly, she rinsed all their dishes,
then put them in an oversize dishwasher.

"I should've taken care of the clean-up,"
Seth said. "You aren't working here yet."

"Oh, of course I'm not," she agreed, but
was pretty confident all she had to do was
say she'd like the position and Seth would
hire her. An uneasiness at being manipula-
tive to get to where she wanted to be nudged
at her, but she offset that by promising herself she'd do a solid job housekeeping, do everything Seth needed help with. She needed
time. Maybe this way, they could both win.
"You made the food. I should do my part. If
I was working here, who would I be working
for, Mr. Caine or you?"

"Me."

She closed the dishwasher and turned to

Seth. "Can I ask how you're related to Mr. Caine?"

"Sarge—he answers to Sarge." Seth exhaled as he leaned back against the counter by the six-burner stove and faced her. "To make a long story short, I came here as a teenager in the foster care system. Sarge and his wife, Maggie, took me in, along with two boys, Ben and Jake, around the same time. Society had given up on us. Sarge and Maggie never did. They became the closest the three of us ever got to having parents."

No wonder he was here. "If you want to interview me for the job, now's as good a time as any. I mean, I feel okay, and it's just a cut, not a concussion or anything."

"If you're sure you're up to it, I'll be in my office for a few hours. Come on in whenever you're ready."

She looked around. "Where's your office?"

"There's two offices here. One is directly across this room past the pool table. That door." He pointed toward a single door straight across the room from them. "That's the ranch office that Sarge used. Libby, my friend who's redesigning the ranch, uses it now. I had an office set up for me in the east wing, the second door across from your bed-room."

"Okay. I'll meet you there in fifteen min-utes," she said, and headed back to her room. She didn't need time to do anything except get her nerves calmed as much as possible. After she'd checked her hair in the bathroom and splashed cold water on her face, being careful not to dampen the bandage, she sat on her bed to just breathe. The view through the back window was stunning with the clear blue morning sky and the rugged land in the distance. It was beautiful country, but her heart was hammering against her ribs.

She exhaled, reached over for her backpack and took a small leather box out of the side pocket that held the photo from the car. She held on to the box and just sat there quietly. It helped her center herself, holding on to it, and reassured her that what she was doing was the right thing. Even if she couldn't fully under-stand Michael's work, and never would, she knew from others who had known him well how brilliant he'd been. Cybersecurity was a top priority for corporations. The attempted hackings were persistent, unbelievably dam-aging and costly for the victims, but Michael had possibly found a loophole—that's what she called it—that would trump 98 percent of hacking attempts. She wanted others to know, for Michael to have a legacy that was worthy of his memory.

The box was worn, a carryover from Michael's college days when it went everywhere with him. It was all she truly had left of him in this world besides the car. The box was something she could hold on to and remember. She exhaled again, then tucked the box under her pillow so it would be there in the night when the loneliness was always worse.

She crossed to the door and stepped out into the hallway, then went to the door across from hers. Before she could knock on it, she heard Seth speaking from behind the barrier. "Owen, I told you I want as little as possible coming at me right now. I'm not available. I'm here for Sarge, period. Handle things the way you want to. I trust you. Just leave me out of it."

Owen? That had to be the VP who had shown her the door at the corporate tower in Seattle. Whatever was going on, it was either frustrating Seth or making him mad, or maybe it was a combination of both. Either way, it wasn't good.

When the silence behind the door remained unbroken by the time Quinn had counted to twenty, she finally rapped on the wood. A moment later, the door opened, and Seth was there, smiling at her. Whatever she'd overheard was obviously finished. "Come on in," he said.

Quinn took a deep breath and stepped into a space that appeared to take up most of the front section of the east wing. With the front and side walls constructed of heavy logs, and the others done in rough plaster, the room's style was somewhat rustic, but it was also touched with futuristic pieces.

From a long glass-topped desk to the left that held two large flat-screen monitors, to a series of strangely shaped naked bulbs suspended from a curving metal track on the ceiling, it looked sleek and modern. A large closed cabinet seemed oddly quaint with heavily carved doors and aged brass handles. The only homey thing in the space was a framed picture on the wall above one of the monitors. A large man and three teenaged boys wearing matching denim jackets were all smiling into the camera. It looked as if they were by a riding ring of some sort, and she knew one of the boys was a very young Seth.

Seth's cell phone on the glass desk, chimed and he glanced at Quinn. "Sorry," he said, as he reached for it and rejected the call. He put the cell facedown by the monitor again and turned to Quinn. A touch of annoyance was in his expression now.

"If you need to take care of something, we can do this later," she offered right away.

He shook his head. "I'm here. You're here. Let's talk."

She felt better about her decision to wait before making any pitch to him. He clearly didn't appear to want to listen to anything to do with his business at the moment. "Okay."

He flashed her that boyish grin and motioned to a stylized chair to her right that looked as if it belonged in some far-off galaxy. It was all sweeping chrome lines that were only softened by dark leather padding to prevent a human body from coming into contact with the hard metal frame. "Why don't you take the recliner?"

She stared at it and wondered if she'd slip

right off if she tried to sit on it. As if he'd read her mind, Seth said, "It won't bite. Trust me. I use it all the time after workouts, and it's great for relaxing. It helps the muscles."

Oddly, Quinn did trust Seth, even though she barely knew him. There was something she sensed in him, a basic kindness and decency, virtues she hadn't suspected she'd find in a self-made billionaire businessman.

"Here goes nothing," Quinn said and went closer to the chair.

He stopped her. "Oh, hold on a minute. I should forewarn you about something before you sit down."

She couldn't help saying, "I'm not going to be transported to the mother ship, am I?"

He chuckled, a low warm sound. "No, but it will automatically adjust to your weight and height as soon as it senses your body on it. It's all automatic and incredibly comfortable. Sit on it and put your feet up on the bottom rests, then your head back on the top support. It does all the work."

"Okay," Quinn said, then cautiously turned to sit. She swung her feet up and onto the padded lower section. She had barely settled with her head on the backrest when the chair did indeed start to move silently as its components slowly shifted along the length of her body. It finally stilled, and despite the strangeness of the contraption, it gave support where she needed, especially in her neck and shoulders.

"So, how does that feel?" Seth asked as he rolled a computer chair over to sit to her right.

Laying in the strange chair with Seth sitting by her seemed an odd setup, more like a patient meeting with a psychiatrist. But it worked, and she appreciated Seth's concern for her comfort. "I feel like a relaxed spaceship captain." She exhaled, nervousness still there despite the comfort of the chair. "I'm ready whenever you are."

"First, there's something I should've asked you before. You never said if you contacted your husband."

Quinn barely kept from grimacing when the throbbing behind her eyes suddenly flared up. She put her right hand over her left and felt the smoothness of the gold wedding band. "Daniel said I'm fine, so there isn't any reason to change plans or worry anyone." She couldn't make herself tell Seth the truth. She couldn't say those words that hurt more every time she had to say them. *Michael is dead.*

CHAPTER FOUR

SETH DIDN'T ASK a follow-up question. Her personal life wasn't any of his business as long as the doctor had her emergency contact number. "Why don't you outline your pertinent work experience for me?"

She kept her eyes on him while she spoke, her right hand staying over her left. "I guess the most important part of my work background is that I did housekeeping in some of the bigger luxury hotel complexes in San Diego while I was in college."

He sat back in the chair and began to swivel slowly from side to side. "Here you'd need to cook basic meals for four people. Regarding cleaning, I just expect this place ordered and dusted. I'll get someone in to do the upkeep on the log walls, so don't worry about that. No need to do any cleaning in here or next door in my workout area. Any questions?"

"Does Sarge have a disability or is he just in temporary care with Julia?"

Seth stilled his chair. "Julia came home with Sarge as his caregiver when he was released from rehab after breaking his leg last year. But he was diagnosed with Alzheimer's before he fell, and Julia's staying to take care of that as it progresses." He actually surprised himself at how calmly he'd just described such a monumental fracture of his world.

"I'm sorry," she said. "I know that has to be hard."

He brushed that aside. "Was that your question?"

"Not completely. I wanted to know if he has any dietary restrictions. I can cook no salt, low salt, nonfat, low fat, vegetarian, even vegan if it's needed."

The list that came so readily from her took him aback. "No, Sarge is basically a meat-and-potatoes man. But check with Julia, just in case." He sat forward again. "Did you do dietary work before?"

Quinn hesitated and Seth saw her swallow before she said, "Not as a job, but I was the sole caregiver for my husband when he was sick." Seth felt blindsided, never expecting her to say that. She stared down at her hands in her lap. "He…had special dietary needs because of his treatments. I learned a lot of specific ways to make food."

"Oh, I'm sorry. I hope he's doing better?"

She seemed to be bracing herself before she said, "Michael passed away seventeen months ago."

The room was dead silent, so devoid of sound that he thought he could hear his own heartbeat.

"I'm so sorry," he said in a low voice. He didn't know what else to say. He tried to gather his thoughts, and all he could think of was Quinn saying she was twenty-seven years old. She couldn't have been more than twenty-five when she was widowed. The photo he'd retrieved from the car for her, which he'd glanced at before giving it to her, was there vividly in his mind. Two people who looked so happy. Then it was gone.

He sat a bit straighter. Quinn was here alone, really alone, and he wanted to offer her something right then that he'd only considered in passing earlier. Now it seemed a very good idea. "Um, well, you know, since you don't have a place in town and you don't have a car, how would you feel about making this a live-in position for a while?" Seth saw her hesitate, and he gave her a second choice before she could answer. "Or I can get a rental car for you, and I'm sure Gabby could find you a room at her B&B when her repairs are done. It's up to you."

She finally looked at him. He couldn't read her expression beyond the shadow of sadness in those blue eyes. "I think staying here until my car is fixed would be a good idea."

He was relieved she wasn't going to leave right away. "Okay," he said.

"You mentioned cooking for four people. Is there someone else besides you, Julia and Sarge?"

"I was including you in the four. Jake and his wife live in the original cabin built on the ranch, beyond the trees where you saw the antelope earlier. But they're down here for meals and sometimes stay in the master bedroom upstairs. They'll be back soon from a trip, so you'll get to meet them then." Jake and Libby had been traveling lately for Jake's new job, setting up teaching centers for pilots. "Ben's in Detroit. He restructures protection systems. He'll be around for the holidays, or maybe sooner."

"What's Jake's wife's name?"

"Jake and Sarge call her by her full name, Liberty, but the rest of us call her Libby. I was friends with her way before she married Jake." He didn't add that he'd never had the good sense to fall in love with her, instead of habitually falling for women who were looking for what they could get out of him. Dating a friend would've been smart, but he loved Libby like a sister. They'd both gone through foster care and understood each other. "They were married this past February. She's the designer and architect for the construction you'll notice going on around the ranch. Any more questions?"

"No. I'll learn as I go," Quinn said. "I mean, if you hire me."

It had been a done deal from the start for Seth. "Consider yourself hired when you feel up to starting."

"I'm ready now. All I do need is a tour of the house to get familiar with it."

"Sure, of course." Seth's first impulse was to offer to be her guide, then she smiled slightly at him, and he almost heard her say, *Michael passed away seventeen months ago.*

"Thank you so much," she said.

He'd never looked at a woman he barely knew who'd just smiled at him and known there was something special about her. It was ridiculous. He stood and headed toward the door. "I'll be right back."

He was out in the hallway with the door shut behind him before he stopped, shook his head and wondered if he was having some late-appearing shock from the accident. Or maybe shock from what Quinn had told him. He had to get away from his reactions to the blonde blue-eyed woman in his office and what she'd just told him. What he needed was to lose himself in a heavy workout or get outside to breathe in cold air and be alone.

He glanced at the entry and Julia was coming out of the west wing hallway. Spotting him, she waited as he headed toward her. "So, how's it going?" she asked.

"Quinn's in my office resting in the recliner."

"And?"

"We agreed that she'd stay here as a live-in housekeeper until her car's repaired."

"That's good, isn't it?" Julia asked.

He hoped it would be. "Of course. Why wouldn't it be?" He made a quick decision. "She needs to be shown around the house, and I have something else I need to do. Could you possibly give her a tour?"

"Sure. Sarge is sleeping. Where are you off to?"

He hadn't thought about that. "Down to find Murphy. I still haven't seen his revised estimates on the outside hay-and-feed storage areas. But I won't go if you need me here."

She patted the monitor clipped to her waistband. "I can hear everything going on with Sarge, so it's all covered."

He glanced at his wristwatch, the one Sarge had bought for him years ago when he'd left for college. It surprised him that it was barely eight o'clock. So much had changed. "Okay, I'll be checking in, and you call if you need me." He reached for his lined leather jacket on the cowhide bench and shrugged it on. Then he sat to put on his boots. "She told me her husband died seventeen months ago."

"Oh, no," Julia said. "Poor Quinn."

"Yeah." He stood. "Please, just give her a tour of the house," he said, then hesitated.

"Julia, do we have any hats around the place? It's cold out there."

"No, I... Hold on." She went back into the west wing and moments later returned holding a black Stetson with a beaded band around the crown. "How about this?"

He stared at the old hat. Sarge had worn a hat like that for as long as Seth remembered. The rule always was, no one touched it. "No, I got in trouble wearing Sarge's hat a long time ago. I don't want to go back there."

"He told me to give it to you. He mentioned something about, 'That boy finally has sense enough to wear a good hat out there.' So, it's yours."

He didn't know why, but he felt unsteady when he took it from her hands. Then he found himself doing what Sarge had done every time he put it on his head. He tapped the crown against his thigh, then put it on, tugging the brim down. It fit exactly.

Julia smiled at him. "From a CEO to a cowboy."

"Hardly," Seth said, hearing a slight unsteadiness in his own voice. "Tell Sarge... I'll take good care of it." He headed to the door, stepped out into the clear cold day and inhaled deeply.

Then headed down to find Murphy, the main contractor for the ranch reconstruction. He needed to focus on the camp matters. That was the most important thing right now, and it was almost overwhelming for him, from the time frame to the scope of it in general. He felt the weight of doing it right for Sarge.

When Seth approached the hay barn that was partially being converted into what the crew was calling *the entertainment palace*— a place for the campers to be if the weather got bad—Murphy was nowhere in sight. So he kept going north to the stables where they were trying to get the extension by the tack room roofed before snow fell. He passed the large riding ring and empty holding pens out in front of the log building and went in through its open double doors.

Stepping inside, Seth caught the mingled scents of damp air, hay, manure and a sweet hint of grain. A restless snort and a few whinnies came from stalls that lined the sides of a wide aisle running front to back through the building. They'd been gradually bringing horses back to the ranch for camp use and so far they were up to eleven, so far, including their personal mounts. They had a long way to go so each camper would have a ride for the week they'd be at the camp. They were still figuring out a good number. Sarge had always done that with the boys as they arrived at the ranch to give them a focus and a way to learn responsibility. It had sure worked for him.

Dwight Stockard, the ranch manager, came out of the side aisle, spotted Seth and ambled toward him. "Hey, there," he called. The man was short and stocky, with slightly bowed legs and thinning brown hair that was partly covered by a beaten straw weave Stetson. He was wearing jeans, boots and a heavy jacket. He glanced at Seth's hat, smiled, said, "Nice hat," then went on before Seth could say anything, "Got a little mare from the Dunbar Ranch yesterday. I think she's gonna be a horse for the younger camper who might need a gentle ride."

"Good," Seth said as he met up with Dwight at the heavy central pole that supported the roof trusses above the cement floor.

Dwight studied Seth. "It don't look like you

got hurt any from running that lady off the road."

Seth didn't even have to ask how the man knew. Dwight had been born in Eclipse and never left, so he was a permanent link in the town's lengthy gossip chain. "No, I didn't."

"That's good. Now, if you're here to ride, I can get Miner ready for you."

Just at the thought of a ride, Seth felt the tension in him lessen. "I think that's what I need, actually."

SETH DIDN'T GET back to the ranch until it was almost five o'clock and getting dark outside. He went into the house to take off his jacket and boots, set his new hat crown down on the bench, then looked into the great room. Quinn was there by the island in the kitchen and looked over at him. He was surprised to see her hair looked clean and silky, falling loose around her face and past her shoulders.

"Did Julia show you around?" he asked across the space that separated them. He wasn't going to go any closer. He needed to learn to keep his distance.

"Yes, she did," she said. "This is a lovely

house, and the bed in the master suite is stunning."

He nodded. "Sarge built all of this and made that bed for Maggie when they moved in here."

"That's incredible."

"It's all unique. One of a kind." This whole place was one of a kind, just like the man who owned it. "How are you feeling?"

"Oh, I'm doing fine."

"Your hair, how did you manage that?"

She tucked the locks behind her ears. "Julia found dry shampoo and she helped me clean it." She smiled again. "It's wonderful to have it close to normal."

"Good to hear," he said. "I need to get in to see Sarge."

"Oh, sure, of course."

He turned and headed into the west wing. When he stepped into Sarge's quarters, he and Julia were at the small table by a side window just finishing a game of poker. He could tell by their expressions that Julia was not the winner.

"Got you good, girl," Sarge announced, then noticed Seth. "Son, I beat her three times."

The big man had been diminished by time, his hair thinning and gray now, and the T-shirt he was wearing with jeans was loose on his large frame. Even though his blue eyes seemed faded a bit, he still had that spark there when he was doing well.

Julia stood and motioned to the table as she smiled. "You take my place and teach him a lesson in humility. I'll be right back."

Sarge laughed. "Sit down, son. I need a challenge."

Reaching for the cards, Seth started shuffling them. "Name your game, sir."

"See you in a bit," Julia said as she left, closing the door behind her.

Sarge sat back. "So, how's the hat?"

Seth was still feeling something he'd decided on the ride was a sense of a legacy. The hat seemed to make everything going on more special. "Thank you. I'll take good care of it for you. If you ever want it back—"

"Son, it's yours," Sarge said. "Now you're here, you need to look more…you know, like this is your place in the world."

He didn't know what to say, so he settled for, "I guess I do."

When Seth reached for the cards, Sarge

stopped him. He sighed. "I think I'll quit a winner."

"How about we take it easy?" Sarge started to get up and Seth helped him over to get on the bed and recline, laying on top of the sheets. "Just relax," he said. "We can talk, or how about some Zane Gray?"

Sarge closed his eyes, then waved that off with his hand. "No, I got some thinking to do, son."

"Oh, okay," Seth said and sat down on one of two chairs by the bed.

Sitting with Sarge as the older man slipped into sleep, Seth admitted to himself that probably for the first time ever, a long ride hadn't cleared his head or even come close to helping him make sense of his life. Being here with Sarge gave him no real desire to head back to Seattle any time soon. And Quinn... He didn't trust himself to make good decisions of the heart. His ex, Allie, had cemented that in his mind. She'd seemed so good, so right, at first. Then she'd turned out to be so wrong. That was two years ago, yet he still felt the sting of his mistake with her.

When he'd walked in the door earlier and looked into the great room, Quinn was there, her blond hair like golden silk. Wearing slim-fit jeans and an oversize sweater, she'd looked up at him and smiled. He'd known right then that the day had been a waste if he thought the ride would tame his reaction at just seeing her.

When Seth caught the scent of cooking food wafting in through the partially open door to Sarge's suite, a hunger he hadn't felt all day was right there. With Sarge still sleeping peacefully, Seth made sure the monitor was on, then quietly left the room. As he approached the archway to the great room, he was stopped by an unexpected burst of laughter. As he went closer, he looked in and saw it was Quinn's laughter. It caught at something in him, the same way her smile tended to do every time it appeared.

He moved back, wondering what he was doing. He'd fallen into whatever it had been with Allie so quickly and made such a bad mistake. He barely knew Quinn, but all she had to do was smile at him. She was also a widow. That had to be so hard for her, and probably something she was working through. He braced himself, then stepped through the archway.

Quinn was putting a basket of rolls by the place settings Julia was laying out at the far end of the long dining table. "I think I would have changed it to Marlin or Milton, or something like that."

"What's so funny?" he asked with what he hoped was a casual tone when he stepped down onto the flagstone floor.

Both women turned toward him as he approached the table. "We were just discussing weird names that parents give their kids," Julia said. "Quinn was explaining her name, which, by the way, if you didn't know, is really Quinton."

"She mentioned that to me," he said, glancing at Quinn and seeing a touch of color in her face. She looked so much better. If it weren't for the bandage, you'd never know she'd been hurt.

"What's your middle name?" Julia asked Quinn.

She smiled ruefully, and Seth knew he'd been really smart to stay away most of the day. "Grayson."

"Grayson?" Seth asked.

"My mother's maiden name."

"So, your parents looked at a pretty blond

baby girl and named her Quinton Grayson?" Julia asked.

"Yes, and then add my maiden name, Churchill. No relationship to Winston."

"That's a great name." Julia glanced at Seth. "What's your middle name?

"I was told it's Liam." He had no idea where his names came from and he had no one to ask.

A chime sounded, and Julia looked at the monitor clipped to the waistband of her jeans. "Shoot, I need to get in there. He's awake and moving." As she hurried across the room, she called back, "Go ahead and eat while it's hot, and I'll get to it when I can."

"Are you sure you're well enough to be doing all of this?" Seth asked Quinn as Julia left.

"Of course. I'll get the food if you get the drinks. I'm not a coffee drinker at dinner. Anything else is okay."

Seth poured a glass of milk for each of them, then put them between two settings that faced each other across the table. Quinn was back with a casserole and a green salad that she put down by a basket of rolls. Before Seth could sit, he heard a thump, then

Sarge's voice carried all the way out to the great room. "I can do that!"

"I'll be right back," Seth called over his shoulder as he took off running for the entry and up the single step. He stopped in his tracks when Sarge came out of the west wing, walking steadily with his cane.

Julia was right beside him, and Seth didn't miss the relief on her face when she saw him. "All of a sudden, he's hungry."

The man's gray hair was combed, and he'd changed into a beige Western shirt with his jeans. Seth noticed his clothes really were loose. "Hey, Sarge," Seth said as he went across to him. "I'm glad you want to come out for dinner."

"Absolutely. I'm starving."

"Me, too," he said as he took Sarge by the upper arm. When he closed his hand around the man's biceps, he almost flinched. There was little remaining of the hard muscles that had been there before. In the three months Seth had been gone before he came back on his sabbatical, Sarge had lost weight and that bothered Seth.

"Well, come on, son," Sarge muttered.

He needed a bit of help going down the single step, and Seth made a mental note to tell Murphy to put a safe transition in before he did any other work. It should've been done a long time ago. Julia called over to Quinn in the kitchen. "There will be four for dinner."

"The more the merrier," she said.

While Seth helped Sarge get seated at the head of the table, he had a flashback to when the older man had sat in that same chair for every meal. "Are you okay?" Seth asked him.

The man turned faded blue eyes to him. For a moment, Seth could almost see that former marine who had stood so tall, teaching him all about life and how good it could be. "I'm glad you came home, son," Sarge said. "I sure missed you."

"I'm glad I did, too." Seth patted Sarge on the shoulder, then took the chair to the man's left.

Quinn brought two more glasses of milk for Sarge and Julia. "Shepherd's pie?" Sarge asked as Quinn took the seat by Julia.

"Yes, it is," Julia said and reached for his plate to serve him.

"Finally, real food," the man muttered as he picked up a spoon and started to eat.

It was fairly quiet at the table for a while,

then after two more servings, Sarge sat back and pushed his plate away. "Now, that was good." Then he glanced at Quinn and frowned. "Who hurt you?"

He'd obviously just noticed the bandage. Seth explained quickly. "She has a cut, and they stitched it up. She made the casserole."

Sarge took that in. "You made that?"

"Yes, sir, I did." She nudged her own half-cleared plate away.

"Well, well," Sarge murmured.

"She's a good cook, isn't she?" Julia asked.

The man glanced at Julia and without missing a beat, his smile was gone. "Well, Missy, she's better than you and them vegetables you try to force me to eat." His eyes narrowed as he looked toward Seth and leaned closer. In a low voice, he said, "I know what to do. You fire her, then you hire the blonde lady. She's my kind of cook."

"Her name's Quinn, and as it happens, you're in luck," Seth said. "I just hired her this morning. So, she'll be cooking for you from now on."

Sarge glanced at Julia. "Now you won't be cooking any vegetables."

Julia took that good-naturedly. "Thank

goodness. We can concentrate on being friends without my cooking getting in the way."

Everything shifted in the blink of an eye as the older man slowly shook his head from side to side and sadness stamped his face. On a heavy sigh, Sarge said, "I don't have no friends. Not me, not one."

Seth spoke quickly, "Hey, come on, you have me and Ben and Jake and Libby and Julia and most of the town. You have a truck-load of friends."

When his eyes turned to Seth again, the sadness had deepened, and it hurt Seth when Sarge said in a dejected whisper, "But I don't have Maggie, I don't. She's gone, son, she's gone."

Seth felt his chest tighten, but before he could do anything, Quinn said, "Sarge, I'm new around here, and I don't know many people. I really don't have any friends, either. Do you think you could be my friend?"

There was total silence, then Sarge seemed to sit up a bit straighter and frowned at her. "I don't know your name, do I?"

"I'm Quinn. I'm from California."

Slowly Sarge's face cleared and a flicker

of a smile seemed to play around the corners of his mouth. "California?"

"Yes. Near Los Angeles. I'm sadly lacking in friends out here."

Seth saw the smile on Sarge's face grow. "Okay, Quinn from California, if it would help you out, I'd be honored to be your friend."

"I'd be honored to be your friend, too," she said.

He suddenly grinned at her. "Deal! Do you know if there's any chocolate chip cookies around here?"

Seth couldn't believe how easily Quinn had cut through the sadness and found Sarge's smile. "I found a whole bunch of them in the pantry in a pink box. How many would you like?" she asked.

"Bring the box, and I'll see about that," he said with a chuckle.

Julia stood and Sarge looked up at her as she asked, "How about you give me a chance to redeem myself at cards? Quinn can bring the cookies in for you?"

"As long as she remembers," he said as he pushed back from the table. Seth helped him to his feet, then Julia handed him his cane.

Seth helped him across the room, then Sarge spoke over his shoulder. "Don't forget those cookies, Quinn."

"They'll be there in five minutes," she called back. Seth went along with Sarge and Julia, helped set up the cards and matchsticks for the game, then headed out. When he stepped into the entry, Quinn was coming toward him with the pink box. "Oh, good," he said as he crossed to her by the cowhide bench and took the package from her. "Thank you for what you did for Sarge in there. He slips sometimes. He knows Maggie's gone, but I'm not sure he understands why. It just makes him so sad."

She shrugged slightly as she folded her arms over her chest. "I'm glad it helped. Besides, I got a new friend out of the deal," she said with a shadow of a smile.

"I'll take these in for Sarge and clean up in the kitchen. Go ahead and turn in for the night."

She sighed. "That sounds very nice, thank you. What time is good for breakfast in the morning?"

"Oh, don't worry about that. I'll be gone

most of the day, and Julia can take care of
Sarge's breakfast. Sleep in if you want to."

She looked down, and her smile looked
slightly forced. "Okay, then I'll see you when
I see you."

QUINN LAY IN BED, tired, yet wide-awake and
wishing she could sleep. Music that was
muffled by the walls had been playing for
a while, and she couldn't quite make out the
songs. She was bothered that Seth would be
gone again tomorrow. She'd have no chance
to talk to him, to get to know him better and
figure out if he could do justice to Michael's
work. Another day was lost to her. She realized the chances of Seth being the one listening to music were pretty good. It was worth a
trip out to the great room to check and maybe
pick up some snacks, too. If she was lucky,
maybe she and Seth could talk a bit.

She got out of bed, wishing she had a robe
with her, but the red sleep shirt she was wearing fell to above her knee. It would have to do.
Crossing to the door, she eased it open, and
at the same time the music stopped. Quickly
she stepped out onto the cold stone floor of
the hallway, hoping she could still catch Seth

if he was there. As she approached the arch and glanced into the room, she saw there were no lights on, and only embers glowed in the fireplace. The space felt empty.

Disappointed, she stepped down into the room to go to the pantry and find something to snack on. When she got there, she took four small bags of caramel popcorn and an unopened bag of marshmallows. Going back out into the shadows of the kitchen, she filled a glass with cold milk, then started back toward her room.

She'd almost made it to the archway when a lamp by the couch flashed on, startling her, and the bags in her hand fell to the floor at her feet. Thankfully, she held a grip on the glass of milk as her eyes adjusted to the sudden brilliance. Seth was standing by the couch, then he came toward her. Before she could retrieve the small bags, he was crouching to gather them up and standing to face her.

"I… I was just… I couldn't sleep, and I…" she stammered, totally caught off guard that she hadn't noticed him earlier. She took the bags from Seth and held them to her chest.

"I thought you'd be sound asleep by now," he said.

It took her a moment to get past her initial shock to realize she had what she'd hoped for. Seth was there. It was just the two of them. "Well, that was the plan. I heard the music earlier."

"I was playing some old songs that Sarge likes, and he wants them played on his equipment out here. Sorry if it was too loud."

"No, it was fine." When he glanced at the things she was holding," she said, "I needed a snack. Julia said I could help myself."

"Lots of sugar."

"It sure is. That's why it's called junk food, and why it tastes so good." Then she jumped in with both feet. "Do you want to share it?"

He took a moment before he said, "Thanks, but no thanks."

She wouldn't settle for him walking out right then, even if she was a bit embarrassed that he'd turned down her offer. "Darn. You do know it's illegal to eat junk food alone at midnight, don't you? Especially marshmallows and caramel corn. Can I tempt you to stay just awhile so I don't break the law?"

He was almost smiling, and she felt close to success, but he still hesitated. "I'm not much for eating sweets at any time of the day or night."

She had a feeling she might not get many chances to be with Seth alone, and she kept pushing, hoping he wouldn't get fed up and leave just to get away from her. "There's lots of cold milk in the fridge," she said as she passed him to go to the ottoman. She put the milk and bags down on the stretched leather, then she hurried back to the kitchen. "Just stay there and don't move," she said, then quickly poured another glass of milk. With it in hand, she went back to Seth still standing where she'd left him.

She handed the drink to him, and he took it. "I appreciate it, but I should get up to bed."

"Okay," she said. "I really didn't want to break the law. It goes against my nature, but I know it's late."

Unexpectedly, Seth stepped toward her. "That junk food law sounds serious, so maybe I could stick around for a few minutes."

CHAPTER FIVE

QUINN DIDN'T HESITATE to sit on the couch at the end closest to the lamp. She exhaled with relief when Seth sat down by her. "About that law, well, most people don't know it exists."

"I wonder why," he asked with a good-natured chuckle.

She shifted, tucking one foot under herself, then tugged at the hem of her sleep shirt in a vain attempt to get it over her knees. "Could you please open the marshmallows for me? I'll destroy the bag."

He put his glass of milk on the ottoman, then reached for the snack and managed to open it. He held it out to Quinn, and she slipped her hand inside and took a handful of marshmallows. "Thank you," she said. "Cold milk, salty caramel corn and marshmallows. Does life get any better than this?"

"Well, that's open for debate," he said.

"Then try it," she urged, and as she dropped

the fluffy white puffs of sugar into her lap, she reached for a bag of caramel corn and tore the top off. After popping a few pieces in her mouth, she chased them with a whole marshmallow and watched Seth's reaction. She loved it that his smile was growing. She'd like a talk with him to be easy and not forced.

"That's a lot of sugar, isn't it?" he asked as she reached for her milk.

After chewing, she took a drink, then finally answered. "I told you. This is perfect junk food. Try the popcorn. It's delicious."

He actually reached for a bag and tore it open. "Here's to junk," he said as he took out a couple of kernels and put them in his mouth.

"Drink some milk with it," Quinn said. "That's a great combination, the salty and the sweet and the milk."

He reached for his glass, took a long drink, then sighed. "Okay, I admit the milk is great, but I'm not touching one of those marshmallows."

"Words no other human being has ever said," she murmured.

He shook his head ruefully. "You either haven't been listening or haven't been around the right people."

She ate some more caramel corn followed by another marshmallow. "So, so good," she said after another drink of milk.

"I don't know how you'll sleep after that stuff."

She leaned forward to put her almost-empty milk glass down on the ottoman, then she rested her hands on her bare knees. There was a single marshmallow in her lap. "I'm already getting a bit sleepy."

He looked genuinely surprised. "You're kidding?"

"No. When I can't sleep, I binge on sugar, and I get tired. That's why I came out here to raid your pantry." She studied him for a moment. "I'm sorry I kept you up. I just…" She shrugged. "Thanks for the company."

"You're welcome," he murmured and twisted the popcorn bag shut before he tossed it over to her. It landed in her lap with the lone marshmallow. "That's all yours." Seth stood, obviously ready to leave without her finding out anything about him, except that he seemed good-natured and he didn't like marshmallows. Nothing that would help her at all later on.

She looked up at him. "Before you go, is there a television I can use?"

"No. Sarge always said it's better to speak with real people instead of watching actors talking to each other with words someone else wrote for them."

She tried to keep him talking. "Okay, well, if it was warmer and there weren't any wild animals lurking in the shadows, I'd go outside and just enjoy the stars and the moon. The sky looks beautiful from my bedroom window."

"I can't promise warmth, but I promise you it will be worth your while in another week or so to go out to moon watch."

She cocked her head to one side. "I thought there wasn't any eclipse coming soon."

"There isn't. But there's going to be a full moon, a super moon actually. It's usually called a harvest moon in October. But Sarge and Maggie called it their Wishing Moon. Maggie always made a wish on it for the boys in the house. She'd never say what she wished for, but she insisted the wishes would come true."

"That's so romantic," Quinn said on a sigh. "I like the idea of a Wishing Moon."

His smile was almost wistful when he said, "Maggie would come back with Sarge, walk in the house and announce she'd made the wishes for her boys. She seemed totally sure that those wishes would become reality."

She was wishing he'd sit back down, but she was afraid if she asked him to, he'd take that as a cue to leave. "I wonder if they did?" she asked, fascinated by the idea of wishing on the moon.

"We'll never know, because she never shared what she wished for. But watching the heavens from here is special. We're not only directly in the perfect path of eclipses, but we have the bonus of clear views of rising super moons and the stars and constellations. They're all spectacular in their own way."

"You're really into astronomy, aren't you?"

"No, but I have a terrific app that's flawless at tracking the heavens around here. It gives information about the moon stages and folklore about the moon and stars."

Quinn stopped breathing for a moment. He had an app? She knew his company didn't do that. They were dedicated to perfecting cybersecurity. She sat forward, shifting to put her feet on the floor, and tipped her head back to look up at him. She had to keep calm and not push. "Julia said something about you being a genius in computer technology. But I thought she said you work in security stuff."

He nodded. "We develop cybersecurity on the international corporate level."

She sat straighter. "Then that app isn't one of yours?"

"Legally it is, but we didn't set out to develop it. It came to us from a third party who offered it to us with a couple of glitches they couldn't iron out. Once we ran it, we agreed to take it on. We made it operable and covered the joint marketing."

Quinn wanted to jump up and down and cheer at what he'd just told her, but she made herself sit very still. "You must have been impressed by it."

"We were. It was a real risk that happened to pay off. Something like that hardly ever works."

She was so close. "But it could happen again," she managed to say nonchalantly, then realized she was kneading the last marshmallow in her hand as if it were a stress ball.

He shrugged. "Sure. I never say never about anything."

The impact of his simple statement hit Quinn and she thought she might cry. Maybe she'd done the right thing after all, picked the right company and the right man and maybe this was all going to work out. The idea of an actual victory was so stunning, validating all that she'd done so far. She felt as if it was within reach.

She looked down at the distorted marshmallow in her grip. "Messy," she said softly, then picked up her glass. She drank the last of the milk, dropped the ruined marshmallow into the glass and slowly stood, trying to kill an urge to hug Seth for what he'd just told her. But she quietly went around him as he stood back to give her room to go to the kitchen.

When she got to the double sinks, Seth was there, putting his glass down by hers on the counter.

While Quinn rinsed both glasses and put them in the dishwasher, she was trying to make her heartbeat slow to a more normal rhythm. She had to think and be very careful. She had to plan her next step, a time when they could talk more and she could try to bring up his company and what they did or didn't do. "I think I'm ready to sleep now," she said as she turned to Seth. "Thanks again."

"Glad I stayed," he said through the kitchen shadows and headed back across the room.

Quinn went with him, and they parted in the foyer. He took the stairs up to the second story, and she headed to the guest room.

Once inside, she brushed her teeth, then climbed into bed. She was still wound up, thoughts flying through her mind about where to go from here on out. As she reached to turn off the sidelight on the nightstand, a soft knock sounded on her door. "Come in," she said as she pushed herself back against the pillows piled at the headboard.

The door opened, and she was surprised when Seth stepped inside. "Sorry, but I thought you might need these." He was holding the bag of marshmallows and the remaining bags of caramel corn and crossed to hand them to her.

"Thank you," she said as he dropped them in her lap. When she glanced up at Seth, he was looking at the picture of her and Michael she had propped against the lamp base.

He surprised her when he said, "Santa Monica Pier."

"How do you know that?"

"The Ferris wheel in the distance. That's iconic. I was there a couple of years ago, and the sun had a golden glow. It's the only place I've noticed that." He exhaled as he looked back at her, hesitated, then said, "I'll let you get to sleep while the sugar's working. Good night," he said and left.

"Good night," she said as the door closed after him.

After she heard the door to his office open and close, silence blanketed the house. But she'd lost the edge that would've helped her get to sleep. She hesitated at eating more marshmallows, then gave up and reached for the bag when another knock sounded. She called, "Come in," and was surprised to see Julia this time.

"Just checking to make sure everything's okay," the nurse said as she came over to the bed.

"Yes, fine." When Julia looked at the bag of marshmallows in her lap, Quinn explained about her encounter with Seth and held the bag out to Julia. "Do you want one?"

"Oh, no thanks."

"Can I ask you something?"

"Sure," Julia said, coming closer.

"Is Seth really as nice as he seems to be?"

The other woman smiled and nodded. "He's a good guy, loves Sarge and would do anything for him. Jake and Ben would do anything for Sarge, too." There was a muffled thud. Quinn looked around, but Julia said, "It's okay. It's Seth. He's in his exercise room off the office. Sometimes he's in there in the middle of the night and those weights clang."

Quinn had a flash of Seth by the car, shirtless. She'd thought he looked strong, which didn't seem to jibe with a sedentary profession like computer coding. Now she knew how he got those muscles.

Julia was talking to her and she caught the last of her question. "…you and your husband?"

She was looking at the picture by the lamp, the way Seth had. "Yes, me and Michael."

"Quinn, Seth told me about Michael, and I'm so sorry. I can't pretend to know what you've gone through, but if you ever need to talk or anything, I'm here."

That offer touched Quinn. "Thank you so much." Julia glanced at the photo again, then back to Quinn with a sad smile. "That's truly a wonderful picture."

"It was taken just before we found out about his leukemia," she said softly, surprised she'd added that, and that the pain, which was always with her, didn't deepen. She was thankful.

Julia cleared her throat softly, then stood. "I need to get back to Sarge," she said. "I hope you can get some sleep."

Quinn hoped so, too.

IT WAS TEN minutes past seven a couple days later, when Quinn stepped outside into the icy morning air with Seth. He was wearing a black Western hat along with his denim jacket, jeans and boots. After two days with Seth gone from dawn until dusk, he'd come to her bedroom door last night and asked her about going into town today. She'd jumped at the chance to get her bandage changed, and to finally meet Henry Lodge and get going on her car repairs. She also would have some alone time with Seth on the ride.

She was wearing the blue jacket Daniel had loaned her with a navy pullover and had skimmed her hair up in a ponytail. Seth, wearing his leather jacket over a red thermal along with faded jeans and scuffed boots, continued to look like a ranch hand, especially when he was wearing the black Stetson. With his jaw showing the shadow of a beard and his hair carelessly combed back, there were no hints of the billionaire businessman in his appearance. She was kind of glad there wasn't. Seth seemed relatable, not like the other executives she'd met. She felt he listened when she spoke. She was looking forward to their drive together.

He started up the old red truck, then turned more toward her, resting his left forearm on the top of the steering wheel. "We'll go see Henry, then stop by the clinic. After that, I need to do a few things."

"I wish I could get the stitches out, but it's too early. A new bandage would be a huge help, though, and I really want to talk to Henry about my car."

"Then let's go," Seth said as he put the truck in gear, flipped on the heater and swung around to drive toward the gates. When they got to the barriers, and were waiting for them to open, Seth brought up something Quinn couldn't believe she hadn't even thought about. "We need to talk about your salary."

She wouldn't take any pay from him, no matter what, but saying she didn't want any wouldn't work, either. Better just to put it off. "We can talk about it later."

He drove out onto the county road and headed east. "Now's as good a time as any." He went on to lay out what he'd pay her. "That's weekly, plus room and board."

She thought that from the amount he offered it would be monthly. "I don't know. That seems too much."

"It's worth it to me to have Julia freed up to concentrate on Sarge. She has a cooking compulsion, and she's good at it, despite Sarge's comments, but that's not part of her job description."

Quinn didn't argue. She just wouldn't take his money. By the time she left, win or lose, she would be in debt to him forever for all his kindnesses. He was a good man, and it bothered her deceiving him on any level. As soon as she could possibly lay out the truth, she'd do it, and hope and pray he wouldn't be angry about what she'd done.

As they got closer to the curve, Quinn felt

herself tensing. "So, what does Sarge do on the land down here?" she asked, not really interested but needing to distract herself.

"Nothing lately, but it used to be mostly cattle grazing," Seth said. He told her about the original entrance to the ranch and about a mess hall and bunkhouse past the old cabin, but she couldn't focus on his words when the blind curve came up. She reflexively closed her eyes tightly, then Seth tapped the horn, startling her, and she took a sharp breath but kept her eyes shut.

A moment later, Seth said, "You can open your eyes now. We're almost to the highway."

She felt so embarrassed he'd noticed what she'd done, but when she looked at him, his attention was on the road in front of them. She grabbed at some general subject to talk about. "It must take forever to see the whole ranch."

He slipped right into the conversation without another mention of her reaction to the accident site. "It's worth the trek. Once the camp's up and running, the boys can ride, hike, fish and swim without having to leave the ranch at all."

He was slowing for the highway when she

said, "You're going to have some very happy campers."

There was a rough chuckle at her intended pun. "That's the plan."

"I don't know anyone, kid or adult, who wouldn't love to ride around here." Quinn exhaled, some of the tension leaving her. "The sense of freedom must be wonderful."

"Do you ride?" Seth asked as he drove onto the highway heading south.

"Yes, but not lately." She and Michael had gone riding most weekends until he got too sick. "I really love it, though."

"When you're up to it, how about letting me show you some of the ranch on horseback?"

She caught herself before she automatically declined his offer. The truth was she'd love to go with him. Plus, if she went riding with Seth, they'd be together one-on-one. There would be no chances for interruptions. That could be a huge help to her in trying to figure him out. "I'd love to go for a ride when you have time."

He nodded. "We'll do it soon"

Quinn looked away from Seth and out at the hints of yellow and pink lingering in the early morning sky. When she inhaled, she caught the scent of pine and freshly turned earth. The wide-open highway had no other cars anywhere in sight. "It's so nice here," she said.

"It seemed like paradise to me when I first got here."

She liked this kind of conversation, with just the two of them, but with no need to face each other. It seemed easier to say what she had to not facing him, to think about what she was doing and why she was doing it—for Michael. "Where did you come from before you arrived here?"

"A lot of places," he said vaguely. "I was assigned here when I was fifteen, and three years later, I left for college and ended up in Seattle. Where were you before Pasadena?"

That was easy to answer. "I was born in San Diego, then my dad got work in the LA area, so we moved there when I was in third grade. I went back to San Diego for college. Then Michael and I moved up to Pasadena."

"What brought you up here?"

She was as vague with her answer to that as he'd been with his answer to where he'd been before coming to the ranch. "I was curious about what this area was really like, and I was between substitute teaching jobs." That was true.

He cast her a quick glance. "So, you just picked up and came?"

"It was a split-second sort of thing. I hadn't even thought about coming here until six or seven days ago."

He kept his eyes on the road as he spoke. "And you didn't know anyone around here before you came?"

"Nope. My parents are in Florida and my sisters are in Alabama and Texas. And I'm here. I mean, Pasadena's been my home since…since Michael and I got married. He was from New York, but he came to California for college on a full scholarship." She didn't know why she'd said that to Seth, but she added, "He was really smart. He was in the world you're in, technology, computers. I honestly never fully understood what he did."

Seth asked, "Really? What was his specialty?"

There it was, sitting right in her lap. "Mostly coding."

CHAPTER SIX

THAT WAS THE last thing Seth had expected. "Who did he work with?"

"He didn't. I mean, he received his graduate degree, but he was diagnosed with leukemia around the same time. He had three companies interested in him."

Some of his best people had been recruited straight out of college. "He must have been good talent."

"He was. He…he loved what he did." He heard her exhale. "It meant everything to him." Then she asked, "Is that the way it is with you?"

He told her the truth. "Yes, for a long time. But I'm working on prioritizing my life differently."

"We all have to do that, don't we?"

"We should, but some of us take longer to do it." He pulled back, realizing he'd gotten into the tough subject of his life. Now that life, in a small measure, included Quinn Lake. He'd fought the attraction he felt around her, partly because he'd assumed at first that she was married, and partly because his choices in the field of romance had been painfully wrong in the past.

But Quinn seemed unique and caring. She was a soft person in a way, with none of the sharp edges he'd seen in any of the other women who'd come and gone, like Allie. He'd run up against a lot of sharp edges in his life, and he was tired of them. But Quinn seemed different, beyond being very attractive. He wouldn't forget how she helped Sarge the other night.

"Thanks again for asking Sarge to be your friend."

"I'm glad he accepted." She exhaled softly. "It's hard when you really love someone and then they're taken away. It's not a…an easy thing to comprehend, much less accept. I can see he misses his wife."

Seth could hear the loneliness in Quinn's voice. "It's been hard for him, and his illness makes it all that much harder. Maybe when he gets to the point of not remembering, maybe then he won't get so sad. I'd hate him to get there, but maybe later on it'd be a blessing to forget."

"You know, no matter what happens with him, I don't believe he'll ever not remember his wife. She'll always be there in some way, even if it's in his dreams."

He wondered if that made loving again even possible. He sure didn't think Sarge, if he were healthy, would ever have looked for love again. But Quinn was twenty-seven, with a long life ahead of her to remember. He stopped that line of thinking and said, "Well, I hope the camp can fill some of the emptiness for him, and bring back good memories of Maggie."

"Oh, I think it will be a very good thing for him," she said as if remembering something not quite sad, but hard to think about. "It'll give him a reason to get up in the morning and to just be here."

Seth wondered what reason Quinn had to get up in the morning after her loss. "That's what I'm hoping for," he said as he regripped the steering wheel and stared down the highway ahead of them.

Thankfully, Quinn asked, "It snows around here this time of year, doesn't it?"

Snow he could talk about, and he would. "We had snow in early August the first year I came here. Then there was three feet of snow on my last day at the ranch before I headed to college."

"When was that?"

"Fifteen years ago."

"Wow," she said. "Can I ask why you didn't come back here after college?"

"I took an offer from a great company in Seattle. Then that work-priority thing set in with a vengeance when I started my own company. My business became my life for almost eight years. But I came back for visits on Christmas or birthdays when Jake and Ben would be here, too. As my company took off, I really got tied down by it."

He wouldn't mention Maggie passing nearly six years ago, and how he'd tried to show up more often after that but had failed miserably by giving in to the pressures of work. "The last time we were all here before Sarge's accident was just over two years ago."

He'd come back to the ranch with Jake and Ben for support after his messy break-up with Allie. He'd never have guessed she would turn from being sweet to vindictive when he'd realized their relationship wasn't what he was looking for. There had been too many lies, too many demands that he couldn't ignore. The break-up had been ugly, with her threatening to take "their story" to the press. He had no idea what story she was talking about, but she hinted at exposing who he "really" was. He had no idea what she meant, but he'd given in and paid her for what she called "her time lost while he'd used her." Seth had had no heart to fight, and she walked away with money, enough to make her smile and leave quietly. He hadn't been open to a relationship since. He might be a genius in technology, but he sure didn't have a clue how to deal with women. "Since then I'd been calling Sarge to keep in touch. We had no idea he'd almost completely shut down the ranch, until his accident," he continued.

Quinn sighed softly. "I'm sure Sarge really appreciated you keeping in contact. Even a phone call keeps the loneliness at bay…at least for a while."

When he glanced at her, she was staring down at her hands clasped in her lap. He knew she was talking about herself again. The picture of Quinn and her husband on the nightstand had shown them glowing with happiness that he doubted had anything to do with the golden California sun.

"Sarge isn't going to be here alone anymore," he said. "I just hope I can make the camp how he and Maggie dreamed it would be. They wanted a place where the troubled kids could come for a time out of their lives. To offer healing, if they could. They wanted to keep giving and helping and caring." He paused, then said, "I just hope I'm able to do that for Sarge."

"You will," she said as if she knew that for certain. "You love him, and I'm sure you felt the same way about Maggie. That makes up for so much. You're doing it to make Sarge happy while he can enjoy it. You understand him."

"Sarge always understood us, gave us what we needed. Like the way he used horses, assigning each of us a ride, and putting the care of the horse in our hands during our time at the ranch. He wanted us to learn responsibility."

"Very smart, and horses are great therapy for kids."

"He did what he could to give us all the

tools to survive in the system when we left here."

"How bad is it in foster care?" she asked.

He wouldn't go into his life before the ranch. Saying what he went through out loud was something he avoided completely. No one wanted to know about a little boy who learned how to not cry by pushing at his nose. A bloody nose was better than letting the other kids see him sobbing. No one wanted a kid who had to think about what he was going to say so no one got mad at him. That was gone, and he wished the memories were gone, too. But they had a way of rearing at the worst times.

He pushed back his thoughts and settled for saying, "The caseworkers try, they really do, but they have heavy caseloads. The kids either have no parents or if they do, they're totally absentee or abusive or useless or locked up. It can be pretty bad. Being in foster care is something you can't understand until you've gone through it."

"Can I ask you why you were in foster care?"

Her simple inquiry brought back more of the past. He remembered thinking he'd never had a mother or father, until a case worker had told him when he was six that everyone did. But he knew he didn't, and he thought he had to be pretty awful to be the only one who'd never had parents. It wasn't until he was ten when one of his counselors had mentioned they'd died in a car accident. He'd been almost been happy to hear that.

"My parents went out for their anniversary. I was told it was snowing and there was an accident. I was about three and was with a babysitter. Child Protection searched for family members to take me, but there wasn't anyone, so I became a kid of the system until I turned eighteen. My real life started the moment I set foot on the ranch, although I didn't know that right away."

"When did you figure it out?"

It was odd that he found telling Quinn about his past was almost easy for him. "It was rough at first, until I realized no one at the ranch was my enemy. Sarge laid down the rules, but they were fair, even the riding rules."

"What were they?"

"Every boy had to ride, respect and care for their horse. I remember the day he introduced me to Chuckie, an old gelding who had one speed—slow. At first, it went well, riding around the training ring, and I felt pretty brave. Then a snake slithered out of nowhere to cut right in front of us. Chuckie turned from old and plodding into a mass of fear and muscle. I think he was trying to jump the fence but didn't make it and plowed right through the rails."

He could almost hear the grimace in her voice when she said, "I'm guessing it ended badly?"

He actually smiled about the incident. "The only blessing was it ended quickly, leaving me with a sprained wrist and scrapes." He was almost living that memory while he told Quinn, and it wasn't all bad. "I thought I'd get time off. But as soon as Sarge could, he got me back up on Chuckie.

"Jake and Ben and I became friends and started riding all over the ranch together. Sarge told me later that going out in the world meant ups and downs, and he never wanted me to stay down for too long."

"A wise man."

"And opinionated," he said with a low chuckle.

"I can tell he understood you, got you on the right path. And you have to admit, he's still pretty opinionated. I mean, he tried to get you to fire Julia right in front of her."

Seth was relieved that he'd found his smile talking about what had been trauma at the time, and that he was actually grateful on some level that it happened. It had centered him more, and he realized that right about that time was when he really began to admire Sarge. "Yes, he understood me more than I understood myself and probably still does."

"Did he and his wife have children of their own?"

Seth saw a sign announcing Eclipse five miles ahead. "No, they didn't."

"That's too bad. Sarge would've made a great dad."

The town was starting to come into view when Seth spoke a truth. "He *is* a great dad. He's my father. He was from day one. For Jake and Ben, it was the same. He's always been there for us."

Quinn was quiet for a long moment, then asked, "Do you believe in some greater plan behind your life, or do you think it's all just crazy coincidences and luck?"

He shrugged. "I never thought about it."

"I've thought about why we get to where we are, and I think this was all planned for Sarge and his wife to find what they wanted—a way to become parents. Then you came here, and they gave you what you needed—to belong and have someone who cared about you, and who still cares. As my mother used to say, you have someone in your life who always smiles when they see you."

Her words hung between them, and he felt as if he'd been given a piece of a puzzle to his life he'd never been able to find on his own—why he'd ended up on the ranch all those years ago. He remembered Maggie smiling when she'd see him. Sarge didn't quite smile all the time, but he always looked happy when Seth was there. "Sarge would try to be stern with us, but there was always that kindness behind what he did. I sure remember that."

"Memories mean so much. It's up to us to never forget to remember, despite what's going on in the present."

Seth knew Quinn was speaking about Michael. Memories were all she and Sarge had left. "I guess so." He had so many good memories of Sarge and Maggie, and he wanted as many more as he could of Sarge before they were all he had. "We're almost to Henry's," he said as they approached a tall red, white and blue sign towering over the highway. Henry's Auto Care & Restoration. He swung off onto the frontage road going south, then took the first right turn.

Henry's place came into view, a long cement block building with a hundred feet of paved parking between it and the road. Strong commercial fencing protected the sprawling storage yard behind it and blocked its contents from sight. Seth drove off the road and across the pavement. Over by the entrance was the tow truck beside Henry's '66 red Mustang. The car looked perfect, probably as it had when it rolled off the assembly line years ago.

"That is an amazing car," Quinn said.

"It's all Henry's handiwork." He shut off the truck, and Quinn was out before he'd taken the key from the ignition.

When Seth caught up to her, she was cupping her hands around her eyes to look through the driver's side window of the Mustang. "Original upholstery," she said with the same awe as someone uttering, *An authentic Rembrandt.*

Seth smiled at her. "I take it you'd give the car an eleven on a scale of one to ten?"

She turned to him, her blue eyes wide. "Eleven? No, it's at least a twenty." Then she colored slightly. "Okay, I know I get excited over beautiful vintage cars."

This banter was a relief after their conversation in the truck. "So, you're a gearhead?" he teased.

"Ah, that would be a no to the tenth power, because that would mean I could actually rebuild the workings and love doing it. I can't and don't. I'm just a fan. Once, I got to sit in a '56 Thunderbird convertible that had been owned by a Hollywood star. It was all original, except for a red pinstripe pattern on the top of the engine's hood."

"I've seen that T-Bird," someone said in a deep voice.

They turned, and Henry was sauntering over to the two of them. He was average height, sturdy, with his dark brown hair caught back from his deeply tanned face in a single braid that fell halfway down his back. Wearing grease-stained gray coveralls, he grinned from ear to ear and wiped his hands on a rag as he spoke to Quinn. "Where did you see the T-Bird?"

"At a San Diego rally about four years ago. Where did you see it?"

"Bakersfield, a year ago. The guy had just bought it from that actor's estate and had it on a flatbed. He wouldn't let it touch the ground." He shook his head with obvious disbelief. "He'd never even driven it."

"What a waste," Quinn said.

"Exactly." Henry stepped closer, offering his hand to Seth. "Good to see you back in these parts again." The handshake turned into a guy hug. Then Henry's attention quickly went back to Quinn as he stuffed the rag in his coverall pocket. "I hope you approve of my work, Ma'am."

"Quinn, please, and I approve," she said with a smile.

He motioned to the building. "Come on inside where it's warmer, and we'll talk about your Beetle."

Within minutes, they were in Henry's office, sitting across from him at a heavy wooden desk. Seth looked around. "This has really been upgraded. Nice."

"Gar Vega, my wife's cousin in Cody, gave me a good deal on the work." With that, Henry turned his attention to Quinn again. "How long have you had the Beetle?"

Quinn shrugged. "My husband had her since high school, and we drove her ever since we met in college."

Now Seth finally understood why the car was so important to Quinn. "You never wanted to do a restoration?" Henry asked.

"We decided against it." Seth noticed her touch the gold band on her finger, as if talking about Michael was hard for her. She obviously still loved him. Then she put her right hand over her left in her lap. "As stupid as it sounds, I just want her back the way she was before the accident."

Henry waved that off with a flick of his hand. "That's not stupid at all. I understand being attached to her."

Seth looked away from Quinn and cut into the conversation. "How do you people get to the place that you assign your car a gender?"

Henry almost rolled his eyes at that. "Simply put, it's a feeling some people get when they sit in a car for the first time." He shifted his chair to look more directly at Quinn. "I'll get her back to the way she looked, nothing more, nothing less. The big question is, do you want your parts to be salvaged originals or new aftermarket?"

Seth asked Henry, "If it were your car, what would you choose for parts?"

"I'm like most enthusiasts of any older car. I prefer salvaged. I work with them all the time."

"Okay, use them," he said.

"They take a lot of time to find, don't they?" Quinn asked.

"Usually, but after I saw the modifications on the engine, I thought you might want originals for her. I contacted a dealer near Dallas who specializes in pre-seventy Beetles. He has everything she'll need right now. He's just waiting for me to call to have them shipped. It won't affect the timeline by very much."

Quinn finally nodded. "Okay, that would be good. Thank you."

Henry nodded and stood. "Now, I'm sorry I've gotta go. I have an appointment out at the Cochran spread in half an hour for a tractor repair."

Seth stood, too. "We're on our way to see Boone at the clinic."

Henry reached for a heavy jacket on a hook

by the desk and put it on over his coveralls as he studied Quinn. "I've got to say, except for that bandage, you don't look too bad for going off-roading in her. Do you have any more questions?"

"What's the timeline?" she asked.

"Three weeks, if we're lucky. I'll put in the order on my way to Cochran's."

"Thank you," Quinn said and quietly walked back outside with the two men.

Henry slipped into his Mustang as he spoke to Seth. "I like the hat. It looks like the ones Sarge always wore."

"It is Sarge's. He gave it to me."

Henry grinned and gave Seth a thumbs-up. "Wow, I'm impressed. How about you two meeting me for lunch around noon, if you're still here?"

Seth looked at Quinn. "How about it?"

"That would be great. I'd love to hear about the history of your Mustang," she said to Henry.

He smiled up at her. "I'd be glad to fill you in on him."

QUINN TURNED TO get into the old truck, just hoping her disappointment wasn't showing on her face. She wasn't sure what she'd been thinking would be the timeline to get the car back, but she obviously hadn't considered it realistically at all. Three weeks, minimum. It hit her like a ton of bricks that she would probably be right where she was for close to a month.

While they headed back toward the highway, Quinn was struggling with the idea that she had to make her extended stay work. She was slowly putting together her plan, thankful for having the opportunity to put a few truths about Michael out there for Seth, no matter how hard it was to bring up the past. Add to that Seth actually taking on an app before with great success and she was on the right track. Now was not the time to panic.

She felt uncomfortable about Seth paying more for the original parts, but he'd said it was his fault. She didn't know about that, but it eased her mind a bit. Maybe her actions during the waiting period—sticking to her plan to help Sarge and be a good housekeeper—would help mitigate things with Seth when she finally opened up about her reason for being on the county road that day.

She had just started to feel settled when she was yanked back to hard reality.

"We'll go to the clinic first," Seth was saying. "Then we'll hit Garret's General Store before we meet up with Henry."

Quinn almost groaned but stopped herself. The general store was owned by the cowboy in the crazy outfit who'd supposedly sent her out to interview for the job. If she walked in there with Seth, one way or another, the truth—that she'd been looking for the ranch and not for a job—would come out. The timing was awful. "What do you need at the general store?"

"Warm boots and some extra winter clothes."

All she could do was not go into the store with Seth, so the owner wouldn't put two and two together too easily. She'd excuse herself to play tourist and go window-shopping so she could keep out of sight until Seth was done. She glanced up as he turned off the highway and merged onto Clayton Drive. Their pace slowed almost to a crawl behind a line of leisurely drivers. Just before Garret's General Store, he turned left onto Wylie Way for the clinic.

When they walked out of the clinic twenty minutes later, Quinn's impromptu visit with Daniel, not Boone, was a blur. All that stood out was the good news she could finally wash her hair the old-fashioned way and she didn't need to use a bandage any longer. She was smiling about that until they were back in the truck, turning onto the main street to park right in front of the general store. Spotting a chocolate specialty shop two doors past it, she decided that would be her target.

Undoing her seat belt, she was ready to get out and disappear, but Quinn didn't even get to the door handle before her plan fell apart completely. There was a knock on the driver's window. When she glanced in that direction, she froze. Farley Garret, with his thinning gray hair, weathered face and wearing an over-the-top red silk Western shirt with fringes all over it, was looking into the truck cab. Without any superpower ability to become invisible, Quinn prepared herself for that moment when everything was over.

Seth rolled down his window. "Hey, there, Farley."

"Hey, right back at ya'." He cocked his head

to one side, studying Seth. "Does Sarge know you're wearing that?"

"Yes, he gave it to me."

Farley grinned. "It's about time." Then he glanced past Seth and saw Quinn. "Well, hello there, darlin'. Heard that Seth ran into a pretty lady but didn't know it was you." His eyes narrowed on her stitches. "You okay? You look pale."

She actually felt lightheaded at the moment. "It's just a cut, but it's healing."

"Well, I'm sure sorry I was the one to send you into that mess. It seems Seth ain't no smooth operator." He added an unneeded sly wink to that statement.

Her mind raced, then she figured a good offense was better than waiting for the first blow to hit her. "Well, I think he's being very nice about everything. He even hired me as his housekeeper."

"Great news." Farley looked away from her to Seth. "So you don't need me to send out anyone?"

"No, not anymore."

"Well, you treat her well, you hear."

Maybe she finally had received a break. Farley Garret didn't seem to be a man bent on giving details or asking for them. "That's the plan," Seth said. "Now, I need some warm boots."

"I've got you covered." Farley stepped back when Seth opened the door to get out. "I sure miss Sarge coming into town and visiting over coffee by the stove in the back. You tell him hey from me, okay?"

"I sure will," Seth said as he closed the door.

Farley smiled in at Quinn through the open window. "You come on back and see me, too, you hear, darlin'?"

"Yes, I will," she said, thankful when both men turned and headed up the steps to the raised walkway. When they were inside, Quinn finally let herself exhale. She hoped, with her being out of sight, she would be out of mind for both men. She figured not following them inside to see what was being said was safer to avoid Farley's questions completely.

Closing her eyes, Quinn tried to just breathe evenly as she fingered the warm smoothness of her wedding band. If she managed to slip past this time, she promised herself that she'd stay out at the ranch and as far away from Farley as she could. As soon as her stitches were removed, she had no reason to come into town again.

Seth was in the store for half an hour before Quinn looked up and saw him stepping out onto the raised walkway. He had two shoeboxes and a large bag with him. He came down the steps and went around to get inside the truck. "That was fast. I'm impressed," she said as he put the bag and shoeboxes on the seat between them.

"I don't like shopping, so it's easy to move fast," he said as he started the truck. He glanced at her, and he didn't look pleased to be done, or pleased at what he'd bought.

"He didn't have what you wanted?" she asked. He tapped the top of two boxes on the bench seat between them, one black-and-yellow hardboard, the other larger and covered in stretched suede. "Half and half," he said.

He still looked off and her stomach knotted at the thought that he might've found out everything. But Farley didn't seem to be a gossip. "What does that mean?"

"I found the boots I needed, then Farley offered me some dress boots he swore I needed, too. They're made out of some special leather with snakeskin in the stitching and welting. I swear, Farley could sell fleas to a dog."

He was bothered that he'd spend too much money? "You can always return them, you know."

Seth shrugged, put the truck in gear, backed out onto the street and headed north. "I'll think about it."

The traffic was slow as they headed north. "We're on our own for lunch. Henry's stuck on the tractor repair. There's a diner up ahead, Over the Moon Burgers, that has great food, or we can go to the restaurant at the Far Away & Back dude ranch. Terrific barbeque."

She felt off balance with the way Seth was acting. Not that he was being rude, but he wasn't the same. His jaw looked tight. "Whichever's closest," she said, wanting to get out of the truck and face Seth. If something was wrong, she wanted to know what.

CHAPTER SEVEN

WHEN QUINN WALKED into Over the Moon Burgers with Seth, she found an eclectic mixture of the Old West, the 1950s and the heavens. The tables and chairs were retro metal and plastic, with red-checked tablecloths and randomly patterned cushions. Rough plank walls held pictures in plain frames, half of them sepia-toned shots of cowboys, cattle and horses. The other half were photos of the moon and sun in various stages of eclipse.

A petite lady in jeans, a red-checked Western shirt and with feathered gray hair came out from behind the long lunch counter to their left. "Seth Reagan! It is so good to see you back here."

"Good to see you, too, Elaine," he said, taking off his hat.

She gave him a quick hug, then stood back. "You be sure to give Sarge my love? I really miss him."

"I will."

She turned her attention to Quinn and frowned at the exposed stitches. "So, you're the lady Seth drove off the road?"

"I… Well, he—" Quinn was cut off by the woman.

"I know. It was the blind curve and the mountain winds blowing through. That combination is bad."

Quinn shifted the conversation. "Seth told me that your food's terrific."

"He should know. He started here in prep and cooking, and he was a pretty good server. He also redid my bookkeeping system that I still use."

"He forgot to mention all of that."

Elaine patted Seth on his shoulder, seemingly oblivious to a tinge of embarrassment on his face. "He's too modest. Now, you two sit wherever you want, and I'll be right with you."

Moments later, they were settled at a table in a far corner of the almost-empty dining area. Quinn had her back to the wall, with a view of the restaurant ahead and the town outside the windows to her left. Seth took the chair across from her.

When Elaine came over and laid menus in front of them, Seth never even looked at his. "I'll have the usual," he said.

Elaine smiled at him. "You bet, but the lady might need a few minutes."

"What's his usual?" Quinn asked her.

"Double burger with everything plus fries and coffee."

"Okay. I'll take a single burger with no onions, fruit instead of fries and hot tea, if you have some."

"I have black or green, and from my personal stash, chamomile or mint."

"Chamomile sounds wonderful." When Elaine left with their orders, Quinn looked over at Seth and couldn't resist saying, "You told me all you can cook is eggs and bacon."

He replied without a hint of a smile, "Honestly, I only cooked for a couple of shifts before Elaine put me in the office doing her daily accounting. The closest she let me get to food after that was when I filled in the one time a server didn't show up."

"You were that bad as a cook?"

SETH DIDN'T WANT to talk about his lack of cooking skills. He didn't want to talk about anything except what he'd learned from Farley in the store. But he wasn't sure how to broach the subject. "Let's just say, I didn't eat anything I made, except the eggs and bacon or cold sandwiches." He put his hat crown-down on the bench beside him.

"Good to know," she murmured. Elaine came with their drinks and set a mug and a small basket with some foil packets of tea bags in front of Quinn.

"It's nice to have another tea drinker around here," Elaine said.

Quinn's smile looked a bit forced to Seth, but the waitress didn't seem to notice as she promised their food would be out soon, then left. Quinn stared down at her mug of steaming water. "Is something wrong?" she asked as she looked back at him.

"What could be wrong?" he countered. Except that she'd lied to him. Plain and simple. And he didn't know exactly how to deal with it, but he had to get this over with.

He watched her pick up one of the foil packets and tear it open. "I don't know," she said just above a whisper.

He looked away from her, down into his coffee mug, then before he could tell her exactly what was wrong, he heard a familiar voice coming from across the restaurant. "Hey, Seth, there you are!"

He turned to see Dr. Boone Williams striding across to their table. The man looked put together as always, in jeans and a thigh-length leather jacket over a chambray shirt. With his dark hair slightly spiked around his clean-shaven face, he was smiling broadly as Seth put his mug down and stood. The doctor's timing couldn't be worse.

"This is a surprise," Seth said as Boone got to their table.

Boone took a chair from a nearby table and put it at the end of theirs between Seth and Quinn. He took off his coat, hung it over the back of his chair, then sat down and looked at Quinn. "So, you're Quinn?"

Seth could tell the man hadn't lost any of his great bedside manner by the way Quinn smiled at him right away. "Yes, Quinn Lake."

"Good to meet you, Quinn Lake. I'm Dr. Boone Williams. I answer to Boone, Doc, or Doc B. Pick your favorite."

"Doc sounds good."

Seth cut in, "You were looking for me, Boone?"

"Yeah. I was at Farley's to pick up shirts on my way back to the clinic from Wolf Bridge. When I saw Sarge's old truck out front, I came on in."

Elaine called from the lunch counter. "Your regular, Doc?"

"Yes, thanks," he called back, then turned to Quinn again. "So, how are you feeling?"

"Starving." She glanced at Seth, then back at Boone. "I've been told they have great food here."

"As long as Seth isn't cooking," he said, and scooted his chair closer to Quinn to get a better look at her injury. He nodded when he sat back. "Daniel did a nice job. You're not going to have much of a scar."

"Daniel's a good doctor," she said, dipping her tea bag up and down in her mug again, and Seth caught her glancing at him. She looked away quickly, a touch of color in her cheeks as he turned back to Boone.

"That he is. So, what do you think of this town of ours?"

"I haven't had a chance to do much sightseeing, but I've noticed that the people are very friendly."

Seth watched the two of them, letting them

talk while Quinn nervously kept dunking her tea back up and down in the hot water. He looked down and tried to sort through his own thoughts. He'd asked Farley to send anyone looking for a housekeeping job out to the ranch. The thing was, Quinn had approached Farley about how to get to the ranch. She'd been looking for something related to the ranch…was it him? Allie had stalked him, waiting in the coffee shop on the ground floor of his corporate offices in Seattle for four days, hoping to catch him "accidentally" during his morning coffee run. That had worked for her, at least for a while until everything exploded. If Quinn was after him like that, how would she know where he was? Why, was it always the money? He felt nauseated.

The food came, and while Boone told Quinn all about the town, she seemed pretty silent, and Seth ate without contributing to the conversation.

"I'd like to see around Eclipse, but I don't think I should take off on a tour around town…" She pushed her plate away, glancing at Seth.

He had no idea what she was saying at first, then he understood. Doc had invited her to go sightseeing. He'd wanted answers from her over lunch, to take care of it here, not back at the ranch. He didn't want Julia or Sarge involved in any way. It didn't help he felt foolish he'd been so taken by Quinn. He obviously never learned, even after Allie, that the people who appeared most trustworthy could be the most conniving. He gave up on the talk there and then. He'd manage to do it privately after she came back from her ride with Boone. "Go ahead," he said flatly.

Quinn frowned at him, then stood. "I'll be right back," she said to Boone, then headed toward a hallway on the far side of the diner.

Seth kept his eyes on her until she was out of sight, then heard Boone ask, "What was that all about?"

Seth turned and ignored the last few fries on his plate. "What was what about?"

"You've hardly said a thing, and you look annoyed that I asked Quinn to show her around."

Seth pushed his mug away. "I don't care about your ride. She can go if she wants to."

"What's your problem, then? You look like you've been sucking on lemons."

"I do have a problem to take care of, but I can do it later."

"Good. Do that. Meanwhile, I'll take a pretty lady for a ride and see where that ends up."

Seth pushed away what was left of his lunch, too, and sat back. "You do that."

"Oh, man, you're jealous?"

"What?"

"I don't know. I'm guessing here," Boone said. "I can't figure out why you'd be acting like this."

Seth shook his head. "I'm not in a good mood. I'm sorry. It's not about you, not at all."

"That's a relief. Daniel told me about Quinn, said she's a widow, pretty, funny, and I thought I'd introduce myself."

Seth sat straighter. He needed to get out of there. "I'm going to head back now. I've got things to do. Tell Quinn I'll see her when I see her."

Before Seth could stand, Quinn was back, and his phone was chiming. He pulled it out of his jacket pocket and glanced at the screen. *Julia.* "Hey, Julia," he said. "What's going on?"

"I had to call the doctor for medication,

and the rule is I need to keep you informed of such a request," the nurse said. "So, Sarge had a rough morning, and the doctor approved a mild sedative for his use. It seems to be working."

"What happened?"

"Sarge was talking about going to find Maggie, then he started to cry." He closed his eyes when he heard her voice break, then she coughed softly. "He's calming down, though."

"I'll be right there."

"No, Seth, I didn't call for you to come back early. I'm just following the rules that you were to be notified about a new medication. You can't do anything about it."

"I'll see you soon," he said and didn't give Julia a chance to argue before he ended the call.

He put his phone away, then looked up to find Boone and Quinn both watching him. "There's a problem with Sarge."

"What happened?" Boone asked.

Seth explained, and Boone nodded. "That's rough, but it's all part and parcel of his illness. It'll pass."

"I'm heading back now." Seth started to get out his wallet, but Boone stopped him.

"I've got it. Just go."

Quinn surprised Seth when she said, "I'm coming with you."

"Oh, no, I don't want…" He stopped what he was going to say. Instead, he said, "I can't ask you to—"

"You didn't ask. I'm offering," she said simply. Then she looked at Boone. "Rain check, Doc?"

"Absolutely," Boone said.

ON THE WAY back to the ranch, neither Seth nor Quinn spoke. Seth felt unfocused and scattered, his mind going from Sarge and his episode to what Farley had told him. He hurt thinking about Sarge crying, being so sad and disconnected because the love of his life wasn't there with him anymore and he couldn't understand it.

He also felt conflicted about Quinn. He'd simply liked her in a way he couldn't remember liking any woman in his past and after only knowing her a few days. He'd liked talking to her, seeing her first thing in the morning, and when she smiled, his world seemed better. But now he was questioning himself for being so instantly attracted to her. He had to take more than a few steps back, clear his head and get some answers from her.

When they were driving up to the house, Quinn broke the prolonged silence. "I'm sure Sarge will be okay. Boone said it happens."

"Yeah, it happens," he murmured and got out after parking. His phone chimed as Seth swung the truck door shut. He checked. Owen was calling, and Seth ignored it as he headed to the porch and took the steps in two long strides.

At the door, he was surprised when Quinn stopped him in his tracks by grabbing his jacket sleeve. He turned to her, glanced at her hand on him, then when she released her hold, he looked up at her. "What?"

She exhaled, then stunned him. "Are you upset with me?"

"You don't—"

"Something's wrong and you need to explain before we go in there." Her voice was low, but her expression was tight. Those blue eyes held his.

"Okay, okay," he said. "You lied to me." He could see it right away in her eyes. It was true. His heart sank.

"Farley told you, didn't he?"

"Yeah, he did. You walked in and asked for directions to this place. He never mentioned a job out here, but you seemed really anxious to get to this area. I guess he gave you an earful about the ranch."

"Yes, I asked him about the ranch. Then after the accident when you mentioned a job, I thought I could get it and have a place to stay for a bit, and it would help you and Julia. I'm really sorry that I took the easy way out, but I needed to—"

The door swung back and Julia was there. "Get in here you two," she said. "I told you not to rush back. He's sleeping."

Seth tossed his jacket onto the bench, put his hat by it, then sat to tug off his boots. "I need to be here." He glanced at Quinn as she stepped out of her running shoes. "You should've gone with Boone."

She looked at Julia. "I want to help."

Julia shook her head. "Thanks, but—"

Quinn never looked at Seth. "I can sit with him while he sleeps or read to him if he wakes up, or whatever you think he needs."

"You mean that?"

"Yes, I do." She stood. "Just take me in to him."

As the two women left, Seth stayed on the bench. What had Quinn started to say? She needed what? Then it hit him. She needed the job. She was in a strange place on her own. But she knew about the ranch. Or maybe she'd just asked for one of the bigger ranches that might need help. He hadn't straightened that out with Farley.

His head was spinning. He knew the lie wasn't much of a lie, nothing like the lies Allie had dished out. It was just one lie, maybe out of convenience. But then again, the first time he caught Allie embellishing something, he'd managed to justify her doing it. He wouldn't be that gullible again. No matter what, he knew he wouldn't ask Quinn to leave yet. He owed her that after the accident he'd caused. She could stay until she was fully recovered from the crash. He'd keep an eye on her in the meantime and stop the foolish thoughts he had about her.

He finally stood and as he stepped into the west wing hallway, Julia waved at him as she went into her room and closed the door behind her. He headed to Sarge's room and the door was partly ajar. He heard Sarge saying, "Tell me about it."

Quinn answered. "Michael and I were in Arizona once and we took a tour around Tombstone. It was terrific."

"Did you see anything about Wyatt Earp or Doc Holliday?" Sarge asked, sounding really interested.

"Yes, sir. They had a lot of things related to them. They had a mock gunfight on the streets, and we saw the O.K. Corral. It was pretty great, but the weird thing was everything was smaller." She chuckled softly. "My husband was over six feet tall, and he had to duck to go in the doors of a couple of houses, and the windows were small. Strange, though, Doc Holliday and Wyatt Earp both were six feet tall."

Sarge laughed. "You know, I've had to duck a lot to get through doors in my life. Now Maggie, she was small."

"She looks beautiful in that picture."

There was silence, and Seth braced himself to go into the room to stop the conversation before Sarge got upset or lost. Then Sarge spoke. "She was the prettiest thing ever. I sure loved her. I still do, you know."

"Of course you do. She'll always be the love of your life."

Sarge sounded relieved. "You understand, don't you? I can tell."

"I do. Michael passed away about a year and a half ago." He thought her voice sounded a bit unsteady, but she kept talking. "Just because he's not here, doesn't mean I don't love him as much as I ever did."

Seth closed his eyes, absorbing her words. Then Sarge was speaking. "Yes, yes, yes," he said in a lower voice. "You know, I don't say much about Maggie around here. I don't want to make the boys sad. They loved her, and I can see that it hurts them if I talk about her."

"Tell you what," Quinn said softly. "If you ever want to talk about Maggie, I'd love to hear more about her. She seems to have been a pretty wonderful person. But I think they miss her, too, and maybe they'd like to talk about her with you. Seth told me about how she wished on the Wishing Moon for the boys."

He chuckled, a low rough sound. "She sure did. She loved them. You know what else she loved?"

"You?"

He actually laughed. "Absolutely. I never figured out why, but she did. What I was talking about was Zane Gray books. She'd read them with me. I was never good at reading myself, but she had the loveliest voice."

"How about I read with you for a while?"

"Yes." Sarge sighed heavily. "Yes, please."

Seth backed up, then walked way. He'd thought it was better for Sarge not to talk too much about Maggie so he wouldn't get upset. But now he understood his mistake. He loved her. It was normal to want to talk about someone you loved. Quinn's words echoed in him. *Just because he's not here, doesn't mean I don't love him as much as I ever did.*

He headed back to his office and called Owen. He was relieved when he found the subject of the missed call had been about an encrypted file he needed unlocked. Seth hesitated, then put in another call to a service company used for background checks on new hires and gave them what he knew about Quinn. With that done, Seth went back to the west wing and quietly looked into Sarge's room. The man was in the bed and Quinn was sitting in the chair to his right. The Zane Gray book was closed on her lap.

He went in and was almost to Quinn by the

time she realized he was there and turned to look up at him. "Sleeping?" he asked.

"Yes," she said in a whisper as she stood quietly.

"I'll take over."

"Okay. Julia said to leave the picture there." She motioned to the picture of Sarge and Maggie, a bigger version of the one Libby had given to him in rehab. It was on a table by his bed where he could see it easily. It showed a large man holding a petite woman to his side, her red hair catching the sun light, and her smiling up at her husband. He knew Sarge would never stop loving Maggie.

He sat down and couldn't take his eyes off the man in the bed. Seth didn't have to think too hard to figure out where he would have ended up if Maggie and Sarge hadn't come into his life. Hate, anger and fear had driven him until the two of them had pulled him off the ledge. Whether that had been a plan or some coincidence, he didn't want to think about where he'd be now if it had never happened.

FOR THREE DAYS after their trip into town, Sarge did well, but Quinn barely saw Seth.

She wanted to explain about her lie, to get things cleared one way or the other. But she never got a chance. He'd popped in, ask how she was, then was gone. She felt as if she'd been shoved into limbo while he spent his time with Sarge. They played cards. Seth read to him, or they just sat on the couch and talked. He even managed to take Sarge for a short outing in Julia's car. When he wasn't with the man, he spent his time in the office or in his exercise room, sometimes far into the night.

She suspected what had happened with Sarge had scared Seth, and other things, less important things, were pushed away for now. Meanwhile, she'd go in and see Sarge when she knew he was alone, and they talked. The older man missed some things, got confused about them, but he surely did remember his Maggie. She knew how much she needed to talk to someone about Michael and how people just seemed to avoid the topic when they got past giving her their condolences. But she was always looking for a chance to talk with Seth when they were alone. She just hoped when that conversation came it wouldn't end with him asking her to leave.

Near dinnertime on the fourth day, Quinn heard, "Hey, there," and looked up from the homestyle potatoes she was making on the stove. Julia was coming down into the great room. "You promised Sarge a real meat tonight." Her neon green running shoes were paired with jeans and a green pullover. As she stepped up by the island, she added, "For my sake, please don't disappoint him."

"There's going to be steak," Quinn said, answering the smile on Julia's face with one of her own. "I wouldn't want him to fire me."

Julia grinned. "You don't have to worry about that. He likes you a lot, and he's going to be thrilled with steak." She leaned back against the granite countertop and glanced at the wall clock in the great room. "He's been sleeping since you read with him earlier, so he'll probably be up for dinner."

"Here or in his room?"

"Oh, I don't know. I'll have to tell you when he wakes up. I just hope he doesn't oversleep or the night will be his."

"That's rough when it means you have to stay awake, too," Quinn said. "I'm up late, so if you need me to take over for a bit, just ask, okay?"

"That's awfully kind of you," Julia said. "But I worry about confusing Sarge or something happening if I'm not close by."

"I understand. I was afraid to leave Michael." The words were there along with an ache deep inside her that lingered, but it didn't seem so intense now. She wasn't certain what was happening, but she suspected talking to Sarge about Michael might be lessening the edge for her. She helped him and he helped her.

"You didn't have any help?" Julia asked.

She glanced over at the other woman. "Michael's parents came out from New York and stayed as much as they possibly could, especially his mother when he had his treatments. They were great, but I still couldn't leave. They offered to pay for live-in care for him, but I didn't want to do that. He needed the people who loved him, not paid help." She stopped stirring the potatoes. "I just couldn't leave or have strangers with him. Maybe I was being selfish, doing that for myself, but I worried about even going to sleep."

Quinn lifted the pan to slide the potatoes onto a serving platter, then put it in the warming drawer of the oven. She heard Julia say,

"I'm glad Sarge talks to you about Maggie. I try, but he closes down, not the way he is with you. I know it's good for him and his memory to talk about her."

"It's good for me, too," Quinn said.

She went to the cupboard to take out the dinner plates and set them on the island. "I guess I'll leave these here, and everyone can get their own plate and cutlery and take it to where they're going to eat."

"If Sarge keeps sleeping for a while, I think I'll eat out here."

"I can do the steaks anytime you're ready for them, so it's not a problem. How about Seth?"

"I don't know. He went down to the stables while you were reading to Sarge to thank Murphy for putting in that graduated step for Sarge at the archway. I should have never called him about the episode when you two were in town the other day. I think it scared him."

Quinn knew it had by the way he'd reacted. "He needed to know. Surprises aren't good," she said, then tried to lighten things up. "You know, I'm getting pretty good at poker."

Julia smiled. "Good, I'm tired of being his

victim." Julia checked Quinn's wound. "You should be able to get the stitches out soon. But with your hair down, you can hardly notice them."

She'd left her hair loose when she'd changed earlier into a white cable-knit sweater and jeans. "I can't wait to get them out."

Right then, the front door opened. "Ah, he's back," Julia said, then headed for archway.

Quinn heard Seth's voice. "How's he doing?"

"Sleeping."

"Let me get cleaned up, then I'll go in and sit with him," Seth said.

"Dinner's almost ready, and since he's sleeping, why don't you eat out here with me and Quinn?" Julia asked.

Quinn didn't hear any response before Seth appeared in the archway. His hair was mussed and he was wearing what she now knew were his usual clothes at the ranch—a long-sleeved thermal shirt, this time a deep blue, paired with jeans.

"Hey," he said across the space between them.

"Hey." She didn't expect him to step down

into the room and walk over to her. He hadn't done that before.

She was surprised when he asked, "How much time do I have before dinner?"

"It can be ready whenever you are," she said.

"Half an hour?"

"Perfect. Just tell me how you like your steak."

"Rare," he said, then turned and left.

Quinn released a breath she hadn't been aware of holding, kicking herself for not speaking to him right then while they were alone. Now, he'd be at the table. She just hoped she could eat. Then Julia was back. "Okay, it looks as if Sarge is awake and raring to go. He wants to eat here at the table. So, he'll get dressed, then we'll come out."

"I can have it ready in half an hour. So, how do you like your steak?"

"Dead."

"Me, too," Quinn said. "Sarge?"

"Bloody." Julia headed back to the west wing.

Quinn was setting the table for four and ready to go out to start the grill when the front door unexpectedly swung open. She looked across the room to the entry, and caught a glimpse of a tall, lean, man holding the door open for a tiny woman with brilliant red hair. They were both laughing as the man bent down to kiss the woman. Quinn was pretty sure she was looking at Jake and Libby Bishop. Then she heard Seth say, "Jake, Libby. I thought you wouldn't be back for another couple of days."

Jake slipped off his leather jacket as he tipped his head to look up at Seth on the second-floor walkway. "We caught a break and finished early in Houston." He tossed his jacket to his left, probably onto the bench. Then he helped Libby out of a forest green jacket. "We weren't going to waste any time getting back home."

Libby was grinning up at Seth. "Boy, it's good to see you. Get on down here. I missed you."

"Give me a few minutes. Where's the beast?"

"We went to the cabin first, and Pax staked out his spot in front of the potbelly stove. He's such a spoiled dog. He chose to stay there instead of going back out into the cold with us."

Jake was taller than his wife by a foot, with

disheveled ash-blond hair. He pushed up the sleeves of the chambray shirt he was wearing with jeans, then reached for Libby's hand. She really was tiny, wearing slim-fit jeans and an oversize pink sweater. "Let's go see the man," she said to her husband and they headed to the west wing without looking into the great room.

Quinn heard words mixed with laughter coming from Sarge's room and she put out two more plates in case Libby and Jake hadn't eaten. Then Seth was there, coming down into the great room. In jeans and an untucked white shirt, with the two top buttons undone and the sleeves rolled up to expose his forearms, he looked different. Maybe he looked younger with his damp hair combed back from his face. Then she realized he was clean-shaven.

She must have stared at him a bit too long, because as he came closer to her, he asked, "Is there something wrong?"

"Oh, no, not at all. I mean…just your face."

His eyes widened. "What about my face?"

"Nothing." She bit her lip, nerves starting to show up. "I didn't mean there was anything wrong," she said quickly. "But you shaved."

"I do that occasionally for no reason at all." He flashed a quick grin and she realized how much she'd missed seeing it. "Just call me impulsive."

CHAPTER EIGHT

SETH WATCHED COLOR touch Quinn's cheeks, and her smile seemed unsteady. "Well, you clean up very well," she said.

She looked good, too. "Did you meet Jake and Libby when they came in?"

"No, they headed in to see Sarge."

"Good, he's been asking for the two of them."

"Can I say something, not for discussion, just to say it?"

He went closer, a bit apprehensively, but he knew he'd been avoiding her. The longer the words weren't said, the less real they'd become. "Okay."

"I apologize for letting you think that Farley told me about the job out here. I should never have done that. I should've just said I would like to have the job when you mentioned it. I'm really sorry, and…" She shrugged. "I'm sorry."

He felt his heart ease at her apology that he could sense she meant. He knew what he wanted and it wasn't for her to pack up and leave. "I've been thinking about it, too." He didn't add how he couldn't stop thinking about it or her. "I'm of the opinion that we need a fresh start, a clean slate. Mistakes can be made, but let's let this go. I'm Seth Reagan." He went closer to her and held out his hand.

She hesitated, then slipped her hand into his. "I'm Quinn Lake. Nice to meet you, Seth."

He found a smile, a real smile as he felt her slender fingers hold on to him. "Very nice to meet you." He took an easy breath and made himself release her hand. "So, you mentioned steaks?"

"Oh, yes," she said, smiling up at him. "Steaks. I have to start the grill, but I need to know how Libby and Jake prefer theirs."

He saw the platter of meat on the island and headed over to it. "Rare for Jake, and well-done for Libby. How do you like your steak?" he asked as he picked up the plate and turned back to her.

She looked at him, then simply said, "Really well done, but no shoe leather."

He liked that twinkle of humor in her blue eyes. "Got it, dead."

That smile of hers came and he knew right then that, despite his trying to avoid Quinn for the past few days, nothing had changed in how drawn he was to her. He hadn't trusted himself to be around her, but he'd been thinking about her more than he should've been. He remembered her tears after the accident. She'd been a total stranger then, but he'd wanted nothing more than to help her. Thank goodness she was smiling now, and things were settled. He put the plate on the table and went to get his boots and jacket back on.

When he returned for the steaks, Quinn was taking some salad dressing out of the fridge and smiling to herself.

"What's so funny?" he asked her before he headed out to the deck and the barbeque.

"I was just thinking that Julia, Libby and I like our steaks well-done, and you, Jake and Sarge want yours rare, if not bloody. Kind of stereotypical male/female, don't you think?"

It was so easy for him to smile. "Sort of sexist, aren't you?"

She countered easily. "No, just smart about red meat."

"Speaking of which, I'll get it on the grill." Seth was still smiling when he stepped through the sliding glass door by the fireplace and onto the deck. The smile fled as the cold—the type that fell somewhere between discomfort and misery—hit him. So he stayed close to the heat while the steaks sizzled. By the time he went back inside, Quinn had put rolls along with a dish of peas and carrots and a green salad on the table. There were six place settings. "Three dead," he called after her. "Three done perfectly."

That soft laugh was there again as she turned to him. "Thanks for your biased opinion. Please, put them on the table close to Sarge's place." He heard voices and looked over as Sarge appeared in the archway. He was doing well using the cane to take the graduated step down into the room with relative ease.

"Smells great," Sarge said. He looked good in a deep green Western shirt, pressed jeans and with his hair neatly combed. Seth felt his heart lift even more when the older man smiled at him.

When Seth saw Jake and Libby follow Sarge into the room, he put the steaks down on the table and crossed to hug each one, happy they were back home. Then he turned as Julia passed him to help Sarge get seated at the head of the table. "Jake, Libby, I want you to meet Quinn Lake," he said. "I told you we needed a housekeeper and she showed up. Perfect timing."

Quinn nodded to the two of them from where she stood near the end of the table. "So nice to finally meet you both," she said. "I heard you have a dog."

"We sure do." Libby smiled. "Pax. He's snuggled up in the cabin being lazy." She and Jake crossed to the other side of the table from her. "This food looks wonderful. All we've had today is peanuts and bottled water," Libby said, then looked at Sarge. "Steak and potatoes, Sarge. Isn't that music to your ears?"

"Beautiful music," the man said with a smile.

Seth slipped off his jacket and tossed it over on a nearby pub chair, then moved to take the seat to Sarge's left. "What do you think you're doing dressing like that?" Sarge asked as he frowned at Seth.

"Sorry, I know I can never look as spiffy as you, but I try."

The older man shook his head ruefully. "Not even close, son, especially wearing that yuppie shirt." He turned and looked at Jake sitting down at his right. "I need to take you boys to Farley's and get you some decent clothes."

Jake agreed right away, obviously not offended. "We'll do that soon, sir. That would be like old times, wouldn't it?"

"Good times," Sarge said, then looked around at the women. "Please, ladies, sit so we can eat."

Libby took the chair by Jake, and Julia sat beside her. Quinn slipped into the chair next to Seth. He looked around the table and it seemed so natural to be there with Sarge at the head, Seth facing Jake and Libby right by her husband. He wished Ben were there and that dinner at the ranch could be like this forever. Seattle was very far away at that moment and not missed. He wanted to be here, with his family. He wanted to be home. For now, he had that, and he promised himself he'd enjoy every second of it for as long as it lasted.

"If you all don't eat up, I'm taking it all," Sarge announced, then waved at the dish of peas and carrots. "Except the vegetables. You all can fight over them."

They laughed at that, and Seth felt a sense of relief. Sarge was Sarge today, and it seemed crazy that a few days ago he'd been so lost.

"Love a family dinner," Sarge said as he looked around the table while Jake cut up his steak for him. He glanced at Quinn. "So glad you could join us, missy."

"Thank you for making me feel so welcome," Quinn said.

It was like years ago when a new kid came to the table and was never made to feel like an outsider by Sarge or Maggie. They were family for as long as they were with them and, for a few very fortunate ones, even after they'd left.

The dinner lasted longer than Seth anticipated, with a lot of talk and laughter. He was surprised at the way Quinn fit in, joking and talking, and the evening was one of the best he'd had in a very long while. When Sarge finished his meal, he asked to sit out on the couch for a while and visit. So they all sat with him, and Seth loved seeing him so involved and enjoying himself. Then he realized Quinn was over clearing the table by herself.

When he caught her eye, he motioned her to join them. She hesitated, then crossed to where Seth sat by Jake on the ottoman. He patted the stretched leather for her to sit down by him.

Libby was by Sarge on the couch with Julia on the other side. "You are a terrific cook, Quinn," Libby said. "Thank you so much for dinner."

"My pleasure," she said.

"Good old-fashioned food," Sarge said and looked at Julia. "Take a lesson from Quinn."

"I definitely will," Julia said good-naturedly.

Jake leaned forward to tap Sarge on his knee. "We sure missed you, sir. As soon as I've finished with my client in Houston, Liberty and I won't be leaving here very often."

Sarge nodded. "Good. This place seems awful empty when you two are gone. Then Seth takes off sometimes, you know." His smile faded and shifted into a quizzical frown. Seth barely saw it coming before

Sarge was slipping away into another place and time. "I don't know where…" He was obviously confused when he spoke directly to Seth. "Where's Maggie, son?"

Libby reached for Sarge's hand to hold it as Seth answered. "Maggie's not here, sir."

The man's faded blue eyes narrowed as he looked from Seth to Jake, then back to Seth. "You…you two could have asked her to come." Then he looked down and seemed to be speaking to himself. "She loves her boys. She really loves them."

There was a painfully awkward silence and Seth could barely breathe. Then he felt Quinn's hand touch his forearm, and he turned to her, but she was looking at Sarge. "Sarge. How did Maggie like her steak?"

Everyone was quiet, and they all seemed to be holding their breaths, the way Seth was at that moment. Then Sarge looked up and his blue eyes met Quinn's. When he spoke, his words sounded more wistful than sad. "She… liked it really rare." He frowned slightly as if remembering. "Yes, rare. She'd say to just pass it over the flames and she'd be happy. She would've loved to be here tonight. She really would have."

Seth found his own voice. "I remember that time you burned her steak. She had fried eggs instead."

Silence, then a laugh from Sarge that broke the quiet tension. "She liked fried eggs," he said, still laughing slightly. "Over easy. She liked them more than steak, so it was all good."

Seth watched him, his face transformed by the humor, and he remembered the way Maggie had eaten the fried egg. Her eyes had been on Sarge all the time as if he were the only thing in her world, and she loved that world, fried eggs and all.

"Maybe we can have fried eggs next time," Quinn said and everyone laughed.

All the tension was gone and Sarge was left smiling slightly with his own thoughts.

"We might try that, Quinn," Sarge said.

"Anytime, just let me know. Or if you want steak again or a good roast or ribs, put in your order. Okay?"

"Ribs?" That obviously pricked the man's interest.

"One of my specialties," she said.

Libby patted Sarge's hand, which she was

still holding in hers. "I love ribs. Totally addicted to them."

Sarge chuckled roughly. "That's my girl, Liberty. We'll have ribs real soon."

Seth wasn't aware he'd covered Quinn's hand on his arm with his, but he didn't pull back. He didn't want to break the connection too quickly. He hadn't felt so secure and grounded in a long time. But he wouldn't try to figure that out now.

"Is anyone up for dessert?" Quinn asked. "There's chocolate or vanilla ice cream."

Jake stood and reached for his wife as she got up. "Thanks, but I don't think so." With his arm around Libby, he spoke to Sarge. "Do you mind if Liberty and I head up to the cabin, sir? We're jet-lagged and need to get some rest."

"You two go ahead," Sarge said, smiling up at them. "I'll take care of your share of the ice cream."

They laughed with him, then each hugged him before they said their good-nights and headed out.

As Quinn eased her hand away from Seth and stood, Sarge smiled at her. "Holding hands?"

Quinn went red, then said, "Just...um..."

Julia stepped in. "None of your business, Sarge," she said with a smile. "How about you and I go in and read a bit. I need to know if the posse goes out or not."

Just like that Sarge let it go. He turned to Seth by him and smiled. "You know, son, that shirt's pretty sharp on you."

Seth felt himself settle as he hugged the man. "You go with Julia, and I'll be right in."

"Don't forget the ice cream," Sarge said, then headed off.

Seth turned to see Quinn crossing to the kitchen. He caught up with her by the sinks in the island. "Thanks for what you did for Sarge." He had to swallow before he could say, "He really does need to be able to talk about Maggie, doesn't he?"

"Yes, he does. People naturally try to avoid talking about the one that's gone. They're afraid of... I don't know," she said on an unsteady shrug. "Maybe they worry it's going to upset the other person, and they aren't sure they can handle that person being upset."

He tucked the tips of his fingers into his jeans pockets and rocked slightly forward onto the balls of his feet. "I thought if I spoke about Maggie, it would make him pull away, you know, going back instead of being here. With us."

"He probably will sometimes, but sometimes he'll smile."

He couldn't move or think of what to say. He felt overwhelmed with relief that Quinn was there, that she had a special touch with Sarge, maybe a common bond that let them understand each other. "Tonight, he smiled."

"Yes, and he seemed so happy to have Jake and Libby here, too."

Seth leaned back against the counter and watched Quinn as she started to finish up clearing the dishes. "He doesn't complain, but I know he misses them when they have to leave for Jake's job. He misses Ben, too."

She started the dishwasher, then finally turned to him. "He still has you," she said softly. "I can tell that means a lot to him."

"It's means a lot to me to have him," he said.

She studied him for a moment. "What was he like when he was younger, when Maggie was with him and you came here?"

"Back then he was this ex-marine who was so strong, but unexpectedly kind and caring and genuine." Seth held to those memories tightly. "He and Maggie made a great team. They backed each other up, and they dealt with things I wish they hadn't had to, with all of us. But they did and changed more lives than I know about."

"I can imagine they did," she said with a soft smile.

"So, how are you feeling?"

She moved around him to go back to the table where she started to push the chairs back in place. "Okay. I'm getting used to the nights around here and the higher altitude."

He went to her and pushed the last chair back in place. Quinn was right beside him now. In her bare feet, if she hadn't been tilting her head back to look up at him, she would have been staring at his chin. She didn't mention her touching him, or Sarge's teasing, so he let it go. "I think I broke a promise to you."

"Excuse me?" she asked.

"I said I'd show you around the ranch."

She shook her head. "No, that was an offer."

He nodded. "Okay, but you said you ride. So what would you think of taking a ride in the morning to see the real ranch?"

"I'd love to."

He wanted to go on a ride with Quinn, out in the open, now that the air had been cleared between them. It wasn't as if he automatically trusted her, but he was closer to trusting her than he'd been over the past few days. He saw nothing but kindness in her, and if she needed a job, she had one. But he'd still take it a day at a time.

"How about first thing in the morning we take a quick run in to the clinic to see if you can have your stitches removed? When we're done, we'll come back and go riding. How does that work for you?"

"I'll be there," she said.

QUINN WAS WAITING for him in the entry at seven o'clock the next morning, and by nine o'clock they were walking out of the clinic in town side by side. Boone had been out on a call again, so he hadn't had a second chance to offer to be Quinn's tour guide. Quinn was perfectly okay with Brenner removing the stitches, and the scar ended up being a thin pink line with tiny spots on either side where the stitches had been.

Julia had lent her a warm pink jacket and

riding boots that fit just right. Seth opened her door as quickly as he could to get her inside. He went around to slip in behind the wheel, then started the truck and flipped on the heater.

Seth pulled out onto the street and headed south, then parked in front of the Addison Law Office. "I shouldn't be long," he said to Quinn. "Do you want to come in?"

"No, you go on in. I think I'd like to walk down Clayton Drive to see the town close-up."

"Great. If I can't see you when I get out, I'll call you on the phone." He took his cell out and handed it to her. "Put in your number."

She did, called herself and when she felt her phone vibrate in her pocket, she hung up and handed Seth's back to him. "We're all set," she said.

Quinn headed down the street, while Seth went in to meet with the attorney about the blind curve. When he left twenty minutes later, he stepped outside and Quinn was no-where in sight. He called her and she answered right away. "Hi."

"I'm done. Where are you?"

"I'm sitting on the top step of the walkway out in front of the diner."

"Okay, I'll be right there."

He'd barely hung up when his phone rang again, but it wasn't Quinn. It was Jake. He had an unexpected problem with his Houston contract and had to get back there as soon as possible or lose it. He and Libby had to get to the airport within two hours. Sarge was doing okay, sleeping, and Julia had said that Cal—Sarge's physical therapist—was coming out for a session, so that was covered.

He wished Jake and Libby were staying longer. He'd really like to talk some things over with Jake, but he knew how hard it had been for him to get work since he'd had to walk away from being a test pilot. He wished Jake luck and said they'd have a long talk when they got back.

QUINN LOOKED UP as Seth pulled in. She smiled from where she was sitting, then stood. She picked up a pink box beside her and a small cup holder that held two paper coffee cups. She got into the truck and put the box and cups down on the seat between them, then closed the door and did up her seat belt.

"Help yourself," she told Seth. "There's some freshly baked muffins and coffee for you." She reached for the coffee cup and handed it to him, then picked up her cup of chamomile tea.

"Thank you." He took a sip and put the cup back in the holder.

"You're welcome," she said as he backed out of the parking slot.

"Stop!" She rolled down her window. "Elaine," she called to the owner who'd just stepped out onto the walkway. "Thanks again for the tea!"

Elaine smiled, waved and called back, "Enjoy!"

Then they were on the main street and Quinn rolled the window up.

"I didn't see that coming," Seth said with a chuckle.

"I just appreciate the tea. All the people here seem so kind, I really mean it. These people who had no idea who I was stopped and spoke to me. Most just said hi, as if they were used to seeing me around town. A genuinely sweet lady told me she was certain you hadn't meant any harm with the accident.

"A teenager stopped to tell me that he was

working with Henry on my VW and was impressed by the engine. I don't have a clue how he knew who I was." She laughed at that. "I feel as if I've landed in a version of Mayberry, where everybody knows my name." She shook her head. "I think I'm mixing up my old TV shows."

"I get the idea," he said, his eyes on the road ahead.

As Quinn sipped more tea, Seth told her about Jake and Libby having to leave early. "Sarge is good, and his physical therapist, Cal, is on his way, so they took off for the airport. "I just hope Sarge understands that they'll be back in less than a week."

"Just remind him every so often that they're coming back soon. Julia said he asks about you every morning when you aren't there, and about Jake and Ben. He only wants to keep tabs on his family."

They drove up onto the highway and headed north. While Seth drove, Quinn sat quietly in the passenger seat, finally saying something when they turned off onto the county road. "Did the attorney think they could fix the road?"

"Burr says there's a pretty good chance the

county will let me pay for the repairs as long as it's done by an approved contractor. I told him to make it happen."

They got to the curve and this time Seth felt Quinn staring at him until they were on the straight road. "I hope he can."

"He's been around here long enough to have friends in high places. If anyone can, Burr Addison can."

When Seth neared the ranch entrance, he pulled between the boulders and put in the code to open the gates. When the way was clear, they headed up the drive. "Do you need to get changed before riding?"

"I need to layer a shirt, I think, but I can be ready in five minutes."

"Okay," he said as he pulled to a stop in front of the house. "Five minutes."

CHAPTER NINE

SETH COULD TELL Quinn was excited about the ride, and as soon as he made sure Sarge and Julia were fine, they headed down to the stables. Julia's riding boots and jacket with its fur-trimmed hood looked great on Quinn.

"What's your timetable for the camp to open up?" Quinn asked as they passed the hay barn and a flatbed truck approached with a delivery.

Seth pointed to the front doors as the driver stepped out. "In there. They can tell you where to put it."

The man nodded, then strode toward the center doors while Seth and Quinn kept walking.

"We're aiming for the week after the Fourth of July this summer. But there's so much to get done. If they can get the roofs on the extensions and the hay storage areas finished, then the inside work can be done during the winter. The same for the original mess hall and bunkhouse, to get them redone and expanded by spring. After we do one season, we're going to reassess what we can do to handle more boys, what expansions we should consider and possibly how to work a girls' camp into the summer schedule."

Quinn paused just before getting to the open stable doors that faced the large riding ring. As Seth stopped with her, he didn't miss what he thought looked like a dismissive expression as she pushed her hands deep into her pockets. "It's going to be so huge," she said.

He had a feeling she wasn't impressed by that. "You don't like those plans?"

A touch of color brushed her cheeks. "I didn't say that."

"No, but you want to. You just don't want to offend me by telling me that. I promise I don't offend easily. I mean, it's just an opinion."

She turned to face him as she exhaled deeply and it misted up between them. "Okay. I assumed it would be simple camping, teaching each boy how to fish and make a campfire and going on hikes and rides and living in tents. The groups of campers would be small, with a low child-to-adult ratio, maybe one to four, as close to a one-on-one experience as possible for the them."

They'd planned on groups of fifteen at each campsite, with two counselors. But as she said it, he realized she'd nailed what had been bothering him subtly all along. The healing he'd found at the ranch had been because of the one-on-ones with Maggie and Sarge, something they worked to make happen for each boy. "In a perfect world, that would be ideal," he said,

She shrugged. "All I know is kids really crave attention. If they're part of a larger group, they'll feel more like a number. I've seen that in my third-grade classes, and boys coming here really need attention. They crave it, and they're in the system. Small groups, I think, could be more healing for them, if that's part of why you're doing this. Trying to make repairs if possible, even for a short time."

All along, he'd been thinking *more* was better. More kids and more features, almost to the point of craziness. He'd thought the more kids they could take in, the more impactful the camp would be. He'd been wrong. Seth knew Quinn had exposed what should be the heart of the camp experience on the ranch, and he'd almost missed it completely. He'd lived through the good and the bad. He should've recognized what the good had been and tried to give that to the campers.

When he took too long to respond, Quinn said quickly, "I know it would cost more per child to have a lower ratio of boys per counselor. But I imagine the camp experience will be the highlight of the kids' summer, maybe their whole year."

Seth was amazed at the passion in her blue eyes when she spoke about the boys. "Why on earth are you working here as a housekeeper and not teaching somewhere?"

She shrugged again. "Because I'm not certified to teach here, and you gave me a job as housekeeper. But I love kids. I always have."

The direction for the camp changed in that single moment. He'd cut down the numbers, restructure smaller camping groups and spread the sites out so the focus could be on interacting with each boy. What was best for the kids was best for them all. "I hope you get back to teaching soon," he said and really meant it.

"Later, I will, but for now I have things I need to sort out in my life before I go back to teaching again."

"I hope things work out for you." She deserved to do what she loved, and he was quite certain from the little she'd told him about her teaching that it was her passion. He moved to go past her and through the wide double doors of the stables. "Come on," he said.

The smell of animals and hay hung in the air, and there were soft snorts and whinnies from deeper in the space. When Dwight came out of a stall halfway down the aisle, he spotted them right away and headed toward them.

"Good morning," he said with a nod. He was wearing knee-high rubber boots along with jeans and a heavy jacket. "I'm Dwight," he said to Quinn. "Are you two here to ride?"

"Yes, we are," Seth said. "Can you get Miner ready for me and find an easy ride for the lady?"

Quinn spoke up quickly. "I can handle a horse." Both men looked at her. "I really can."

Dwight tipped his head toward her. "Ma'am, don't worry. I'll get you an interesting mount." Dwight started off farther down the aisle. "Jerry Moore sent over another horse. She's not touchy, and the best thing is, she likes being ridden. She's about eight, medium size and a good gait. Her name's Angel." A chestnut with a white muzzle stuck her head out over the half door they were approaching.

Seth glanced at Quinn. "What do you think?"

Stepping closer, she reached out to stroke the animal's muzzle. "I think she's perfect."

"We'll take her," Seth said to Dwight.

Ten minutes later, he and Quinn were walking their saddled horses out of the stable. Seth led the way to the open gate of the riding ring. "Let's take a few turns so you can get a feel for your mount."

Set could tell Quinn didn't want to trot in circles to warm up. "I promise you, I can ride."

"I'm sure you can," Seth said in a tone that probably sounded a little patronizing. He wanted to make sure it was safe to go up into the higher land. He took the reins for her horse from her. "Get on up," he said as he steadied the mare.

Quinn hesitated, then seemed to think better of arguing. In very short order, she managed to get in the saddle safely. "Ready," she said.

Seth led both horses into the ring, then handed Angel's reins back to Quinn. After he mounted Miner, a strong-looking buckskin, they rode slowly around the large enclosure until they passed the open gates to start on a second circuit. "I really can ride," Quinn said impatiently.

"I believe you, but you said it's been a while."

"Yes, but riding a horse is like riding a bike. Once you do it, you don't forget how." They were approaching the open gates again. "I was seven when I first rode a horse, and that horse wasn't afraid of snakes."

Seth laughed, remembering what he'd told her about his own first ride, and Quinn gave him a mischievous look. The next instant, she nudged Angel and took off through the open gate. They passed the holding stalls on the southern side of the ring heading west.

"Hey, there!" Seth called after her. "Wait for me." She kept going but seemed to slow as he came up from behind, but she didn't stop. "Okay, okay, you win," he said as he drew alongside her. "You definitely can ride."

Quinn brought Angel to a full stop as they approached the pastures and a hay lean-to that had just been built. The land was fenced and cross-fenced, spreading out in front of them. Beyond, to the west, the ranch flowed into open grazing areas that climbed up into the foothills off in the distance. The beauty of the land was staggering.

When Quinn turned to Seth, she was almost glowing with pleasure. He knew right then he'd just been existing over the past few years, running through unremarkable dates, with work at the center of his world. Since he'd started the plans for the camp last year, he'd redirected his focus, and then Quinn had burst into his life. He felt it expanding, moving away from business and meaningless things.

"I'm sorry about taking off," she said, not looking sorry at all. "I couldn't help myself. But you're the guide. So, where are we going?"

Seth pulled himself out of his unexpected moment of self-awareness. He pointed ahead. "We'll go west, past the fencing, then swing

north and finally curve back down this way."
He wasn't sure what was going on with him,
but things were definitely shifting. What
drew him to Quinn wasn't just her looks or
her stunning smile. It was more than that.
She seemed to fit into his new world. She was
friends with Julia and Sarge. He knew Libby
and Jake liked her. Seth loved her insight into
the camp matters. It seemed to be falling into
place somehow, despite the breach about her
lie. That was fading and starting to seem like
an overreaction on his part. "Just stay with
me. No taking off on your own, okay?"

When she nodded, he started off, and she
paced her horse with his. "How long have you
been riding Miner?"

"He's one of the first horses Dwight
brought in with the starter group about eight
months ago. I've been riding him since then."

"There's no more cattle on the land?"

"No, that comes after we have enough good
horses for the campers. Most of the open grazing land was cleared for cattle when Sarge
ran them here." Seth explained to Quinn how
Sarge had selectively cleared grazing land,
using the wood he cut for the construction
of the buildings and fencing. He strategically

left scattered stands of trees for shade and to block winds that gusted down from the higher ground. "His master plan was developed without wasting any of the cut trees."

They rode on at a good pace, Quinn falling into silence as she seemed to be taking in her surroundings. As they approached a sprawling stand of old growth, Seth stopped Miner and Quinn pulled Angel up by him. "What now?" she asked.

"We'll take a shortcut through the trees just up there." He nodded toward the north and started in that direction. He glanced at Quinn as she followed toward an opening in the thick mix of pines and leafless deciduous growth. "It's only wide enough to ride single file."

"This is an adventure," she said with a smile.

He wouldn't argue with that. He'd gone this way so many times in the past, but it felt as if he was doing it for the first time. Having Quinn there changed a lot of things. He started off, and she was beside him until he took the lead into the trees, then she slipped back to follow. The silence was almost eerie, broken only by the sound of dried branches and pine needles being snapped under the horses' hooves on the rising ground. The cold seemed deeper.

When they broke out into a narrow clearing on higher ground, Quinn came up beside Seth again. He glanced at her, and her face was touched with high color from the cold. "We'll head north for half a mile, then leave the horses and take a short hike, if you're up for it."

"Yes, sure, of course," she said.

He kept going toward a cluster of leafless trees. "Here we are," he said and dismounted.

Quinn adeptly got down off Angel, and as she secured the mare to a strong branch next to Miner, she asked, "Where are we hiking to?"

"You'll see when we get there. Are you staying warm?"

"Not warm, but comfortable," she said.

"Good enough." He started off, leading the way due north over hard uneven ground through a scattering of brush and trees. He found the path that had been packed down over the years by kids and adults climbing to the same spot he was aiming for. The day was going better than he'd expected, and he knew the woman with him was responsible for most of that.

When the path narrowed, Quinn slipped back to get behind Seth. He glanced over his shoulder to check on her, and she was keeping up with him just fine, until their eyes locked. She stumbled right then and pitched forward. He twisted around and grabbed for her arm just in time to keep her on her feet.

She managed to stay up, her breath misting into the air, then she shifted as he let go of her.

"I thought you were stopping, so I—" Then she cut off her own words and a smile touched her lips. "I'm good to go."

"That's good to know," he said, his own smile coming easily. "We're almost there."

Quinn moved to go around him, and he stopped her.

She turned. "You said we're almost there."

"We are. Close your eyes?"

"Excuse me?"

"Close your eyes, and don't open them until I tell you to." When she still hesitated, he added. "I want you to get the full impact of what I'm going to show you. Now, give me your hand and close your eyes."

She studied him, then finally took his offered hand and shut her eyes. "I don't see this ending well," she murmured. "Pun intended."

Her hand was freezing. "You're not supposed to see, period. Trust me. No peeking, okay?"

"No peeking," she said as her hand tightened slightly in his.

"We'll take it slowly." Seth started off with her, telling her when there was a rise or an uneven part in the ground, then he helped her clear the final step. "Don't open your eyes yet," he said as he let go of her to go around behind her and rest his hands on her shoulders.

Carefully he positioned her to face south and a bit east. "I know California has a lot of great scenery, but I want you to see the best view in all of Wyoming, if not the country." He moved back and went to her side again so he could watch her reaction. "Okay. Open your eyes."

Quinn blinked, then Seth saw what he'd been hoping for. Her lips formed a soft O as her blue eyes widened. "Wow."

QUINN TRIED TO take in the world spread out in front of her from where they stood on a rocky outcropping high in the foothills. The land flowed out for what seemed like forever in every direction, over grazing land, to fenced pastures, then to the ranch buildings and the main house. Over it all was a sense of peace, so tangible to Quinn that it almost took her breath away.

She focused on the main house and its relationship to the hay barn and stables to the northwest. With everything in miniature, the trucks and a tractor sitting behind the stables where the lean-to was being built looked like children's toys. "It's unbelievable," she breathed.

"Some of the best times I remember having were right here, coming up to watch the sunrise alone, or being here with Ben and Jake. I didn't realize how much I missed it until I came back this time."

"I'm not sure I ever would have left if I'd lived here," she said honestly.

"Well, we all left. First, Jake enlisted in the army, then Ben headed to college. I was the last one. After all Sarge did for us, none of us were around for him when he really needed help."

She heard the regret in his voice, something she knew all too well, and she turned to him. He was squinting into the distance. "You were all building your lives. I'm sure that Sarge understood that."

"He always understood." Seth pushed his hands deep into his jacket pockets and exhaled roughly, his breath puffing up into the air. "I can't change things in the past, no matter how much I wish on the moon I could. Here and now is all that I have any control over."

She shared something she'd learned when she'd been alone those nights after Michael had passed. "We all have regrets, a ton of should-haves, would-haves, could-haves." She felt that guilt about Michael; it was why she was so driven to keep her promise to him, no matter what it took. Sometimes a small lie could help the greater good. She knew she was trying to rationalize what she'd done since meeting Seth, but she couldn't go back. Not now. "All we can do is keep going. Maybe, somewhere along the way, we get a chance to do something for the person the way you are for Sarge and Maggie with the camp." That's what she'd been doing for Michael, making herself keep going. That's all she could do now.

Seth turned toward her, his eyes meeting hers, and there was something there that she didn't understand. Maybe the same thing that had made her lose her footing on the way up to the ridge when he'd looked back at her. He moved closer, and unexpectedly he took her right hand with his left. "Let's move back a bit," he said.

She looked down and saw the toes of her boots were less than three inches from the edge of the ridge, and beyond that the earth dropped dramatically straight down the steep side of rough rock and brush for maybe fifty feet. "Oh," she said, instinctively moving back a half pace as she tightened her hold on Seth. "Wow, I never even looked down."

"It's safe enough," he assured with an easy smile. "You weren't in any danger. I just wanted you to be aware of your surroundings."

"I am very aware thanks to you." She looked back at the sprawling view. "This is beautiful," she whispered.

"Yes, beautiful," he echoed, and when she glanced at him, he was looking at her.

"I'm glad you brought me here." It was a good memory to take with her when she left.

She felt a tendril of her hair that had come free of the ponytail flutter against her cheek. But before she could brush it away, Seth let go of her hand to gently tuck her hair back and behind her ear. His hazel eyes lingered on her face, then he blinked and said, "I'm glad you came with me." He drew his hand back and motioned toward the trail. "I guess we should head down."

As they walked back to the horses, Quinn stayed behind Seth. She'd never forget these moments on the ridge, good memories. She hadn't had too many of those in the past seventeen months. But that was all they would be. She took a deep breath, part of her wishing they could've stayed longer, then she thought about Seth holding her hand on the brink of the ridge. Maybe it was a good thing they were going back now. She couldn't even begin to think about his touch on her cheek. She pushed that away. She was here for Michael, just for Michael, and nothing else mattered to her.

When they were back in the saddle riding eastward along the trees, Quinn broke the silence that had hung between them since they'd left the lookout. "Aren't we heading back?"

"Yes, I'm just taking a different route," Seth said as their horses kept pace on the hard ground. "It's more direct."

When they were past the trees, he motioned to his right. "We'll go that way, and it should bring us out close to a path that goes south and back toward the stables."

They rode on, nearing another group of bare trees and skirted them to the west. Quinn spotted two long buildings in the distance that she'd seen from the lookout. Trucks were parked by both, and the sound of hammering and sawing hung in the air.

"The mess hall and the bunkhouse," Seth told her before she could ask. "If we had kept going east, we would've passed them, then the old cabin on the road that leads to the original entry gates to the ranch near the blind curve."

He motioned to another thick grouping of trees halfway below the two buildings and off to the southwest. "Those trees block the view of the stables and hay barn from here. The trail's pretty overgrown, but we can ride it."

They went the way he indicated, cutting

through the brush, and when Seth finally stopped, they were nearing the open back doors of the stable. Quinn sighed, wishing the ride could be longer.

"Are you getting tired?" Seth asked.

"Oh, no. I was just thinking that this is all so uncluttered, so silent and peaceful." She looked up at clouds that were darkening the sky as they crept closer. "It feels like the first time in forever that I've really been able to hear myself think."

That brought a sideways glance from Seth and his tone was touched with teasing. "So, you're hearing voices?"

She liked that tone of joking in his voice and the humor that touched his hazel eyes. "No, I just meant life gets so noisy, and when there's a peaceful pause, it just…" She shook her head. Her peaceful pause had been on the ridge until Seth had taken her hand and brushed at her hair. She'd felt something then that she couldn't define, but it confused her. She was here for Michael. But seeing Seth look at her like that… She shook her head. "Never mind, I'm being silly."

"Not at all. That's why I go to the lookout. I can think up there most of the time." He dismounted and led his horse through the open back doors of the stable.

As Quinn followed, she realized that today was the first time she'd really enjoyed something since Michael had passed. Just that thought made her pause, and she rationalized it was the riding. Being out in the open with the freedom that brought was wonderful. But she didn't deny that Seth had also been a source of some of that enjoyment.

He was a good-looking man, a kind man, a generous man, and a forgiving man whom she liked being around...maybe more than she should. But that was it. There wasn't any more. She didn't want to go where her thoughts seemed to be tumbling together. She had to focus, take the second chance Seth had given her and fulfill her promise to Michael.

THEY WERE BACK at the house by midafternoon, and Seth went to his office. Quinn went to talk to Julia. Sarge was on the bed with Cal, who was flexing the man's legs. The physical therapist, wearing jeans and a T-shirt, had a shaved head and a muscular build. "So, how did the ride go?" Julia asked.

"It was wonderful. We went up to a viewing ridge and I saw the overhead view of this land. It's incredible."

Sarge looked over at her. "It's going to snow."

That had come out of the blue. "You think so?" Quinn asked.

"I guarantee you, Quinn. Snow."

Julia nodded. "He's usually right. I don't know how he does it."

"Well, I'd love that. I never saw snow when Michael and I visited his parents in New York. We went in the summer. We never got there in the winter."

"When it snows here, it really snows," Julia said.

Cal turned to Sarge. "How about resting for a bit and we'll do more after lunch?"

"Okay, if you're too tired," the older man teased.

Cal laughed at that. "Yeah, I'm old and my arms ache."

Sarge let Cal settle him as Julia spoke to Quinn. "Where's Seth?"

"In his office, I think."

"Okay. I'll see him later." The woman looked tired, and Quinn understood that completely.

"Do you want me to tell him something?"

"If you talk to him, just tell him to come in here when he gets a chance."

"Sure, I'll do that," she said, then left while Sarge had a late snack.

Quinn found Seth in his office at his computer. He looked up when she came into the room and smiled. "That was a good ride."

"I loved it. I was used to riding trails near Griffith Park in Los Angeles. I've never been riding on land like this."

"It's unique," he said.

"Oh, Julia wants to see you when you get a chance." As he got up, she went closer. "Before you go, I want to say something and if I'm out of line, just tell me, please."

"What is it?"

"She's exhausted. I don't think I've ever seen her take time off. If it's all right with you, I can stay with Sarge for a couple of hours while Julia goes out for an early dinner or something?"

He swiveled his chair to face her more squarely. He shrugged. "I guess so, as long as Sarge is okay with it."

"I'll take care of him. I like visiting with him, and I'm sure it would be okay for a few hours."

Seth didn't look noticeably disconcerted by the man's tone or question as he came over to sit by Quinn. "Just checking on you." He looked at Quinn. "Sorry for being so long."

"Not a problem. I've come to love Zane Gray's storytelling."

Sarge smiled. "Told you so. *Riders of the Purple Sage*. The best of all his books."

"I can take over now," Seth said.

Quinn looked up at him and couldn't tell if things had gone well during his call or not. "If you don't mind, I'd like to finish the last few pages of this chapter. But you're welcome to stay and listen."

He pulled the other chair over beside hers, then looked at the tray. "Is that coffee still warm?"

She put the book in her lap and turned to the side table to pick up the mug. "Warmish, but not hot," she said as she shifted to hand it to Seth. "But the sandwich is pretty good."

"Thanks," he said as she handed him a napkin and the sandwich. He settled with his food and drink. "Go ahead."

Quinn kept reading but was very aware of Seth beside her. When she chanced a look at him, he was watching Sarge, who seemed riveted by the story. After ending the next chapter, Quinn asked. "Another one?"

"Thanks, Maggie, no," Sarge murmured as his eyes slowly closed. "I need to get busy on the hay barn roof. Snow's coming."

"You rest for a while, then we can talk about the hay barn," Quinn said and waited until she was certain he was asleep before she turned to Seth. His attention was still on Sarge. "He's good," she said softly and took the now-empty mug from Seth's hand. "You can go and take care of your business, if you need to."

Seth shook his head. "No. I'll take over here," he whispered.

"I'm feeling brave. Do you think it would be okay if I go for a short walk near the house? It's getting late, but there's still enough light out."

"Sure, of course."

She had a thought. "If I run into an animal that isn't a cat or dog, what do I do?"

He leaned closer and said in a low voice, "On that off chance, just stay very still, and let them leave on their own. When you can, back away slowly. Take your cell, and call me if you see anything."

"Okay," she said, a little less sure about the walk now. "I won't be gone long." Maybe she wasn't all that brave after all and would just sit on the porch.

In her borrowed boots and jacket and with her phone in her pocket, Quinn stepped out of the house five minutes later into the cold of the late afternoon. The sky was heavy and darkening. She flipped her hood up over her hair, pushed her hands in her pockets and stood on the top porch step to look around. She couldn't see anything moving, so she cautiously went down the steps and decided she would go as far as the hay barn.

She started off to the west on the gravel drive and kept going to a curve that swung slightly north and up. The hay barn was first, a large mostly log building with a high roof covered with green metal sheets. There were no sounds of any work being done now, and no vehicles were parked by it. But the double front doors had a gap of about two feet between them. Curious about what they were doing inside, she decided to take a quick look.

She slipped through the opening and into a vast space with strings of work lights illuminating the central area. The smell of sawdust and hay hung in the cold air. A loft, maybe ten feet deep, ran around the wall halfway between the cement flooring and the massive trusses that supported the roof. Stacked lumber and an array of power tools partially obscured a wide area in the middle of it all.

Silence echoed around her, but as Quinn turned to leave, that silence was broken by a shuffling noise. She jerked around, looking for anything that could have made the sound. Then it happened again, and she thought it came from ahead and to her right. Whatever was there was hidden by the stacked lumber and a huge circular table saw.

A wild animal must have made its way inside while the doors had been left open, and Quinn did what Seth told her to do. She stayed very still, then ever so slowly started to back toward the exit as quietly as possible. She reached in her pocket to take out her cell and glanced at the screen to pull up Seth's number. But she stopped when there was another sound that she knew no animal could make, a muffled sobbing.

She pushed her phone back in her pocket, hesitated, then cautiously went to her right and over to the large saw. She leaned forward to look over it. There was no wild animal, but a small child was huddled in the corner where the log walls butted into each other. She couldn't be sure if it was a boy or girl. Their face was hidden, pressed against bent knees, and they cried as if their heart would break.

"Hello," Quinn said, keeping her voice calm and low. "Can I help you?"

The crying stopped on a sharp intake of air, then ever so slowly, the child looked up at her. Shaggy auburn hair with sawdust clinging to it framed a boy's face that was pale and tear-streaked. He looked to be maybe six or seven years old. His blue eyes were slightly swollen from crying, and he stared up at her with both fear and defiance in his gaze.

"I'm Quinn," she said in a voice she'd used with troubled kids in her classroom. She didn't go closer.

He blinked rapidly, then finally spoke in a small unsteady voice. "I'm looking for a man called Sarge who lets kids live here and ride horses and stuff."

A runaway? How could a child so young get all the way out here? She cautiously took a single step, trying to ease around the saw.

"Sarge is my friend. He lives up at the big house."

That made the boy sit up straighter as he scrubbed his face with the sleeve of a blue corduroy jack he wore with faded jeans. His clothes looked as if they were at least two sizes too big for him. "You know him for real?" he asked.

"For real," she said, slowly taking another step closer. "He's a very nice man." Only a few feet separated them now. "I could take you to meet him, if you'd like?"

He eyed her skeptically. "You're not lyin', are ya?"

"No, I'm not. I promise."

The touch of defiance grew in his expression. "Tell him to come here."

"He can't do that. But I can take you up to him."

He took his time before he slowly stood, a small wiry kid maybe a few inches under four feet in height. "Okay, but you'd better not be lyin'."

She knew offering him her hand wouldn't be welcome, so she didn't. "I'm not. Follow me," she said, and he did silently all the way back up to the house. He didn't falter until

Quinn stepped up onto the porch. That was when he stopped at the foot of the stairs.

"I'll be waitin' right here."

"It's cold out here, and it's really warm inside."

"I'll wait," he said stubbornly.

She played her trump card. "I have some good spaghetti in the house along with cookies and milk. But if you aren't hungry..."

He looked torn between standing his ground in the freezing cold or getting food and warmth. It only took a moment for him to grudgingly agree. "Okay, I'll come on in." He trudged up the steps and followed her into the entry, stopping in his tracks when he spotted the stuffed mountain lion head on the wall to his left just inside the door. "Wow, that's... that's..."

She closed the door behind them. "Scary, huh?"

"No, it's awesome," he said almost reverentially.

"Awesome," she echoed, then motioned to him. "Take off your jacket." She shrugged out of hers and laid it on the cowhide bench, then the little boy put his down by it without her telling him to. The T-shirt he was wearing was so faded that she could barely make out a picture of some cartoon character on it, and his running shoes had probably been white at one point but had turned a stained gray. "Come on, and we'll get that food for you first. Then we can check on Sarge."

They'd barely stepped down into the great room when Seth unexpectedly spoke from behind them. "Hello, there." Quinn turned toward him, but the boy stood absolutely motionless before he cautiously turned away from her and toward Seth.

"I thought I heard you coming back," he said to Quinn. "Who do you have with you?"

"We haven't been introduced," Quinn said.

"What's your name?" Seth asked. When the child kept silent, Seth came closer to crouch down to get nearer the boy's eye level. "I'll just call you Kid, okay?"

"No," the little boy said quickly and firmly.

"Then how about Buster or Bubba?" Seth sounded serious. "Your choice."

"I'm not Buster or Bubba. I'm Tripp."

"I'm Seth. Welcome to my home." He looked past Tripp and up at Quinn. "So, am I supposed to guess how you went for a walk and came back with your friend?"

"I found him in the hay barn, and he's hungry, and I promised him spaghetti. He was asking about Sarge and wants to meet him."

"You do, do you?" Seth asked Tripp as he stood up.

"I want to see him real bad," the boy said.

"While Quinn gets the food for you, I have to go and check on Sarge. If you want to come with me, you can."

The boy turned to Quinn, looking small and vulnerable next to Seth. "Can I?" he asked her uncertainly.

"Sure."

Seth turned and headed to the west wing with the boy following two paces behind him. She went to quickly heat up leftover spaghetti and pour a glass of milk. She was just setting cutlery on the table by the food when the boy and man came back side by side. The two weren't exactly buddies, but they seemed more easy with each other now.

Tripp spotted Quinn by the table. "Sarge is real tired, so he's gonna sleep now, but he called me *boy* and said he has horses."

"He does have horses," Quinn agreed as she headed for the pantry. "Sit down and start eating while I go to get the cookies."

By the time she was back from the pantry with the pink box and paper napkins, Tripp had a good share of his spaghetti eaten. She glanced at Seth standing near the boy, then she took a seat across the table from Tripp. "Is there a problem with Sarge?" she asked Seth.

"No. The problem is Tripp won't tell me how he got here and why he came. He said he'll only tell you."

Tripp stopped eating while Seth was speaking and stared silently down at the remaining food on his plate. "Oh, okay," Quinn said. "Tripp, you can finish eating, then we can talk."

"Thank you," he said politely, never looking at either of them before he started eating again.

Seth took the seat next to Tripp, and Quinn watched both of them. Seth sat silently as Tripp ate quickly, as if he were afraid that the food would be snatched away from him. When he was down to his last bite, Quinn handed him some napkins. While he wiped his face and hands, she nudged the milk closer to him. He dropped the used napkins on the table by his plate, then reached for his drink.

"So, you saw Sarge?" Quinn asked after

giving the boy a chance to take a drink and put his glass down.

"I sure did. He was real nice. Can I have a cookie now?"

"Sure." Quinn opened the box by her and handed him one.

After dunking it in his milk, he ate it in two bites. Then he drained his glass. "That was real good. Thanks, Ma'am."

"Please, you can call me Quinn."

He nodded.

Quinn didn't know if Seth had much to do with small kids in his life, but he was beyond patient with Tripp. "Quinn is an expert on anything made with sugar," he told the boy.

"Wow." Tripp looked at Quinn, blue eyes wide with obvious admiration. "Awesome."

"Now that you've had some food, how about you tell Quinn how you got here and why you came?"

Tripp shrugged, then started to speak quickly as if to get it over with. "Okay, I don't have nowhere to go, so I wanted to stay here."

"How did you get here?" Quinn asked.

He looked uncomfortable now. "I didn't want to go with Mr. E in the van. Then this big truck was there, and some guy was talking about how come Sarge helped kids. He said Sarge was real kind and had horses. So I sneaked into his big truck with hay and stuff and hid. Then I got here." If that was true, he had to have come in on the hay truck Seth had directed to the barn when they were going on their ride.

"Did this Mr. E know you didn't get back into the van, or did he leave you on purpose?" Seth asked.

He shook his head. "He didn't know nothing."

"How old are you?" Quinn asked.

"Six."

Quinn didn't miss the way his chin lifted slightly. But she couldn't forget the sobs she'd heard when she found him. It still tugged at her, and she found herself hoping more and more she could really help him.

Seth exhaled. "Who is Mr. E?"

"A guy."

"Who?" Quinn nudged in a soft voice.

"I'm Tripp Allan Martin, okay?" He was getting upset and his voice raised. "That's me, Tripp Allan Martin."

"Okay, that's good." Seth stood, obviously aware a meltdown might be in the boy's near future. "I need to go back and check on Sarge. You stay here with Quinn."

The boy looked at Seth as he left, then turned to Quinn. "Why's Sarge in bed?" he asked in a half whisper.

"He's getting old and forgetful, and there's a lot to remember in his life."

"I bet he's a hundred and his head's full of stuff, huh?"

The boy seemed awful small to be out in the world alone. "No, he's not, but he is a lot older than you are."

"I'm not so young," Tripp said with his chin lifting again. He'd learned passive defiance somewhere along the way—not getting in anyone's face or yelling at them but making sure they knew what he meant.

By the time Seth came back into the great room, Tripp had grown silent. Seth crossed to the table but didn't sit down as he spoke to the boy. "So, is there anything else you want to tell Quinn?"

Tripp looked down at his empty plate, then unexpectedly blurted out, "I came here 'cause I don't have no one who wants me. Okay?"

Quinn could see that Seth almost flinched at the boy's words, but kept his voice low when he asked, "Where are your mom and dad?" The boy scrunched his eyes shut hard and didn't answer. But Seth persisted. "Where are they, Tripp?" When he got no response, he glanced at Quinn.

She reached across to lightly touch Tripp's hand, which he'd clenched into a fist on the tabletop. "Tripp, we want to help but we have to know who you were with."

He started jiggling nervously in his chair, then she saw him swallow. "Mr. E," he said without opening his eyes.

"Who is Mr. E?"

"Not my Dad" was all he said before he finally looked at her again.

"Why did you run away from Mr. E?" She hated where her imagination was going as she tried to fill that blank in on her own.

"I didn't want to go. A new kid told me if I got out when he didn't know, I could go find a place to be. I heard that man in the truck say Sarge lets orphans live here." He stilled, then looked right at Quinn and announced, "I'm an orphan."

"You aren't an orphan if you have a mom and dad. Where are they, Tripp?"

She waited, then he finally whispered, "They're in heaven."

She glanced at Seth who was staring at the boy, and the pain she saw in his expression tore at her. "They...they died?" she asked and had to bite her lip.

"Yeah."

She got up and went around the table to get closer to Tripp. "Why were you with Mr. E?"

"He says he's my foster dad, but he lied. I'm an orphan, right?"

All Quinn could do was nod and fight an overwhelming need to hug Tripp to her. Just six years old and he'd lost the two most important people in his world. Even after her loss, she couldn't imagine what that would do to a small child.

Seth cleared his throat and crouched by Tripp on his other side. "So, Tripp Allan Martin. You got out, and you ran away?"

Quinn watched the boy turn to Seth. "Yep. Sure did."

"Listen to me, Tripp." Seth had his full attention. "When I was little, my parents were gone, and I went to a foster home. I ran away, too. I thought I could find a place where people really wanted me."

Tripp gasped. "That's how come you got here?"

"No, I didn't get to come here for a while after that. I went back to another foster home, quite a few, actually, then I was brought here."

Tripp seemed to shrink as he started to shake his head back and forth hard. "No, no, no, I won't go back. Mr. E's gonna be real mad, and I hate that place."

When the little boy began to tremble, Seth reached for him and pulled him to his chest. The man scrunched his eyes shut the way the boy had moments ago. "It's going to be okay," she heard Seth whisper roughly. "I promise it's going to be okay." Then Seth slowly opened his eyes and met hers. "Max is on his way. My cell is in the entry on the bench. Use redial and you'll get him. Tell him I need to speak with him before he comes inside."

"Okay," Quinn said, unnerved by the unnatural brightness in Seth's hazel eyes.

"Thank you," he whispered hoarsely and kept holding onto Tripp.

"I'm sorry," she heard the boy say in a muffled voice. "I'm real sorry."

"No, it will be okay," he murmured. "I promise you, it will."

A roar of an engine sounded at the front of the house followed by the blare of a horn. Quinn moved quickly, ignoring Seth's cell phone on the entry bench to hurry outside. She saw a large white SUV with a light bar on the roof and ran down through the falling dust to get there as the sheriff opened his door to step out.

"Seth wants to come out to talk to you before you go inside." She hugged herself against the cold as she stood by the man's open door.

Max nodded without argument and sat back in the driver's seat. "Tell him I'll wait right here."

She hesitated, then said, "The boy, Tripp, he's so little, and I think he's been through a lot."

Max nodded. "Yeah, a whole lot, including his parents signing away their parental rights."

Her heart sank. It was worse than she'd even thought. "He thinks they're dead."

"That's probably the easiest way to tell him instead of saying they didn't want him. He's been up for adoption for almost two years, but he had some interest until the people knew he has learning problems and is really shy. I guess he's had all he can take. On top of that, his foster parents don't want him to go back to their house. Apparently, he's too disruptive."

CHAPTER ELEVEN

QUINN STAYED INSIDE with Tripp and kept an eye on Sarge while Seth went out to talk to Max. She tried to think of some way to distract Tripp that didn't involve more cookies. Then she had an idea. First, she checked on Sarge, then took the monitor Seth had left on the table for her and led Tripp into Seth's office.

She left the door open and let Tripp sit in the space captain recliner. When the chair sensed his slight weight, it automatically started adjusting for him. It shocked him at first, then he laughed and scrambled off. He got right back on to make it adjust again. Quinn loved to see him laugh. His face lit up. He was an endearing child, trying to survive any way he could.

"This is kind of like a spaceship, huh?"

She watched him cock his head to one

side, then he said, "No, it looks like a real fancy car."

She couldn't see a car, but she agreed. "I guess so, sort of a super car. Do you like cars?"

"Yeah, I sure do. But all Mr. E has is an ugly brown van."

"I love cars, and I used to go to car shows."

"They got car shows?"

He was all into it now. "Yes, and they bring really crazy cars there sometimes. Sometimes they're weird. They had a truck that had such big wheels—it was so high off the ground that you had to use a ladder to get inside it. They call it a monster truck."

His eyes widened. "Wow. A monster truck. Did you fall out of it?"

She laughed as she reached for one of the computer chairs and pulled it over to sit so she was at eye level with Tripp. He came closer, and he gripped the arm of her chair with one hand. "No, I didn't, but I heard that one of the guys who drove it into the show grounds— you know, where they were letting people come to look at them—he fell out of it when he forgot how high he was off the ground."

Tripp suddenly looked serious. "Did he get into bad trouble?"

"No, and he didn't get hurt. But I bet he felt pretty embarrassed."

"I think he did," the boy said solemnly. "How come you like cars, being a girl and all?"

"I always liked cars. I got married to a man who loved computers, but I got him to love cars, too."

He was staring at her, enthralled, and she kept talking. "The last show we went to, there was a car that was so long it had to come on a really big flatbed truck. It was called a super limo. It was purple with glitter in the paint and gold trim around the windows and on the tire rims."

He was smiling now. "You're kiddin'."

"No, we got to ride in it."

He came even closer. "You did?"

"Yeah, and it had hydraulics that made it go up and down while we were in it." She made the motions with her hands. "And I almost got sick."

He giggled at that. "It's 'cus you're a girl, huh?"

"No, but this girl does have a sensitive

stomach," she said as she brushed at his hair to keep it out of his eyes.

She was startled when she heard Seth speak from behind her. "She thinks the car she drives is a girl, Tripp. What do you think about that?"

Tripp giggled again. "Nah, but I bet trucks are boys, huh?"

Seth reached for the other computer chair, pulled it up beside Quinn and sat down. "Some are, but some could be girls."

"Yeah, they could be, huh?"

"Now, we need to talk, you and me, and…" Seth glanced at her. "Quinn, too, if she'd like to stay?"

Before Quinn could agree, Tripp reached for her hand. He squeezed it tightly. "Stay, please," he said, just shy of begging, and any traces of laughter were gone.

She didn't know what was happening, but she didn't want to leave the boy or the man right then. "I'll stay."

"Okay, we have to talk about what you did," he said to Tripp.

Suddenly, Tripp pulled away from Quinn and stood facing Seth, his small hands clenched at his sides. "Please, please, don't send me back, please."

"You're not going back to Mr. E's house," Seth said.

"For real?"

"I will not let them send you back there." Seth reached to take both of Tripp's small fists in his hands and leaned closer to him. "I'm friend's with Max, the sheriff. He's a very good man, and he's coming in to talk to you in a minute. But before he does, I have to explain what's going to happen. You won't go back to Mr. E's house, but you will have to go to the head office in Cody, you know the big building where you go once a month to talk to the doctor?"

Tripp was dead still. Then his eyes narrowed as he snatched his hands free from Seth and said one word. "No."

"Where does he have to go?" Quinn asked.

"Family Services," he said without looking away from Tripp. Then he spoke to the child again. "Please, let me explain. You'll go back there with the sheriff, then in a week, Mr. McFarland, your caseworker, said that you can come here and stay if you want to."

Tripp quickly shook his head. "Naw, you're lyin'."

"No, I'm not lying."

Quinn could tell Tripp wanted desperately to believe Seth, but the boy simply shrugged and said, "I don't lie. You can tell Sarge that I don't lie." He crossed his arms in defiance and didn't say anything else.

"You'll stay in the play wing for a week that's beside the offices. Then you can come back here for a couple of months, if you want to."

His eyes slowly got bigger. "For real?"

"Yes, but only if you want to."

Tripp was very still. Then he started jumping up and down and clapping his hands. "Yes, yes, yes! I can come back! I want to! I want to! Please!" The boy became still, his short-lived joy gone. He seemed to deflate. "Then I go away again, don't I? I always go away again."

Quinn couldn't stand the touch of fear in the boy's expression now. She took his hand again and moved her chair to get closer to him.

Tripp kept silent as he looked back at Seth, but his hand tightened like a vise on hers.

"Mr. McFarland will ask you if you want to come here for a couple months, and it's up to you. You can choose."

Tripp looked wary. "I can?"

"Yes, you can. It's your decision. I mean, you hardly know me, and you might need time to see if that's what you want to do. But it's up to you."

The boy was starting to shake again, and Quinn thought he might go into shock. Instinctively, she drew him slowly closer, and her heart melted when he leaned into her. She put her arm around him. "He's telling the truth, ain't he?" Tripp asked Quinn in a low shaky whisper.

"It's true," she said, her eyes never leaving Seth, who held her gaze with his. "He really means it."

"It's just one week," Seth said. "That's seven days."

Tripp hesitated, then finally said, "Do I gotta go there now?"

Seth nodded. "Yes. I'm sorry. It's the rules, but I'll be there to pick you up when they say you can come back."

"I have to sleep at the bunkhouse room there, too?"

"Yes."

Tripp stood straighter. "I kind of don't like the bunkhouse, 'cus kids cry and all, but I guess it's okay." He took a breath and moved away from Quinn to stand in front of Seth again. "Just…don't forget me, please?"

"I'd never forget you," Seth said, his voice slightly unsteady. "I promise."

Quinn swiped at her eyes and smiled at the boy. "No one could ever forget you, Tripp Allan Martin."

AFTER MAX DROVE off with a stoically re-signed Tripp, Quinn stood by Seth at the bottom of the porch steps. Both were without their jackets, yet neither one looked away until the white SUV disappeared from sight over the rise. "What just happened?" Seth asked in a low voice.

"You just offered one little boy something I suspect he never had before in his whole life—hope."

Seth stood very still as her words sank in. Hope. If he could give Tripp that gift, he'd do whatever he could to make sure the boy never lost it. He turned to Quinn, who was hugging herself and shaking from the cold.

"Come on inside." He didn't hesitate to put his arm around her shoulders and hurry with her up and into the house. He let go as they both sat on the cowhide bench and finally took off their boots.

"I hate that he had to leave, even for a week," Seth murmured. "I can tell he's been lied to so often, or at least he thinks he has been. I have to make sure I keep my word to him." He glanced at Quinn. "Max knows his caseworker, Lou McFarland, and got an agreement up front because of Tripp's circumstances. They'll let him come back here after a quick check on us, then he can stay while they do a full vetting to release him for two months of foster care here. Max made that happen. I owe him. I wish I could've promised more, but I'm not here permanently, and I'm not set up for long-term care for him."

Quinn shifted to face Seth a bit more. "So, you really did run away when you were a kid?"

"Yeah. I told you my parents were gone, and I had no family, and I was in my second foster home, and I hated it. I can tell you that Tripp saw living with Mr. E not as a moment in time that would pass. He saw it as a forever situation. All I saw growing up were people who pretended to be my family and weren't, so I went looking for a place where I could belong. Like Tripp was trying to do."

"They sent you back to the foster home?"

He stared down at his hands on his knees. "No, they took me to another one, then another and another. By the time I ended up here, with Sarge and Maggie, I was pretty angry and resigned."

"I'm sorry," she said on a soft sigh. "I can't even imagine…"

"Be thankful you can't," he murmured. "I've worked for years to try to forget all of that, and I was getting there. Then I was looking at Tripp shaking and scared, and I knew what he was doing, what he was thinking, how scared he was and how lost he felt." Just saying that out loud reinforced his need to protect that small boy from all of that, a child he'd known only for a few hours.

Quinn was silent for a long moment, then he could feel her staring at him. "You know I mentioned some plan behind our lives before."

He didn't want to hear some esoteric statement, not even from Quinn. He kept his eyes on his hands pressing against his knees. "Let me guess. This is all some cosmic plan? You're here to find Tripp, and I'm here with all that misery in my past. Is that close to what you're about to say to me? Or maybe you think Tripp wished for all of this, and there it was for him."

"I'm sorry," she said in a low voice.

He hadn't meant to be sarcastic, not after what Quinn had done. "No, no, I'm sorry. Go ahead, say what you want to. I'll listen."

"I was thinking, seeing you with Tripp, that maybe those memories you want to forget are what makes you able to see so clearly what he's going through. I don't know too many people who could understand what his life has been like. Good or bad, your life made you who are at this moment. Our lives do that to us, and it can be pretty awful. But in the end, there's always some good that comes out of it."

She'd spoken softly, and he wanted to look at her, but he couldn't. "Sarge said that even burning your hand can be good if it stops you from touching the stove again." He swallowed to ease the tightening in his throat. "I guess you're both saying the same thing."

"I think so. Whether this is all some sort of plan or a child's answered wish, or just plain coincidence, you're in Tripp's life now. Whatever help you need with him or with Sarge while I'm here, just ask."

He hadn't thought anything out, except to get Tripp in a safe place for a while. He didn't even know what to ask for, but he had a singular thought that Michael Lake had been very fortunate to have Quinn when he was in such great need. "Thank you," he said, then stood. "I should check on Sarge."

"Of course," she said and touched his arm.

When he looked at her, she held out the monitor.

He took it but hesitated as he looked down at her. "I don't know what I was thinking of, that I can help a kid I've only known for a couple of hours?"

"Sometimes that's all the time you need with a person to know you want them in your life, that they belong there."

That summed up what Sarge and Maggie had handed to him all those years ago. They'd given him a place to belong, and he'd been more than a challenge for them.

"Max mentioned that Tripp has some learning disabilities," Quinn said.

"MacFarland explained that he acts out and can't focus, then he gets angry that he can't."

"He's been in kindergarten and first grade, and believe me, even kids that have so-called *normal lives* in that age group can be a handful. But I've always thought, if a child feels loved and wanted and is the center of the world for just one person, that could change everything."

He never had one person like that in his life until he had two of them who made him feel special and wanted. "I'm going to do that for Tripp if I can." He turned to head to the west wing but stopped at the entrance to the hallway and glanced back at Quinn. "Quinn, I do think you were supposed to be there to find Tripp." He surprised himself admitting he believed that.

QUINN CROSSED TO the staircase and sank down on the second step up so she could see out the front window and watch the driveway as night fell. When Seth had said she was supposed to be there, she had the strangest thought. Maybe she wasn't here to get Michael's work acknowledged. Maybe the plan had always been for her to find the little boy and make sure he met the man who could change his life. She knew that Tripp being brought into Seth's life trumped what she wanted when she came to the ranch. It was all about a child.

"Is that Julia?" Seth asked as he stepped into the entry and drew her attention to the window.

Headlights flashed and the big white truck was there. Julia got out, hurried up and onto the porch, then the front door opened. She stepped inside and was beaming as she swung the door shut behind her. "Hello, everyone," she said as she slipped her jacket off. "How's Sarge?"

"Everything's good." Seth studied Julia. "From your smile, it looks like everything's good with you, too."

She laughed at that. "Better than good."

"I was just going to start a pot of coffee," Quinn said. "Do you two want some?"

"If Sarge is sleeping, I'd like to sit down with a good cup of coffee and unwind," Julia said.

After Julia checked on Sarge, the three

of them sat at the dining table with coffee and what was left of the cookies. While Seth told her about Tripp, Julia listened intently, then sighed. "Quinn, bless you for taking that walk."

"I came really close to not even going on the walk," she admitted.

"Thank goodness you did," Julia said, then glanced at Seth sitting beside her. "So, you're getting set up to foster him?"

"For a couple of months. At least he can have a break from that life for a while."

"That's a huge commitment, especially to a young child. I mean, I love it, but are you sure you can do it with everything going on in your life?"

Seth sat back, ignoring his coffee. "I'm not sure about anything, except I want to try. I'm here with Sarge for at least that long, and you know, Seattle isn't where I want to be now. They don't need me, not with Owen at the helm. So, I can be here for both Sarge and Tripp."

"At least for now, you're cleared for it," Julia said.

He shook his head slightly. "I'm cleared

until February. But it's my business. I started it and it's mine."

"What are you getting at?" Julia asked, and Quinn wanted to know, too.

"I don't know. I really don't." He looked dead serious.

"You're thinking of not doing that with Tripp?" Quinn asked.

"Oh, no, that's a done deal, but I think I'm not going far enough. Two months. That's going to go by in a blur, then Tripp will go back to the system. Sarge told me once that Maggie wanted to keep all the boys that came through here, and when they left, it broke her heart every time."

"I can imagine," Julia said.

He stood, hesitated, then looked from Julia to Quinn. "I need to talk to Owen," he said. "I'll be in the office."

He left and Julia looked at Quinn. "What was that all about?"

Quinn knew some of it. He didn't want Tripp back in the system, but there was no way for him take on Tripp on a permanent basis and still work in Seattle and care for Sarge here. "He's made a connection with

Tripp. When it comes time for him to go, it's going to break his heart."

Seth surprised both women when he came back into the great room. He sat down and said, "I've decided to try to do long-term fostering with Tripp. He won't have to go back to his old life."

Quinn was thrilled, but how would he do it? "You mean that?"

"I sure do. I talked to Owen and told him that I'm not going back to the company."

"What?" Quinn asked, shocked.

"You're just walking away?" Julia asked.

"It's not that simple. Lots of paperwork and getting things realigned, but I can do anything they need from here. It's all on Owen now, and I'd go silent on all things business. I think it's been coming since Sarge's accident, but it's gathered momentum lately. I belong here, not in Seattle."

Julia smiled. "Sarge will be thrilled if you aren't heading back to the city all the time."

Quinn sat in stunned silence, hearing Seth's words but unable to deal with them. He was letting Owen Karr take over, the man who didn't have time to even listen to her presentation for Michael's Shield. If she could have, she would've stood and excused herself. But she wasn't sure her legs would hold her at the moment.

It couldn't be over just like that. It couldn't be. She'd gotten so close. She just needed more time, but if Seth was out of the loop, she didn't know what to do. She closed her eyes for a moment to process that. It hurt to be so close to a possible win for Michael, but she couldn't just give up.

"Quinn?"

Seth startled her, pulling her from her thoughts. Then she felt a touch on her arm and Julia was speaking to her. "Are you okay? You look pale."

Things had changed so abruptly. She was surprised that the world wasn't spinning out of control. "I'm...okay. I think it just hit me that... I...almost didn't go down to the hay barn. What would've happened if I hadn't?"

Seth had come around the table and crouched by her chair. "But you did. That's what counts. You went and you found Tripp. Now he's safe."

When Seth said those words, something settled in her. *Tripp is safe.* "Yes. Yes, he is," she whispered.

"Everything's the way it should be," he said, his hazel eyes holding hers.

"You believe that?" she asked as Julia watched the two of them.

Seth touched her hand. "Yes, I do." He covered her hand with his, gently squeezed it, then let go and stood.

"I'll be in the office calling MacFarland to tell him I want full vetting for fostering without a time limit. Max might be able to reach him again." He looked down at Quinn. "How about another ride in the morning? I can show you the campsites."

"Yes, that would be great."

CHAPTER TWELVE

AN HOUR BEFORE NOON, Seth was alone in his office. He'd showered and changed into a fresh gray thermal and jeans after coming back from his ride with Quinn. She'd been excited to find snow upon meeting him in the entry that morning. She'd motioned to the side window by the door. "Sarge said it was going to snow, and bingo! Snow. Real snow!" He smiled now thinking of it—though he hoped the snow wouldn't cause cloud cover during the Wishing Moon.

The day had been good so far. Their ride had been low-key, just wandering up into the foothills so he could show her where three of the campsites would be come spring. She seemed intrigued by everything, including the snow, and he felt more and more settled that he might be doing this right this time. But he still had that unease that maybe this was more his doing than reality.

Her approval meant a lot to him, more than it should, and he felt uneasy about that. He knew he had growing feelings for her, feelings that were only strengthened by her interaction with Tripp. Now he was thinking about being here permanently as soon as he could figure out the legal ramifications of stepping back from the company. It would take time, but meanwhile, he'd be here most of the time with Tripp and Sarge. Quinn would be here, too.

When a soft knock sounded, he swiveled around to face the door. "Come on in."

Quinn was there and crossed to hand him a slip of paper. "Julia asked me to give this to you for when you go into town the next time. She said there's no rush."

He glanced at the list, then back at Quinn. "Tell Julia I'll go now," he said. "I want to check in with Burr to see what he managed to find out from the county about the blind curve."

"Okay. Thanks again for the ride. I love what you're going to do with the campsites."

"Thanks for your input," he said. "Next time I'll show you the bunkhouse and the mess hall."

"That would be great. Have you heard anything about Tripp?"

"Max left a message that McFarland expedited background checks for the quick placement. So his stay at the office might be more like four or five days." He was pleased about that. But the full-time fostering would be a lot more difficult to put in place. "You know, I've never been impressed with my money. It's always been a byproduct that happened to come from me doing what I love. I never used it to step to the head of the line for anything. But with Tripp, he had parents who literally signed him away."

He grimaced with disgust at what they'd done to their son. "Then his last foster parents didn't want to take him back. He's had no serious inquiries for adoption, and unless something is done, he's lost. I'm not above making it easier for him if I can. Money's just money, but this is his life."

"Maybe you should call and see if you can talk to Tripp, so he knows you haven't forgotten about him?"

He remembered a time when he was small, and no one seemed to remember him. Four

or five days back then would've felt like forever. "I will."

"Tell him hi from me, okay?"

"Don't go yet," he said and made a call on
his cell. "Hey, Max, I was wondering if you
have a number I can call to talk to Tripp?"

"This is your lucky day. Hold on," the sheriff said.

There was a pause, then Seth heard the
boy's voice over the phone. "Hello?"

Seth smiled at Quinn and pulled the phone
back to put it on Speaker. "Tripp, it's Seth.
What are you doing with the sheriff?"

"He came and got me to go for a ride in the
police car and he let me put on the siren," he
said. "It's really, really loud."

"Wow, that sounds great," Seth said.

"Max is going to get me a badge, so I'll be
like his deputy, too. When I get big, he said I
could work with him if I wanted to."

Seth watched Quinn listening to the boy.
She was smiling, and he was glad she was
there. "You'd better not arrest me when you
see me," Seth said.

He'd made a joke, but it obviously wasn't
funny to Tripp, who said quickly, "No, no,

no, I wouldn't. I never would. I promise. I really promise."

He cut in. "Hey, Tripp, I know you wouldn't. That was a joke."

There was silence for a moment, then Tripp asked, "When are you coming to get me?"

"As soon as Mr. McFarland tells me I can. But soon."

"Can Quinn come, too, please?"

"Why don't you ask her? She's right here."

He nodded at Quinn, and she said, "Hi, there. It's Quinn. Is that you, Tripp?"

"Yes, me, Tripp Allan Martin. You remember me, huh?"

"I'll never forget you."

"Max came and got me out of the office."

"Good, that's so nice of him."

"You'll…you'll come to get me, too?"

She closed her eyes. "Yes, I'll be there with Seth as soon as Mr. McFarland says you can come back here. I promise."

There was silence on the phone, and Quinn opened her eyes to look at Seth.

"Hey, Tripp. Are you okay?" Seth asked, his eyes holding Quinn's as he spoke to the boy.

"Yeah, but I… I just…" There was another

long pause, then Tripp said quickly, "You still want me, right?"

"I sure do," Seth said. "Where are you now?"

"Where Max lives. His place is real huge, and he's got a black horse called Thunder and all kinds of rodeo stuff."

"Have you ever ridden a horse?" Seth asked.

"No."

"Would you like to?"

"I don't know how," the boy said in a small voice.

"When you get here, we can see about teaching you, okay?"

"Are you lyin'?"

Seth closed his eyes. "Tripp, let's get something settled right now. I will not lie to you, ever. I promise you that."

"I'm sorry," he said in a small unsteady voice.

"Hey, I'm not mad. I just want you to understand that what I tell you, it's always going to be the truth. Got that?"

"I got that," he said a bit more firmly.

"Now, you go and see Max's place and have a great time."

"He says he's got a donkey called Morris. That's a real weird name, huh?"

Seth chuckled and looked back at Quinn, who was smiling a bit herself. "Very weird. I'll call you tomorrow, I promise. Okay?"

"Yes, please."

"Let me speak to Max again."

Max came back on the Speaker. "He's one happy kid."

Seth was so pleased Max was helping with Tripp. "Riding along with you as shotgun has to be great."

"No, I mean about you taking him."

"I just couldn't let him go back, Max. Thanks for what you're doing for him."

"I'm happy to do it," Max said. "Maybe I'll even get to be Uncle Max someday. I gotta go."

Seth ended the call. "He's having fun with Max," he said, then stood. "I forgot how tough it can be for a boy like Tripp to trust anyone." He looked at Quinn. For a moment, he hadn't trusted her over a single lie. He really was the product of the boy he'd been. Trusting anyone had been a rare thing in his life, but now, with Quinn, he thought he might be getting better at it. He wasn't all the way there, but listening to her talking to Tripp about cars while he stood just outside in the hallway, and her reading to Sarge looking happy to be doing it, had shifted so many things for him. Maybe he could actually outgrow his past. He hoped so.

He watched Quinn lower her eyes to stare at her hands in her lap. Then she asked in a low voice, "When did Sarge win your trust?"

That made him pause. "I don't know. Somehow, I just knew it, that I could trust him. But there was no major moment that I remember. He was just there, and he always kept his word."

"You'll make that happen with Tripp," she said meeting his eyes again.

"I hope so," he said. "I'm going into town, but I'm thinking I should get things for Tripp for when he arrives. I don't even know what I need to fix up the bedroom upstairs for him. Then there's clothes, books, games and a computer."

He exhaled, then knew what he did need. "I'd really appreciate it if you could come and help me figure out the basics. You're used to kids around his age and you'd know more about what they'd like than I do."

QUINN WANTED TO go with Seth so badly after talking to Tripp, but she hesitated. During the night she'd made a huge decision to stay at the ranch until she saw Tripp safely settled with Seth. She couldn't approach Seth about Michael's work, not now. But when Tripp was home, she knew that was when she'd leave for Denver. Seth never had to know why she'd shown up that day at the blind curve. "I don't know."

"It would be a huge help for me. I'll have to pick up what Julia wants at Farley's, and he carries all the clothing a kid on a ranch would need. What size do you think he'd wear?"

She sure didn't want to face Farley again, not with him knowing she'd lied to Seth. But she could do one thing. "Can I call Max?"

He didn't ask any questions but handed her his phone. She hit redial and Max came on. She explained what she needed, then hung up. "He's going to find out Tripp's clothing and shoe sizes, then text the information to you."

"That's great." He hesitated, then said, "You will come, won't you? Julia mentioned there's a specialty store on the southern edge of town that caters to the dude ranch crowd.

It has everything you'd need to make a Western bedroom for a kid."

"Okay. I'll come, and while you go to Farley's I'll find the boutique and see what they have," she said.

He studied her. "Oh, I understand. I never told Farley anything about how you got here. He did all the talking that day."

She almost felt dizzy with relief. "Okay. When do you want to leave?"

He flashed that crooked grin. "Ten minutes ago?"

The drive into town was easy, talking about colors for everything and old and new toys. Max sent the clothing sizes and the measurements for Tripp's feet. Quinn found out Seth only remembered having one toy when he'd been small, a set of plain wooden blocks he'd taken with him from foster home to foster home. They'd disappeared somewhere along the way.

Three hours later, they were on their way back to the ranch with Julia's order and everything else needed to transform the almost bare bedroom upstairs. There were clothes for Tripp, a heavy denim jacket and a pair of Western boots along with running shoes.

Even a kid-size hat that was a lot like the one Seth was wearing. When they pulled up to the log house, they unloaded the truck and took everything upstairs.

Quinn unpacked the bedding with cowboys on it, and Seth wanted to make up the double spindle bed right then. One thing led to another until the room was transformed. Quinn stood back to study the results of what she and Seth had done together, and she sighed with satisfaction. The room was full of everything horses and cowboys, and a large dose of cars, too. From the comforter to the pillows and the pictures above the headboard, the West was alive and well in that room. The lamps on the small nightstands had bases with rearing horses and the leather shades had branding patterns on them.

A high dresser against the log wall at the front was full of clothing, and a wooden chest at the foot of the bed held extra blankets and pillows. The shoes were sitting on the floor alongside the bed. A shelving unit that had been original to the room held books and another lamp. On the two lower shelves, she'd set up the plain wooden building blocks she'd found and several model cars she'd hoped Tripp would like.

As she and Seth stood there, he touched her shoulder. "You did a great job. He's going to love all of this. The cars are terrific, and the blocks, they're just like the ones I had."

She smiled at him and admitted, "I actually got them for you, but maybe you can get Tripp to share."

He was quiet, and when she looked at him, he said in a low voice, "Thank you."

"I saw them and thought you should have them," she said. "Maybe Tripp will end up in construction and he can practice building things with you. Make a town and use the cars. Maybe we can get an old red pickup truck."

Seth chuckled. "I'm no builder, but ask me to run AutoCAD programs or do coding, I'm a whiz."

"We all have our gifts," she murmured, then glanced at the shoes by the bed. "His feet are pretty small, aren't they?"

"I hope he likes those boots."

"He's going to love those boots." She was so grateful she'd been able to contribute in some way to help Tripp and Seth in their new lives. "Best of all, he'll love being here with you."

She felt him come closer to her, and his voice was low. "Thank you for all you've done for Tripp and for me. Julia was right, you know."

"About what?" she asked as she turned toward him and felt her breath catch.

His hazel eyes held hers, and he was so close she could feel his breath brush her face. Then his gaze dropped to her lips. "She told me we make a good team," he whispered as he bent toward her and kissed her. The contact was gentle and lingered as she closed her eyes. She felt overwhelmed by a feeling she hadn't known could exist in her life anymore. She thought she'd lost it forever. But it was there—a sense of connection with a man, a connection she wanted. Seth gently cupped her chin.

When she forced herself to open her eyes, she knew she shouldn't be standing right there, looking up at a man who was proving her heart hadn't been permanently broken. Then a sense of betrayal she suddenly felt for Michael was almost suffocating her. She had no right to feel anything or want anything more from Seth. She owed him, period. She'd lied to him. Nothing could change that. But she couldn't lie to herself. Most of all, she'd promised Michael, and she had to keep moving.

Seth whispered, "I didn't know someone like you could come into my world." His words shattered something in her, and she turned away.

"I… I should get things started in the other bedroom so it's ready for you to use when Tripp takes this room." She blindly began to pick up stray packaging and push it into an empty box. "I'll get rid of this." She didn't look at Seth again before she walked out of the room and headed straight downstairs.

She hurried through the quiet house to the mudroom off the kitchen and dropped the wrappings in a trash can by the door to the back deck. But she didn't leave the space. She sank down on a bench that ran along one wall and buried her face in her hands.

She'd felt nothing for any man after she'd met Michael, not until Seth had been there. She'd slowly began feeling things for a man who was becoming far too important to her, making her almost forget Michael, and that scared her. She inhaled unsteadily and clenched her hands until they ached.

It had seemed a simple plan a long time ago, to just be here and help Seth any way she could, then explain about Michael's Shield and either win or lose. But nothing was simple about her time here with Seth, not one thing. There was no reason to stay. She wanted to, but she couldn't. Something in her didn't want Seth to ever know about the real lie she'd lived here. She'd leave. But that thought didn't make her feel any better at all.

CHAPTER THIRTEEN

SETH STOOD ALONE in the newly done bedroom, wondering why he'd been so impulsive and kissed Quinn. No, he knew why. He'd wanted to kiss her, period. But kissing her at that moment had obviously been wrong. She'd looked confused and hurt, which he hadn't intended. Then she'd turned and walked away, leaving him doubting if he'd ever get anything to do with matters of the heart right. Maybe his initial intentions had been right—help her until she was well and had her car, then let her go. The thing was, he actually didn't know how he'd let her go.

He finally went to check in the bedroom directly across the walkway from Tripp's new room, but Quinn wasn't there. He left and went downstairs, pausing when he heard things being moved in the kitchen. Through the archway, he saw her doing something at the stove with her back to him. He wanted to talk to her and figure everything out. Instead, he turned and went to see Sarge and Julia.

It was an hour later, when Sarge had beaten Seth in a third game of poker, that Julia came into the room. She crossed to the bed where Sarge had stretched out to rest and Seth was getting ready to read him some Zane Grey.

"Well, who won?" she asked, smiling at the two men.

Sarge gloated a bit. "I skunked him."

She patted Seth on his shoulder. "How humiliating."

"It sure is," Seth said, then asked, "Where's Quinn?"

"She left dinner in the warming oven, then took me up to show me Tripp's room. You two did a great job. It's perfect."

"So, she's still up there?"

"Maybe, or in the master bedroom. She mentioned cleaning it in case Libby and Jake wanted to stay up there when they come back."

"Thanks," Seth said and left the room.

When he got upstairs, Tripp's new room was empty, but as he stepped out into the hallway, a creaking sound came from the open double doors to the master bedroom. There were no lights on inside, and he went through a short hallway lined with closets and out into the room beyond, a smaller version of the great room below it.

He stopped by the massive poster bed Sarge had made for Maggie fifty years ago out of trees off the land. Then he caught movement in the shadows near the stone fireplace on the back wall. As his eyes adjusted, he could make out Quinn in Maggie's rocking chair. She was facing the back window by the hearth.

"There you are," he said, going over to her.

"Yes, here I am," she said softly through the shadows, but didn't stop the slow rocking.

"What are you doing?"

"Thinking."

"Do you do that often?" He knew it was a stupid attempt at humor to ease the tension he felt between them. It didn't work.

She sighed. "No, but I probably ought to."

He went over to sit on the raised hearth, facing her through the shadows. "Are you okay?"

"Fine, fine," she murmured.

"Oh, it's that way, is it?"

"What?"

"You're mad?"

There was silence, and it was the loudest silence he'd ever heard. When he couldn't take it any longer, Quinn finally half whispered, "No, I'm just trying to figure things out."

"What things?"

"Life. It gets complicated."

He'd kissed her. He knew that had complicated everything. "I'm sorry."

Quinn finally glanced toward him, but the shadows in the room made her eyes unreadable. "It's my problem," she said. "Was there something you needed?"

"No, except to tell you the Wishing Moon is tomorrow night."

"When's the best time to see it?" She didn't sound too thrilled.

"The app says at nine o'clock. As it climbs higher, it diminishes in size."

She spoke quietly. "Thank you."

"As I said before, the cabin's where Maggie loved to make her wishes. Another option that's closer is the hay barn loft."

"I guess the hay barn would be the best place for me to go." He didn't hear any excitement in her voice, just an agreement she'd go.

"Just make sure you wear warm clothes."

"I will," she said, and added in what seemed like an afterthought, "Dinner's in the heating drawer."

Food was the last thing on his mind. An impetuous kiss had shifted everything. He hesitated, then stood. He didn't want to be in there with her any longer. He couldn't keep fighting to try and make conversation, and the silence made him nervous. "I'll be in Tripp's room if you need me."

Then he walked away from her. Life changes were coming at him in a rush, and he felt slightly dizzy from their impacts. He just needed to be alone.

THE NEXT MORNING, Seth was on the Donovan ranch in a stall by a double riding ring with Max and Tripp. The boy was sitting on a gray donkey, the one named Morris. Seth was by him, his hand over Tripp's on the saddle horn. He could tell, despite the adventure of sitting on the animal, Tripp wasn't at all easy with it.

"Do donkeys race like horses?" he asked Seth.

"I bet they have donkey races. What do you think, Max?"

"I think if they have frog races, there has to be donkey races. What do you think, Tripp?"

"I guess." He was in a faded blue shirt and torn jeans with old running shoes on his feet. His corduroy jacket didn't seem heavy enough to protect him against the cold. Seth wished Quinn was there with him. But after the kiss and her reaction, he'd let that go for now. It was too complicated, with him being worried about repeating past mistakes and Quinn still loving her husband so much. No matter what went on, his feelings for her just kept getting deeper and he had no idea how to stop that happening.

"Seth?" Tripp was saying. "How come Quinn didn't come with you?"

"She was busy," he said vaguely.

"Oh, okay," the boy said as he leaned closer to Seth. "Can I get off now?"

Max said, "Hold on a minute. Give me your phone, Seth."

He passed it over after unlocking it, then Max said, "Smile, you two!"

He took a picture, then passed the phone back to Seth who looked down at it. "Pretty handsome guys, don't you think?" he asked Tripp as he showed the picture to him.

The little boy looked at it and a huge grin showed on his face. "We are handsome guys."

Both men laughed, then Seth turned to Tripp and held out his hands. "Yes, you and me," he said as the little boy went into his arms and hugged Seth tight around his neck.

"Thank you for not forgetting me," Tripp whispered.

Seth closed his eyes and hugged Tripp to him. He didn't know how he could love the boy in such a short time, but he surely did. "I never will. Never."

"What about Quinn. She'll forget, won't she?"

Seth carried Tripp out of the stall and headed over to stacked hay bales by the huge bar. He sat down, kept Tripp on his lap and knew he had to explain a bit to the boy. "Quinn, she's only been at my ranch for a while. She's really great, you know."

"Yes, she is," Tripp said with one arm around Seth's shoulders and his other resting on Seth's hand at his waist. The boy needed contact, and Seth was even more sure he'd made the right decision to leave the company and be here. "She really likes you, and she'll be at the house when you come there. But I'm not sure if she'll stay there after a while."

Tripp moved enough to shift and look Seth right in the face. He frowned. "She's gonna go away?"

"I don't know. I hope not, but you have to let people do what they want to do. Did you know Quinn came from California?"

"Really?" His eyes grew wide. "Like the beach and everything?"

"Yes, the beach," he said, remembering that photo of Quinn and Michael. "That's where she usually lives."

"Then can we go and see her there?"

"I don't know. We could ask her. For now, she's at the ranch and really happy that you're coming there to live."

Tripp hugged Seth again, burying his face in his neck. "That's good," he whispered.

Seth closed his eyes and knew he could pretend he wanted Quinn for Tripp's sake, but that was only a half truth. He wanted her to stay, to give him time to figure things out, but he didn't know how to make that happen.

QUINN DIDN'T SEE Seth when he finally came back to the ranch after dark. She heard him arrive, then silence fell on the house. After calling her mother and father, needing to just hear their voices, she picked out her clothes to wear to see the Wishing Moon. At eight thirty, she was dressed in a white sweater over a thermal, along with jeans and heavy socks. She had just pulled her hair back in a ponytail when a knock sounded on her bedroom door.

She opened it, and her heart lurched when she faced Seth in a black flannel shirt and jeans. He looked her up and down. "I see you're ready to go to the hay barn."

"Yes, I am," she said.

"Okay, let's go," he said and headed down the hallway.

She hurried after him. "Where are you going?"

"To the hay barn with you," he said without stopping.

Oh, she hadn't expected that. After the kiss, she felt awkward just walking beside him. Seeing the moon with him seemed far too much. "You don't have to."

"No, I don't, but I want to. It's time to get there if you want to see the moon the moment it clears the earth. Maggie said that's wishing time."

When they were in the foyer, Seth sat down on the bench and reached for his boots. Quinn didn't know to how stop him without being rude. And she wouldn't be rude. So she sat on the edge of the bench, keeping a distance from him to put on her boots, then reached for her pink coat and slipped into it.

Seth stood and put on his leather jacket, then his black Stetson. "Come on, time for you to make a wish," he said.

She went to the door with him, and out into the cold night. The moon was more than half-way visible above trees to the east, its light already making itself felt over the land, reflecting off the lingering snow. They headed side by side down to the hay barn in what for Quinn, was an uneasy silence.

As they approached the building, Seth went ahead and opened the front doors enough for them to step through. There was darkness inside, and Seth led the way in and to their left through the heavy shadows. As her eyes adjusted, Quinn could make out an upright wooden ladder attached to the front log wall just past the sliding doors.

"Do you want to go first?" Seth asked.

Quinn stepped up to the ladder, grabbed the heavy two-by-fours on the sides and went up slowly toward a hole cut in the floor of the loft. At the top, she stepped up and out onto plank flooring. The hint of moonlight seeped in around the frame of the closed delivery doors. Seth came up and went past her to slide the doors open. Moonlight streamed into the darkness.

Seth turned to her. "It's your choice. Sit on the edge of the doorframe and dangle your legs or sit back a bit if you feel more comfortable."

"Where do you like to sit?"

He smiled ruefully at her. "On the hip of the roof, but that's not an option. Is it?"

"No, it's not," she said and moved closer to the doors. She dropped down to sit on the floor, then scooted toward the opening. As soon as she eased her legs over the side, she knew she was in the right place. The moon to the east was huge and had just another quarter to go before it totally cleared anything on the earth that could block its light. "Wow, this is great," she whispered.

Seth sat down by her and she inched far-

ther away from him. He didn't act as if he
noticed, but he had a blanket in his hand.
"I had Murphy leave this here in case it got
colder." He shook it out and laid it across her
legs, then pulled part of it back over his own
legs. He took off his hat and laid by his side
on the edge of the blanket.

It was cold, but there was no wind, and the
night had a sense of peace about it that Quinn
tried to gather to her, but she couldn't push
away the memory of the kiss. She kept her
eyes on the moon, startled slightly when Seth
shifted. She felt his body heat on her right
side. Staring up, she said softly, "I had no idea
it would be this beautiful." She could sense
Seth watching her as she tipped her head back
farther to look higher into the eastern sky.

"It is pretty amazing," he said.

"More amazing than the view from the roof
hip?" She never took her eyes off the moon.

"Okay, I have to admit that sitting up there
comes close. But as an adult, I have to also
admit it's dangerous. I'm thankful Sarge and
Maggie never knew we did that."

She glanced at him, his features defined by
the moonlight and shadows. "I have a feeling
Sarge knew exactly what you all were up to."

Seth denied that. "No, he never called us on it, neither did Maggie."

"I'd bet he never let on to Maggie, but he understood that you boys had to find your own way. So, Maggie didn't worry, and you all survived."

So MANY THINGS Sarge had taught them came by his actions with them and for them, not against them. But what Seth couldn't understand was how Quinn seemed to know Sarge so well. "You're probably right." Seth was quiet for a moment, hesitating, then he told Quinn about where he'd been all day. "I went to see Tripp at Max Donovan's parents' ranch today. I know I should have asked you to go, but I wasn't certain you'd want to."

"Why would you think that I wouldn't have wanted to?"

He exhaled in a rush, his breath lifting into the air between them. "I made a mistake and stepped over the line with you. I know that upset you, and it was wrong."

She looked taken aback as if she'd never expected him to say that. "Seth, I…" She bit her lip, then said the truth. "I would've loved to go and see Tripp, but you're the one who's taking him in, and you need the time with him before he comes here." She shrugged. "I just hope you both had fun."

Seth held her gaze, then said, "We did. He rode a donkey." He reached in his pocket for his cell, then opened it and tapped the screen a couple of times before turning it toward her. "Tripp on Morris the donkey. He was a bit scared, but brave." He watched Quinn study the picture, then she looked away, and he sensed she was upset. "Could you send that to me?" she asked, her voice slightly rough.

"Sure," Seth said as he drew it back, regretting it so much that he hadn't taken her with him. He texted her the photo. "Next time you should come with me, and especially when I go to pick him up," he said. "Tripp really wants to see you again. He's worried you won't remember him."

Quinn looked down and was quiet for a moment. "Can I ask you something I've been thinking about?"

He didn't know what to expect, but he nodded. "Go ahead."

"Is it true that they can remove a child from a foster home for any reason if they think it's justified?"

"They do have all the power."

"I mean, if he's happy here, I can't imagine how it would affect him if they decided he had to leave."

The image of Tripp when he'd thought he'd have to go back to another foster home came to Seth. The feeling of the boy shaking while Seth hugged him hurt to remember. There'd been no one in his own life to hug him when he'd been afraid like that, when he'd felt as if he was never going to be wanted by anyone, when he'd been totally lost. He knew that was the moment he'd connected with Tripp. He wouldn't let the boy face the fear of another foster home, then another, no matter what he had to do.

"Once he's here, I'll find a way to make sure that doesn't happen to him." Seth had always known that fostering was supposed to be a stopgap measure for a kid, not a permanent situation. That was the nature of the service. He looked at Quinn. "I won't let Tripp be up for grabs in the system."

"I'm so glad he has you fighting for him now," she said just above a whisper and her breath faintly misted into the night.

"Answer me something?"

She nodded and he asked, "Would you foster him if you had the ability to?"

She didn't hesitate. "From the moment I found him crying, I just wanted to make him smile. I always wanted children, but my life just... Well, it didn't work out. Now I'm not in any position to help anyone very much. But if I realistically could, I would do whatever it took to care for him and protect him."

Quinn took his breath away in so many ways. "I thought so," he murmured.

"Can you imagine if he were out here now, watching the moon? He'd remember this forever and have a good memory to help blot out some of the bad ones.

He could see her smiling almost wistfully. "I like that idea. One good memory gets rid of one bad memory."

He knew that happened. His scattered early memories were blurry, but he knew they were bad. His memories of life with Sarge and Maggie at this place were vibrant good memories that overshadowed the ones he hated. He stared out at the night. This memory would be a good one, no matter what happened in the future.

They sat silently together, Quinn never

looking down, while Seth faced his growing feelings for her, things he'd never felt for any woman who'd come into his life before. Nothing even close. And Tripp was in that mix. Right then, he wasn't looking back at what had been but attempted to look into the future, at what might be. As the moon rose above the earth, he felt Quinn shiver against his arm. "Cold?" he asked.

"A bit."

He did what he'd wanted to do since he'd first sat down by him and she'd moved slightly to keep from making contact. He slipped his arm around her shoulders and tugged the blanket up higher for both of them. "Body heat," he said, thankful that she didn't jerk away from him. But she didn't come any closer, either.

The night was an odd combination of light and dark as Seth felt each breath Quinn took. "The moon's clear of the earth. It's wishing time." He watched her close her eyes, then become very still. When she finally opened her eyes, she sighed.

"Done?"

"Yes," she murmured as she turned to look

at him. "How about you? Did you make a wish?"

He'd wanted to as silly as that sounded, but he hadn't. "I've learned to not count on wishes," he said matter-of-factly.

"I made my wish, so now you have to, too."

Her scent, something that was elusive but gentle and warm, lingered around him and he found himself faltering, then agreeing. "Okay," he said, and closed his eyes. His world became all about Quinn, about possibilities, about her breathing, the slight unsteadiness as she exhaled.

He found himself actually making a wish and hoping that for once it would come true. "Done," he said as he looked at Quinn again.

"So, what did you wish for?" she asked with an endearing hint of a smile.

"You know the rules. You can't tell a wish without losing it."

"You're right, but promise me that if…no, when it comes true, you'll tell me."

"I will *if* it ever comes true," he murmured.

Quinn looked back at the moon as it rose higher. His breath tightened as he skimmed the sweep of her throat, the tilt of her chin and when he realized he was clenching his free hand, he forced himself to ease it open on the blanket over his thigh.

"If you wished you'll do well with Tripp," she said in a soft voice, "that's a given. He'll do better than you could even imagine being with you."

He knew right then that he'd almost missed the whole point of what he wanted for Tripp. He wanted the very best for the boy. He should have known that when he'd felt Tripp shaking in his arms. He didn't want any half solution or anything temporary. He didn't want a constant fight to keep Tripp with him, a fight that would probably never end. He knew what he had to do probably when Tripp hugged him at the ranch, though he was just admitting it to himself now. He wanted to make Tripp his son. Then they could never take him away.

"I'm going to talk to Burr when we discuss the blind curve and get a recommendation for an adoption attorney who would know their way around adopting a child out of the foster care system."

Her eyes widened, and she gasped, "Oh, my gosh, do you mean that? It's been only days that you've known Tripp."

"You were right, that sometimes a person comes into your life and from the start you know they belong there forever." That's the way it had happened with Quinn, too. He couldn't imagine not having both Tripp and Quinn in his life.

"That's wonderful," Quinn said, then the next thing he knew, she was hugging him.

He wrapped her in his arms and held on to her. "Thank you," he whispered.

She eased back to look up at him. "For what?"

The question hung between them, until he finally answered her honestly. "For helping me remember what it was like being in Tripp's position where nothing was certain from day to day. The only thing a child in the system wants is forever. Thank you for reminding me."

Seth couldn't even define what that meant to him. He knew he should just let go of her, but he couldn't make himself do that. And she didn't move away. Her eyes held his and her lips parted softly. He felt her warm breath on his face when she exhaled, and he slowly moved closer to her. He hesitated until she lifted her hand and touched his face gently.

He couldn't turn back. He didn't want to turn back, and he went even closer until his lips were on hers. Then he could taste her, feel her heat, and she slowly slipped her hand around to the back of his neck.

The kiss became real, with Quinn responding this time, and it grew between them, shattering whatever promises he'd made to himself about going slowly, taking time, giving her time. He drew her closer, then framed her face with his hands. Gently he kissed the healing scar, and she trembled at the contact. "I'm so sorry you got hurt," he murmured.

When he spoke again, his voice wasn't quite steady. "I don't know how you and I found each other at all, but the possibility of a master plan doesn't seem so crazy anymore. I was so worried you couldn't…that you wouldn't want…" He tried to find the words. "I thought you were still working through your life, you know, and that has to be hard for you. It's a lot to figure out."

He was surprised when a tear escaped and ran down her cheek. He brushed at it with his thumb and whispered, "No, no tears."

She slowly moved back until he lowered his hands. "I can't. I can't do this. I thought… I'm sorry." She was breathing quickly now and turned from him, freeing herself from the blanket to scramble to her feet. "I'm so sorry," he heard her whisper again as she looked everywhere but at him.

The moonlight had lost its intensity as the moon rose higher, and he couldn't quite see her eyes now. All he knew for certain was the woman standing there was ready to run. Before he could think of what to say or do, Quinn turned and headed for the ladder. He got up, grabbed his hat and went after her.

He went down quickly, and by the time his feet hit the concrete floor, she was out the open doors and gone. He hurried out, saw her heading down the driveway, and jogged to catch up with her. "Slow down," he said. But she ignored him, so he reached out and caught her by her arm. That stopped her immediately, but she didn't turn to him, or try to free herself.

He was lost. He couldn't say he was sorry for what had happened. He wasn't. "I think we need to talk."

Quinn shook her head. "No, we don't. I don't know why I did that. I'm confused and forgot," she said in a slightly breathless voice.

His wish had been that he could kiss her one more time and have her want it as much as he did. It had barely come true, before it had been shattered. Reality still trumped fantasy and wishes. It always did. The reality was Quinn was in love, but not with him. Michael was still her love. He always would be. "Let's get back," he said, drawing his hand away. The really stupid thing about the whole mess was he envied a man he could never meet, a man he could never compete with, but whom Quinn loved. He knew right then that she always would.

AS THEY NEARED the house, Quinn finally found the ability to breathe evenly, despite the tightness in her chest. She never looked at Seth as he walked beside her. Her hugging him, she understood. She was thrilled that he was going to give Tripp a forever home. But the kiss… She didn't understand why she'd gone closer, why she'd needed to kiss him, to breathe him in. Then he'd said, "I don't know how you and I found each other at all. *I thought you were still working through your life.*"

They'd found each other because of her

manipulations and her lies. Michael was part of this, too. She cared about keeping her promise. It was what had kept her going for so long. But now she found herself caring for Seth and she had to let that go. She'd let him believe what he did about her reasons for being here, and he was honorable enough that he'd never kiss her again.

But what really hurt was the simple fact that she thought about fighting, explaining things to Seth, trying to get him to understand. Maybe he would, but most likely, he'd never trust her again for anything. She couldn't fight and win. The loser would be Tripp. He'd be torn by her disappearing, and Seth had enough on him with Sarge and Tripp and getting away from the company.

She'd do the right thing and leave after Tripp got here. She'd explain to him that she'd remember him forever, and that maybe they could write to each other. Although, she doubted Seth would want her to have any contact. Her throat tightened. An uncomplicated break was the best way for her to walk away. Maybe she was a coward, but everything just hurt too much. She'd leave knowing Tripp was safe and happy.

She took a deep breath as the moon rose higher and became smaller in the night sky, and it seemed to take forever before they got up on the porch and the entry door to the house. "I am really sorry to give you the wrong idea," Quinn said in a tight voice she barely recognized as her own before Seth could open the door.

"Please don't," Seth said, tension edging his voice. "You made your wish, and that's what's important."

She started to shake for some reason and tried to stop it by hugging herself. He studied her for a long awkward moment before he opened the door to go inside. She didn't want to say anything else or try to explain the unexplainable to him. She'd never tell him how his kiss had shattered every truth she had believed about her life after Michael was gone.

"I'll go to bed, if that's okay?"

His eyes flicked over her. "Sure. Good night."

Quinn knew she couldn't sleep, but she needed time alone. She turned and headed to her room. The moment she had the door closed behind her, she leaned back against it, then slid slowly down until she was sitting on the floor.

Pulling her legs to her chest, she wrapped her arms around them, then pressed her forehead against her knees, taking almost the same position Tripp had been in when he'd felt all was lost in the hay barn. She'd never felt more lost.

CHAPTER FOURTEEN

As SETH HAD watched Quinn close the door to her room, it felt very permanent to him. A stopping of whatever he'd let himself feel. He headed for his office, passing her room without glancing at it, knowing that he had to get away and not just for a ride or a drive. He needed to not be around Quinn so he could think and breathe. Now was the right time for him to go back to Seattle one last time and take care of unfinished business before Tripp came home. He checked the clock. It was just ten thirty.

Once in his office, he called a jet-leasing company out of Cody, and they assured him they could get him wheels up by 2:00 a.m. to fly him to Seattle. Then he sent a message to Max. Any news on Tripp?

As late as it was, Max's answer came right back.

McFarland says to give him three more days. No promises, but he's trying.

Keep me in the loop. Heading to Seattle. Will call Tripp at ten in the morning. Back late tomorrow.

His next message went to Owen: Coming back. I want this settled now. He put in his flight information, then added, Put Conrad on standby for flight back tomorrow afternoon by three.

When Julia told him Sarge was doing well, and with Quinn there and Cal coming out to the ranch in the morning, everything with Sarge was covered. One burden had been lifted, but a bigger one still hovered over him throughout the day as Seth sat alone in his private living quarters in the corporate tower in Seattle. He silently watched the city far below. Life was everywhere, but his life wasn't in Seattle anymore. He'd talked to Tripp earlier and just making contact with the boy had underscored that he was doing the right thing for Tripp and Sarge and himself.

Now he was waiting for Owen to show up. He'd been gone over two hours, and Seth was anxious to get answers. Lately, he often seemed to be waiting for a corporate decision about his life. This was the last time he'd have to do that. This one was the big one. He turned toward the door to the executive office when it finally opened. Owen came into the room. "Hey, it's done."

But Owen wasn't smiling. Seth's heart sank. He didn't want a fight with the board over his new demands. "Did it turn nasty?"

Owen sank down on one of the chairs by the window and motioned Seth to the other one. "They were not happy you weren't in there, and dealing with me didn't seem to be what they wanted."

"Too bad. I'm sure you did everything right."

Shadows under Owen's eyes gave away the fact that he probably hadn't had a good sleep for a while. Despite that, his buttoned-down white shirt, red tie and navy pants did look nearly perfect.

Owen exhaled. "They finally left. Do you want to hear the board's terms and final answer?" he asked without giving away anything in his tone, good or bad.

Only if it's good news. "Okay."

"I'm glad you told me I could let them know about Tripp. I think that kind of mollified them and explained how you could even think about stepping back from the company. Personally, I think you adopting the kid is pretty great."

"I still love the company and want it to grow, and I want to leave it in good hands. But my life's in Wyoming now."

Owen nodded. "I understand. I just never thought you'd ever leave."

"Me, neither," Seth admitted with a slight smile of relief. "But the day has come, and from now on, decisions and operations are up to you and your team. The board did agree that you're now CEO, right?"

He smiled a bit at that. "I will be after the full board meets and does what they need to do. It's a formality."

Seth could feel more of the pressure leaving him. "Good. That makes this a whole lot easier for me."

"You'll get the notice along with the paperwork in a week or so. They agreed with the existing stock shares. Actually, they agreed to all your terms, even your continuing use of the corporate jet. It's all on the way to Legal, but before you leave, they need a few signatures."

More relief swept through Seth. His demands had been extreme, but those were the terms he had to have. He was just thankful it had gone smoothly. "Thanks for handling all of that," he said. "I don't know what I would've done without you all these years."

"Thanks for trusting me." Owen, who hardly ever showed emotion, almost blushed as he stood. "All my best to Sarge, and good luck with the little boy." He held out his hand.

Seth stood but ignored his hand and gave the man a hug. As he stepped back, he said, "You're a good man, Owen Karr. Come on up to the ranch and we'll go riding."

"If you know a good riding instructor," he said with a laugh, then patted Seth on the shoulder. "Just go. Don't worry. I've got this."

Later that day, Seth was in the corporate jet heading to Wyoming, officially out of the business side of his company. He took out his cell and called Julia. She answered after two rings. "I'm on my way. How's Sarge doing?"

"He had a good night. So far, so good."

He heard laughter in the background. "Sounds like a party going on."

"Boone just brought Quinn back."

"What?"

"They went out for a drive earlier this morning."

There was more laughter, which he knew came from Quinn. "Oh, well, the weather cleared so tell Sarge I'm on my way."

He put away his cell and settled back in the seat. Now he was heading home and not looking back.

They landed through heavy gray clouds at the Cody airport, and the old red truck was right where he'd left it. Driving that truck was part of coming home, too. By the time Seth was pulling between the boulders and through the gates at the ranch, he felt a sense of freedom that had grown steadily since the takeoff in Seattle. He didn't know what was going to happen in his life, but he'd be with Sarge and Tripp through it all. He'd back off from Quinn, and maybe the old saying *time heals all wounds* might prove true. He really hoped so. He didn't want to lose her.

As he topped the rise in the driveway just before five o'clock, he was surprised to see the gray VW parked by the porch steps. He didn't know how to feel now that Quinn had her car and her wound was healed. Before the truck had come to a stop beside the small car, the front door opened and Julia stepped outside. Seth was out of the truck when she called, "So glad you're back."

He got his luggage, then headed up the steps to her. "How's it going here?"

"Pretty good," she said.

Once inside, he put his bag on the stone floor, stripped off his jacket and tossed it onto the bench. He looked around, hoping to see Quinn, but she wasn't in sight. "So, how did things go in Seattle?" she asked.

He'd left the black hat at the ranch and when he saw it laying on the bench, he knew he'd missed it. "I'm not going back for the foreseeable future, if at all," he said. "Max called and said that Tripp might get cleared sooner than we thought, but no promises. Where's Quinn?"

Julia shrugged. "She headed down to the stables. I haven't seen her since."

"Is Sarge awake?"

"He's snoring."

Seth grabbed his bags and headed upstairs to change. "We'll talk in a bit," he called back over his shoulder.

QUINN LED ANGEL back into the stables through the rear doors and out of a growing wind that brought a biting cold with it. A new hire of Dwight's, a young, lanky guy named Gill, met her just inside the doors.

"Ma'am, I'll take her for you and clean her up, if you want?"

She hesitated, then handed him the reins. "Thank you. I appreciate it."

He gave her a slight tip of his hat and said, "My pleasure, Ma'am," before he headed off with Angel. Quinn kept going through the building to the open front doors and barely took a step outside before she ran into someone in her path. Hands gripped her shoulders to keep her on her feet, then she was looking up into hazel eyes.

"Hey, slow down," Seth said.

For a moment, she felt a surge of pure happiness that he was there, but then reality hit her. She made herself take a step back. He pushed his hands deep in his jacket pockets. "I didn't know you were back."

"I just got here, and I was looking for you." She blinked. "Why?"

"Julia said you were riding."

"I was, but it was getting really cold and it's going to be dark soon, so I came back."

"Good thing you did. There's that feeling in the air that a storm's coming," he said with a glance up at dark clouds starting to gather overhead. "I saw your car's back."

The small talk felt awkward to her. "Henry really did a good job on her. He even figured out how to put in a working heater and brand-new three-point seat belts."

"I told you Henry's terrific. Julia said you were out with Boone, so you got your guided tour?"

She'd been so thankful that Boone had asked to go see the area. "Sort of. We went for a ride, then Henry called when I got back here. So Boone dropped me at Henry's after we had lunch at one of the dude ranches. It was nice." Pushing her hands into her jacket pockets, she went around Seth to start toward the house. He was right beside her. "I hope things went well for you in Seattle."

"Let's just say things are settled," he said. "How was your ride with Boone?"

"Good. It's really beautiful around here," she said. "But I had a lot of time to think on the ride."

"About anything important?" he asked her.

"Yes. I think—no, I know—I've been confused and terrified at losing Michael all over again if I…keep going. I've never figured out how to just be alive without feeling guilty."

Seth was silent, and when she looked at him, he was staring straight ahead. "I can see how you could feel that way," he said.

"I need to figure things out. I have to make sense of my life. Michael told me to have a good life, but I'm not there yet."

Seth was silent as they approached the house and went inside. Quinn slipped off her jacket, then sank down onto the bench to take off her boots. When the second one dropped onto the stone floor, she looked up. Seth came closer, then crouched down in front of her. He took off his hat and laid it beside her. A foot of space separated them, but her awareness of the man was overwhelming.

"Good news," he said. "McFarland might be able to shorten Tripp's stay at the headquarters by another day, and Burr found an attorney in Casper who's done a lot of work in adoptions with the foster care system." His face lit up. "As soon as Tripp's here and settled, I'm going to contact that attorney and see what I have to do to get the process going."

She felt the sting of tears behind her eyes. "That's wonderful." She blinked rapidly. "I hope it all works out."

"Whatever I have to do, I'll make it happen," he said with real determination, then added, "Secondly, I want to apologize to you."

She swallowed hard, knowing what he was going to say, but hating having to listen to it. She lowered her head and stared down at her boots laying between them on the stone floor. When he touched a forefinger to her knee, she didn't move. "I didn't mean to upset you," he said. "I'm not good at this sort of thing, and I know life's complicated for you."

Complicated? He had no idea how complicated and wrong her life was right then.

She heard him take a breath. "I know the time's not right, that you're still sorting through things in your life." His voice dropped lower. "I saw Maggie and Sarge together, and I'm pretty sure their relationship was the same kind you and your husband had. It's never over, it can't be. I want you to know that I understand that as much as I can. Take all the time you need, and do whatever you have to do, but don't forget I'm here."

The silence between them was heavy, and Quinn felt the tears silently slip down her cheeks. Seth thought he knew. He was offering to wait, to let her figure it all out, but he didn't know that he'd shown her that she'd been standing still since Michael died, focusing on keeping her promise to him. By doing that, she'd actually isolated herself behind Michael's Shield, using it as her protection from ever being hurt again.

She could hear each breath Seth took as he waited for her to say something. She kept her eyes down. "You don't owe me an apology," she whispered. She remembered her response to his kiss and felt heat rising in her cheeks. "I don't even know what I need. Can we leave it at that for now?"

"However you want to play this out," Seth murmured, and she knew right then that if things were different, she could feel so much for him. She made herself look up, ignoring the tears still falling. "Thank you," she managed as she got to her feet.

She couldn't bear what he was offering her

when she didn't deserve it. "Remember. Don't forget I'm here," he whispered.

She headed quickly toward the east wing. Once she was inside her room, she made it to the bed and sank down on the edge of the mattress. She looked at the picture by the lamp and whispered, "I love you, Michael. I always will."

Her phone vibrated in her pocket and she took it out. Her mother had texted her, but before she opened it, she looked at the last picture she'd received, the photo of Seth and Tripp. Their smiles made her heart skip, then the reality of what could have been crashed down around her. She fell back onto the bed, curled up on the blue comforter and silently cried.

When there were no tears left, she slowly got up and made herself go into the bathroom to splash cold water on her face. She'd promised herself she'd leave quietly. She would. She just didn't want Tripp to think she'd forgotten about him.

Then she had a remarkable thought. If she went to Denver and the final company wanted Michael's work, if that was settled and her promise had been kept, maybe sometime in the future she could come back to the ranch. Maybe she could see Seth and Tripp and Sarge and know they were okay. Maybe, just maybe, she could make sense out of her feelings for Seth and the boy who would be his son.

That helped her breathe a bit easier, knowing she might not be walking away forever. When she finally headed out, Julia was stepping into the entry. She saw Quinn and motioned behind her. "Seth's in there if you're looking for him. It's almost seven and no one seems hungry, so don't worry about dinner. I'm going in to play some poker with Sarge and hope I don't lose what matchsticks I have left."

"Good luck," Quinn said, then she went down into the great room and saw Seth. The side lamp was on, and he was on the couch, his feet propped up on the ottoman with his head resting against the sofa back. She thought he might be asleep, then he turned toward her.

"Hey," he said softly. "Come and sit down."

She stopped by the end of the couch. "Do you want something to eat?"

"No, thanks. I want you to sit down."

She gave in and crossed to sit on the leather cushions between him and the arm of the sofa. What excuse should she use to justify leaving as soon as Tripp was here? Personal business, a family emergency, a job offer in Pasadena? "So, you aren't going back to Seattle?" she asked.

"No, I'm not going to drag Tripp back and forth with me or leave him and Sarge here while I'm gone."

"You'll be stepping back from it all?"

"I did this morning and the board agreed. My executive VP is going to take over as CEO. My time will be my own, and it'll be spent here. I want time to be here with Tripp, to try to do for him what Sarge has done for me."

That smile was there, slow and easy, touching his hazel eyes, and her heart lurched. "Wow, just like that, you changed your life?"

"It wasn't that simple." He shrugged. "I wanted things to change. So I took care of everything I could on this last trip. I settled my future with the company, and I'm straightening out my private life."

"What do you mean?" His life seemed pretty well laid out so far.

He hesitated, then shrugged again. "I've had a past that's pretty messed up. I mean as an adult, as in relationships. It took me a while to realize that no matter how I went into a relationship, I always carried heavy baggage with me."

"Baggage? You were married before or…?"

He shook his head and said, "Oh, no, nothing got that far. I'm talking about my money, what I have. Anyone can read a financial magazine and find out Seth Reagan's worth, and I've just happened to come into contact with more than one woman who saw dollar signs when they saw me. The last one, a couple of years ago, I swear, I thought I knew her, but… I found out I was wrong again." He actually looked embarrassed as he shook his head ruefully. "All Allie wanted was what she thought I could give her—money. She had me believing her for too long before I figured out what was fact and what was fiction with her. I was just a means to an end."

He sat forward, hands clasped, elbows on his knees, then he glanced sideways at Quinn. "It was all my fault." She almost flinched at the look of disgust and self-anger in his eyes, and her heart was hammering. He exhaled heavily. "Live and learn, and I'm here now, taking control of the life I want."

Quinn never wanted him to look at her the way he looked when he talked about Allie. She'd played him. Not like that woman had, but she knew he'd probably see it that way. She'd been right to plan on leaving without saying a thing to him about Michael's Shield. She'd go quietly, very quietly and directly to Denver.

They both jumped when Julia yelled, "Seth! Help!"

Seth was on his feet immediately and took off running toward the west wing. Quinn hurried after him and stopped at the door to Sarge's room. Julia was crouching beside Sarge, who was on the floor slouched back against his bed, his legs splayed out in front of him. He looked fine, if a bit rumpled in his jeans and T-shirt, but Julia was flushed.

"He decided to lay down, and I thought I had him positioned, then I turned to get his pillows. The next thing I knew, he was sliding down between the rail and the footboard and onto the floor."

Sarge smiled up at Seth standing over him. "Hi, there, son. Glad you're back."

"Sarge, why did you do this?" Seth asked, as he hunkered down by him.

The man smiled slyly. "Because I wanted to."

"Can I help?" Quinn asked from the doorway.

Julia waved her closer. "Yes, please," she said as she got to her feet.

The three of them worked together and finally got Sarge safely back on the bed, lying on top of the blankets, with the rails readjusted. The older man looked pleased, as if he'd had an adventure, while Julia and Seth just looked stressed out. Julia touched Sarge's shoulder. "Promise me you'll never do that again."

He looked up at her questioningly. "Do what?"

"Never mind. Are you comfortable?"

"I would be if you'd quit fussing over me."

"Okay. I'll quit," Julia said and stood back.

"Good," Sarge muttered and closed his eyes.

Quinn was watching Seth watch Sarge. Then he said, "Sarge, is it okay if I go and take care of something?"

There was no response at first, then Sarge

slowly opened his eyes and looked up at Seth with a certain sadness in his faded blue eyes. "Are you leaving again?"

"No, I'm staying here for a very long time. You'll get sick of me being around."

"Never, son, never," he murmured.

Seth moved closer and bent down over Sarge. Quinn heard him say, "I hope you know how grateful I am for all you've done for me."

Sarge smiled up at Seth. "You're my boy. I'd do anything for you," he said, then closed his eyes again and sighed. "Maggie and me love you and your brothers."

Seth stayed there without moving, then Quinn saw him close his eyes for a second before he straightened up and turned. Without looking at Julia or her, he strode out of the room. Julia caught Quinn's eyes and motioned toward the door with her head. "I'll be fine. You go."

Quinn went out into the hallway and hurried back to the great room. Seth was on the couch, leaning forward, his face buried in his hands. She didn't hesitate going to sit beside him. Even though Sarge was fine, Seth wasn't. She almost couldn't bear it. Fighting

the urge to rub his back or take his hand, anything to lessen what he was going through,
she asked, "Are you okay?"

He didn't move for a long moment, then
finally sank back into the soft leather of the
sofa. Raking his fingers through his hair, he
said, "Is it going to be like this forever? I
won't see it coming, then it hits me like a
sledgehammer. What if Tripp had been here?"

"It won't be easy, but it'll be worth it,
knowing you're doing the best you can for
Sarge, because he'll know that, too, whether
you think he does or not. I think Tripp would
have laughed seeing the way Sarge thought
it was all an adventure. And Sarge wasn't at
all upset that he ended up on the floor. He
didn't get hurt," she added. "Besides, I think
Tripp should see how much Sarge loves you.
He needs to see that relationship."

"I know, I know," he said.

"Can I get you a drink of something?" she
asked.

She wasn't certain he'd heard her until he
finally said, "No, thanks, but could you sit
here with me for a while?"

She wouldn't leave him alone, not until she
had to. "If you want me to." She was angry

with herself, wishing she'd never lied, never manipulated, no matter how well intentioned.

Seth reached for her hand, lacing his fingers with hers, then he closed his eyes. "I want you to," he said.

CHAPTER FIFTEEN

QUINN STAYED WITH Seth as he fell asleep, still holding her hand, and she didn't move. She knew she wouldn't let go of him until he broke the connection himself. She'd stay right there and wait, no matter how long he needed her to be there. She never wanted to leave him, and she'd have to live with that. When his hand tightened slightly on hers, then he shifted back, turning toward her as his eyes slowly opened. A sleepy smile shadowed his lips. "You're still here," he whispered.

"You needed to sleep," she said.

"What time is it?"

"It's around nine o'clock."

He shifted to sit up and leaned forward, letting go of her to rub both hands roughly over his face. "Sorry, I just meant to rest for a few minutes. I didn't get much sleep last night."

"That's okay," she said, thankful he looked better and less stressed.

"I need to check on Sarge."

She stopped him before he could get up. "Julia said to tell you Sarge is fine. He doesn't even remember the fall."

He exhaled and sank back again. "Good." His hazel eyes studied her, then he said, "Whatever brought you to this place, I'm glad it did."

His words left her breathless. He'd never know what brought her to this place and into his life, not now. But maybe someday when she'd kept her promise to Michael, she could come back and the truth wouldn't be as destructive as it would be right now. She wanted to believe that was a possibility.

Before she could say anything, Seth spoke again. "I have a confession to make."

She blinked. "What?"

"I've been thinking about how things happen, and I'm convinced life isn't a bunch of random acts that happen to connect in some crazy way. There has to be a plan at work."

She felt sick to her stomach.

A chime sounded, Seth hesitated, then reached to take his cell out of his jeans pocket. He checked it, then looked at Quinn. "I'm sorry. I have to make a quick call to the office. There's so many loose ends to tie up." He hesitated, then cupped her chin lightly. "Just remember where we left off okay?"

Quinn wouldn't forget anything about Seth.

A few minutes later, Seth was on a video call with Owen. The man's expression didn't bode well for the reason he'd made contact. "What's going on?" Seth asked, anxious to get back to Quinn.

Owen was sitting behind the glass desk in the executive offices, the city at night behind him as he spoke. "Apparently, you requested a background check from Platt-Overton on a new hire?"

Seth was blank for a minute, then remembered asking the firm about Quinn. "Oh, yes. I hired a housekeeper for the ranch and wanted a quick idea about her background. How did you know?"

"I was checking your shared files to archive them, and I found the report."

Owen was nothing if not thorough. "Okay."

"So, is she living there, or does she come and go?"

He had no idea why Owen cared one way or the other. "It's a live-in arrangement for now."

"So, her name's Quintin Lake?"

"Yes. She goes by Quinn." He wanted to cut this short. "Why are you so interested that you're calling me at this time of night about a housekeeper?"

"I'm interested because I know her."

That got his attention. "What?"

"She was here on the same day you left for the ranch the last time. Do you remember me telling you about some guy I was meeting about a program that would redefine cybersecurity?"

He remembered. "Yes, I do."

"He turned out to be a she, and if your Quinn Lake is a blond lady, that's who I met."

Seth just stared at the monitor.

"I got rid of her, but she left an outline of a project called Michael's Shield that she wanted to offer for a buy-in."

Seth felt as if someone had punched him in the stomach. He remembered that second night when Quinn questioned him about coauthoring projects and going outside his company for ideas. Her husband had done coding, was a genius at it, supposedly. He never thought anything of it. But now he knew Quinn had been on the road that day intending to find him. He didn't understand how she could've even known where he was, but she'd been coming after him to sell him something called Michael's Shield. It always boiled down to the money. At least when it came to him it did.

"I'm sending the background-check dossier to you now." Owen looked down, then back up. "It should be there."

Seth checked his inbox and nodded. "I have it."

"What do you—" Owen started.

Seth cut off the call with a "Talk to you later." He quickly pulled up the attached file and clicked it to open it. It came right up. Requested: B.G. scan for Quintin Grayson Churchill Lake.

When he'd finished the first three pages of the seven-page report, he stopped reading. He knew that Quinn had been married to Michael Lake. Truth. She'd taught third grade at Dale Brady Elementary School in Pasadena. Truth. She'd married Michael Scott Lake right after graduation, then taught for six months before she'd walked away to be caregiver for her husband as he fought leukemia. Truth.

After her husband had passed, there was little available about Quinn, except her taking a string of substitute teaching assignments until six months ago, presumably when she'd left California and started traveling. She'd finally made her way to Seattle. When he'd been in the building, targeting him to try to sell her husband's work.

She hadn't simply lied about the job—a lie he'd talked himself into forgiving her for by minimizing it to get past it. His stomach clenched and for a moment he thought he was going to be physically ill, then it settled into a knot in his gut. He'd wanted to believe her, and had actually come to trust her. He wasn't sure of much of anything right then, except she was out there waiting for him.

WHEN SETH DIDN'T come back right away, Quinn crossed the great room to the sliding doors to look out at the night. Only slivers of moonlight broke through dark clouds roiling across the heavens. Seth had said a storm might be coming, and it looked as if he'd been right.

"Quinn?"

She turned as Seth stepped down onto

the flagstone floor, carrying some rolled up paper in one hand. He looked serious as he came over to her, stopping with just a few feet of space separating them. "Bad news?" she asked.

He stared at her without blinking. "Yeah. Bad." His voice sounded oddly flat.

She quickly asked, "It's not Tripp, is it?"

"No. I was on a call from the company."

"Oh, then I'll leave you to do what you need to do."

He shook his head. "No. We need to talk."

His eyes were narrowed on her, as if he couldn't quite look fully at her. Uneasiness prickled at the nape of her neck. "Talk about what?"

He was silent for a long tense moment, then he stunned her. "You said your husband was great at coding. You neglected to tell me about Michael's Shield."

For a horrifying moment, Quinn felt as if she'd faint. Quickly, she brushed past him and went over to the couch. There was no running away from what she had to do, so she sat down and tried to catch her breath, hoping she could put the right words together.

Then Seth was standing over her. "I… I can explain about Michael's Shield."

"I'm sure you can," he said in a voice devoid of anger or any other emotion at the moment.

There would be no explaining anything. She knew that by the way Seth was looking at her, hard, without any softness in his eyes. "How did you—"

He sat down on the ottoman and held the papers in his hand out to her. "This is the background check on you. We do it with all new hires," he responded as he tossed the papers onto the couch beside her.

Clasping her hands to make sure they wouldn't start shaking, she said, "Seth, you need to understand—"

"What I understand is you came to corporate headquarters to sell me something your husband had developed. Owen Karr sent you on your way, but somehow you found out about me coming here, and you followed me." He exhaled in a rush as his expression grew taut. "I have no idea how you found out about the ranch, but I know that some grand plan didn't have a thing to do with anything between us."

"When you assumed I was looking for that job, I thought, just maybe, if we got to know each other—"

"Got to know each other?" he asked. "So that's what you call what you were doing, getting to know me? Here I was thinking you..." He pushed that away. "It was all a lie."

Quinn felt as if she was fading away, losing her grip on everything around her. There was nothing to hold on to, nothing to stop what was happening. The kind, gentle man was gone, and the child who had never trusted anyone was there full force, angry and hurt, and it was worse than she'd ever thought it would be. "No, it wasn't. I know I should've told you right away, but I...didn't know how to get anyone to listen to me. And I thought if I got to know you, I'd understand you better and..."

Words caught in her throat as she realized he was looking at her with pain now. No explanation would take that away. He'd never trust her again. She had to leave. She'd done enough damage here. She certainly didn't want Tripp around this mess she'd made. She'd leave humiliated and broken.

"I'm sorry, so sorry," she managed to say.

Seth leaned toward her, only inches separating them, and she didn't know why she wasn't crying. "When were you going to tell me, Quinn? Or were you going to play me until I got so tangled up in you that you could've asked me for anything, and I'd have given it to you?"

Those words hurt in a way she'd never experienced before. He wasn't shouting. He wasn't threatening. He was just saying something that he totally believed she was capable of doing to him. "Stop," she whispered unsteadily. "Please."

He spoke as if she'd said nothing. "Keep looking for someone to buy your husband's work, because I have no interest in anything you're offering."

Something broke in her. "If I'd told you right at the start why I was on the road that day, you wouldn't have listened to me. You would've done the right thing by my car and with the medical stuff, then walked away. All I wanted was one person to listen to me, and look at Michael's work, and no one would. None. I tried so hard. But I did this all wrong. I know I did."

He grimaced. "I guess we'll never know

what would've happened if you'd been truthful from the start."

He stood and reached into his back pocket. He pulled out his wallet, took money out, then pushed it toward her. "This should cover what I owe you for services rendered." She stared at several hundred-dollar bills. "If it's not enough, bill me."

She stood abruptly, ignoring the money, almost colliding with Seth, who stepped back quickly to avoid the contact. "I'll get out of your way in the morning. Just...tell Tripp that I—"

"Don't worry. I won't tell him about your lies," she heard him say.

Her heart was breaking. "Please, for his sake, tell Tripp I'll never forget him."

She saw him swallow hard. "I'll protect him."

Quinn made it to her room, closed the door, then sank down on the side of the bed in the room filled with night shadows. She heard footsteps in the hallway, followed by Seth's office door opening then closing hard. She was shaking when she took Michael's box out from under the pillow and held on to it for dear life. It was her only lifeline. Then she remembered the picture by the lamp base. Laying the box back by the stack of pillows, she reached for the photo.

"I'm so sorry. I ruined everything," she whispered to Michael as she pressed the picture to her chest. "I tried my best."

She knew right then that she couldn't stay there until the morning. She had to get out of there before the whole world around her shattered.

She turned on the bedroom light, found all of her things and pushed them into her backpack, then put the picture in her jacket pocket to keep it closer before she shut the light off again. She sat there, waiting until she finally couldn't hear anyone stirring, then she slung her backpack and leather bag over her shoulder and braced herself. Opening the door, she paused, then headed for the entry.

Quickly and quietly, she put on her jacket and boots, then turned, ready to leave when Seth appeared in the entrance to the east wing. He stopped, and stared silently at her, obviously not aware she'd be there.

"I'm leaving. I want you to know I never meant to hurt you or Tripp." She barely recognized her own voice. "I'm sorry about every-thing."

"So am I," he finally said and walked down into the great room.

She headed to the front door, pulled it back, then stepped outside. She stopped in her tracks after she pulled the barrier closed behind her. It had started to snow, large flakes falling silently in the bitter cold of the night.

She never looked back as she hurried down the steps and over to the Beetle. She tossed her things across to the passenger seat, then she got in and closed the door. She started the engine and turned on the heater. Swiping at the snow clinging to her hair, she made a U-turn and headed off through the snowy night toward the gates.

When she drove out onto the county road, the wind came without warning, picking up quickly and pushing at the small car. Losing Michael had been the most painful thing she'd ever lived through. She couldn't go any-where in this world and find him again. But even though she'd know where Seth would probably be in the years to come, she'd never know how he was, if he was happy or how things turned out with Tripp. There was no way she could ever come back here. That was truly another horrible loss.

SETH TURNED TO the entry as the door shut behind Quinn and then he headed back toward his office. His muscles seemed jerky, and he felt disassociated from reality some way. He didn't get very far. He nearly fell into the wall in the hallway, just trying to breathe as the images of Quinn beat down on him. He'd been angry with Allie and walking away had been a relief. But the pain he felt right then at the loss of Quinn stunned him. He couldn't move. He had no idea how long he stood there before he realized Julia was there talking to him.

"Seth?"

He slowly managed to turn toward her voice. "Quinn left," he said in an unsteady voice.

"She's going to town at this time of night in the snow?"

"I don't know where she's going, but she won't be back."

Julia came closer, obviously surprised. "What are you talking about? She never said anything about leaving. The last I talked to her, she was beyond excited about Tripp coming here." He flinched inside at her words. "I don't understand what happened."

He hesitated, then went into the entry and dropped down on the cowhide bench. Julia followed him to stand over him as he gave her a quick version and ended with, "It was all a lie, everything she's said and done since she got here."

"She lied about what?"

"Farley sending her out here on a job interview. She never mentioned she was coming here to sell me a program her husband developed. She could've told me the truth then but she didn't even try."

Julia frowned at what he'd said, then he saw understanding mixed with compassion on her face. "Let's see, she'd been in an accident, took a hit on the head. Her car was almost destroyed, and you think she should've given you a presentation of her dead husband's work right then?"

"Julia, I—"

"She lost her husband, Seth. A man she truly loved from what I can tell." She spoke with real emotion. "She probably lost part of herself, too, then she tried to make something happen from what he left behind."

Seth opened his eyes and stared at his hands clenched together. "What should I have done? Told her everything was just fine, that I'd invest tons of money in what could be a worthless package?"

He looked up as Julia put in a call on her cell. She shook her head as she pushed her phone into her jeans pocket. "Her phone's going right to voice mail. She shouldn't be out there in that poor excuse for a car in this weather. You shouldn't have let her leave like that."

"She didn't ask my permission to go," he muttered.

"For the record, I think you've just made the worst mistake of your life. Now, I need coffee," she said as she turned and stepped down into the great room. Almost immediately, she was back without coffee and holding the dossier and the money he'd tried to give Quinn. "What's all this?"

"Her background check and her pay for the work she did here. She didn't want it."

She motioned him to move over, then dropped down by him and put the money on the seat between them before she started to go through the report. Finally, she rolled the seven-page document up and set it down by the money. "Did you read it?"

He wouldn't admit he'd stopped because he was afraid of throwing up. "I stopped in the middle."

"You stopped too soon. You missed the part where they found out about Michael's leukemia and she married him despite his illness. She was there with him through all of it." She shook her head. "She was never looking for what she could get out of you. She was trying to leave a legacy for Michael, the way you're trying to leave a legacy for Sarge and Maggie. Fortunately, you have the money to do it yourself. She needed help."

She stood and left the papers with the money beside him and headed toward the east wing. "I'll be right back."

A legacy. His shoulders hunched as he felt the impact of what he'd done, driving Quinn away and out into the storm. She wasn't Allie. She was kind and cared about people. She'd never asked for anything.

Julia came back. "Here," she said. "It was half hidden under the pile of pillows on her bed."

He looked at a small leather box she was holding out to him. "What is it?"

"I don't know."

He took it from her and opened the worn clasp to look inside. There were four thumb drives and a sheet of folded paper. He took the paper out, opened it and Michael's Shield was printed in bold black lettering at the top of a list of ten of the best tech companies in the country. The first eight were crossed out. His company was the ninth. He glanced at the thumb drives that were labeled simply one through four.

He refolded the paper and put it back in the box with the thumb drives, then closed the box. Quinn had left behind what looked like the very reason she'd tracked him down. Seth stared at the box and hated what he'd done. A legacy. He knew that need to do something for a person he loved, to help people remember them and what they'd done with their lives.

He felt physically sick again. That scared boy who couldn't trust anyone was still there in him, and he knew how destructive he'd been with Quinn. "I'll go and try to find her," he said, but Julia stopped him. "No, that old truck isn't good in this weather. Call the sheriff and see if he can find her."

"I'll go. You call Max and ask him to be on the lookout for her VW. He's seen it before, so he'll recognize it on sight."

He got ready, then spoke to Julia before he left. "I'll call if I see anything, and you call if you hear anything."

"Be careful," she said.

Seth went out and off in the old red truck. Julia was right that the truck wasn't snow friendly, but if he took it easy, he knew he'd at least get to the highway.

It was just past four o'clock in the morning when Seth had pulled off the highway, barely able to see in front of him, through the still falling snow. He'd planned with Max to head toward Cody while one of Max's deputies headed south, so they covered the full length of the highway in both directions. When he'd met up with the deputy, they agreed he'd head back toward Eclipse and the officer would go back north and check the frontage roads.

He'd made it to the off ramp for Henry's business, turned onto the side road and stopped. A call chimed. Max. He answered it quickly. "Did you find her?"

"No," the sheriff said. "But her car's been found at Bobbie Denton's gas station, just off the street in his side parking."

She'd made it town. "Where's she?"

"Don't know. The car's dead, no sign of an accident, and it's been here long enough for the snow to almost bury it."

Seth swallowed hard. "I'm on my way."

By the time he made it onto Clayton Drive and saw a gathering of vehicles by the gas station in the rays of the breaking dawn, his nerves were shot. He'd never known a fear like the one that had all but consumed him during the night while he searched for Quinn. He pulled up by the sheriff's SUV as people dispersed to cars nearby or headed off walking down the street. The snow had finally stopped. Max spoke before Seth could ask anything. "No sign of her, and whatever tracks would have been there, were buried long ago." Seth looked around at the town, then closed his eyes. "At least we know she got this far," Max added.

He exhaled. "You said earlier Brenner's at the clinic. Boone's still in Cody?"

"Brenner said he hasn't heard from him."

Seth tried to think rationally, but all his

mind seemed to zone in on was Quinn out there somewhere alone. "What's in her car?" he asked.

"Nothing much. Just the key she left under the driver's mat. Come on," Max said as he went to his SUV. "Let's get in where it's warm and we can talk."

As they settled in the idling SUV, Max asked, "We've checked with everyone you told me Quinn would trust to help her. Nothing."

She sure hadn't tried to contact him. "You never talked to Boone, right?"

"No, I didn't think it would help with him gone and all. She'd have to try reaching someone close by."

Seth took out his own phone and called Boone. It rang four times before a groggy voice came over the line. "Dr. Williams."

"It's Seth."

There was prolonged silence on the other end, then he heard Boone clear his throat. "What do you need?"

"Quinn's missing. They found her car abandoned by Bobbie's gas station and there's no trace of her."

"Oh" was all he said.

"Did she call you last night?"

"Sorry. No, she didn't. Why did she go out in the storm alone?"

"She wanted to leave. I've been up all night trying to find her."

Boone was silent for a long moment, then said unexpectedly, "You don't deserve her."

"Who do you think—" He stopped himself. "Boone, how did you know she went out on her own, that she left like that? You said you never talked to her."

"No, I said she never called me last night."

Seth closed his eyes as the truth hit him. "Where is she?"

"I'm technically her doctor, so I can't discuss my patient with you. I have to go and get over to the clinic." The line went dead.

CHAPTER SIXTEEN

SETH LOOKED AT the phone in his hand. "He hung up."

"Well, did she call him or not?" Max asked.

Seth sank back in the seat. "He said she didn't."

Max frowned at him. "That's it?"

"No, he told me she's his patient and he can't talk about her with me."

Max frowned. "What's that supposed to mean?"

"He knows what happened. He knew about her driving off in the storm."

"Well, where's he?"

He realized he knew exactly where Boone was now. "He's at home on Twin Pines getting ready to go to the clinic."

Max put the SUV in gear and made a U-turn to head south on Clayton Drive. "It sounds as if I need to talk to him."

When they got to Twin Pines Road, the

large SUV took the deep snow easily all the way to the end of the long cul-de-sac. They parked as close as they could to the two-story farmhouse where Boone had been raised and trudged up to the snow-covered porch. Seth got to the door just as it opened. The doctor was there in a T-shirt and pajama bottoms.

"Get in here and be quiet," Boone said in a low voice. He stepped back to let them into the large living room that occupied most of the front of the old house.

"Where is she, Boone?" Seth asked.

"Keep your voice down," the doctor said.

"She's here?"

Max stepped in. "If you can't talk to Seth about this, come on into the kitchen and talk to me. I've got people out scouring the town for her in the cold and snow. If you know something, you'd better share it with me."

Boone held up his hands in a gesture of surrender. "Okay, okay. Call your people off. You don't need them."

Seth couldn't remember being as angry with Boone as he was right then. He took a step toward him. "I thought you were my friend."

"I'm a better friend than you can imagine."

The doctor shook his head. "I came back from Cody last night when I heard there was going to be snow, and I didn't want to be stranded up there. I got to town around midnight and saw Quinn walking near Farley's. Her car had stalled and wouldn't start up again."

Seth stared at Boone, his anger being almost smothered by relief. "She's here, isn't she?"

Boone looked pained. "Just know that you don't have anything to worry about. But she asked me not to tell you where she is." He glanced between them. "You two should leave."

Seth felt broken as Julia's words echoed in his head. *You've made the biggest mistake of your life.*

"Okay," he finally managed to say. "Just please, do me a favor."

"I've done all I can." Boone moved closer to Seth and put his hand on his shoulder. "I'm sorry. I stepped over the line saying as much as I have."

He'd leave for now and give her space so she could rest. As long as she was with Boone, she was safe. He looked at Max. "Drive me back to the truck."

Max nodded. "Sure."

Quinn had been the best thing to ever come into his life and he knew he wasn't going to just walk away and lose her forever. "Tell her…" He had to stop to clear his throat. "Boone, take care of her, and please, just…" He stopped. "I'll go for now."

Then both Boone and Max looked past him toward the back of the large room. He turned and Quinn was there, barely three feet away from him in her red sleep shirt. Her hair was tousled around her face. With everything he had in him, he fought the raw need to hold her and stayed where he was. He closed his eyes a moment, then exhaled as he looked at her again. "You're okay?"

She bit her lip, then nodded. "Yes."

QUINN FOUGHT AN overwhelming sadness. Seth had done the right thing, the way he always did. He was some sort of hero, coming out to find her in a horrible storm. Honorable to the end, even if he hated what she'd done. Her heart ached at the mess she'd left. She reluctantly looked away from Seth to the sheriff. "I'm so sorry. I truly didn't mean to scare anyone."

"I'm glad Boone found you," Max said. "All's well that ends well."

Quinn could feel Seth staring at her and her heart pounded in her chest. "I should've left a note in the car," she said.

Max took out a two-way radio and spoke into it. "Subject found safe on Two Pines at Doc Williams's house." He smiled at Quinn but spoke into the radio again. "Pack it in. Everything's good. Thank you, all."

Quinn knew she'd done more damage by running, and there was no way she could take any of it back. But what she could do was not cause any more problems for Seth or this town. "Could you thank everyone for me for being so kind," she said to Max.

"Absolutely."

A chime from a cell phone sounded, and Quinn finally looked at Seth as he pulled his cell out of his jacket pocket. He glanced at the screen, opened it, then unexpectedly held it out to Quinn. "It's for you."

She didn't understand until she saw Julia's name as the caller. "Julia?"

"Quinn, is that you? Oh, my gosh, I've been so worried since Seth left to find you.

Then he didn't call, and I thought he must be in trouble."

"Seth's okay," she said. "My car broke down in town."

"As long as the two of you are safe, all's right with the world. You can fill me on what happened when you get back here. Tell Seth to be careful driving home."

She stammered, "I… I will," but she knew it would be Seth taking that trip alone. When she'd left Seth hours ago, it had been unbearable, and now she had to do it all over again. She didn't want to. She wasn't sure she could survive leaving him again. All she wanted was to be with him, to have the lies gone, and him smiling at her again.

Max spoke to her. "Your car's fine where it is for now, Quinn. I can give Henry a call to check it out if you want?"

"Thank you, yes," she whispered.

"Okay." The sheriff hesitated as he looked at Seth. "Do you still want me to drop you back at your truck?"

Quinn finally made herself look at Seth as she held his phone out to him. "Don't…don't forget this."

He took it from her. "Thanks," he said as he pushed the phone back in his pocket.

"Julia, she…she said for you to be careful driving back home." Quinn tensed. She just couldn't do it. She couldn't say goodbye, then watch him walk out the door.

Max turned to Seth. "Let's get going."

Before she could do anything, Seth surprised her. "No, I need to speak with Quinn alone."

She felt her whole body stiffen. Boone asked, "Is that okay with you, Quinn?" If she said no, she'd lose everything. If she said it was okay, she at least had a chance. She nodded. "Yes."

"Take the room you were in," Boone said to her. "I'll start some coffee."

Max headed for the door. "Call me when you need a ride," he said over his shoulder to Seth, then left.

Quinn turned away from Seth and crossed to the still-open bedroom door. She needed to sit down. Her legs were shaking, and the last thing she wanted was to fall over. Seth was right there with her, then swung the door shut behind them while she crossed to the old-fashioned sleigh bed and dropped down on it. She didn't know what to say or do, so she silently sat there, trying to breathe as she looked up at Seth.

Seth undid his jacket and came closer, standing over her. She hated that. As if he'd read her mind, he crouched down in front of her. He was so close she could see fine lines at his eyes that she hadn't noticed before. "You don't have to say anything, just hear me out, okay?"

She looked down, her hands clasped so tightly together that they almost ached. "Okay," she whispered.

Then he shocked her. "You forgot Michael's box."

"What... How?" She reached for her backpack on the floor and pulled it up onto the bed to unzip the side pocket. Then she remembered, holding it, looking at it, then worrying about the picture. She'd been so distracted by everything at that point she'd left the most important thing in her life behind. Then it hit. It was important, but something else had taken over, something more important now—the life she was trying to make for herself.

"Julia found it in your room."

She closed her eyes, willing herself not to

cry, and pressed a hand to her mouth. Her whole life, which had been so focused since Michael passed, was almost unrecognizable to her now.

"Just nod if I'm correct. Michael's Shield is what your husband thought could revolutionize cybersecurity. From what I'd guess, it's a firewall that's designed to respond to the individual attempts on the system. It's probably got a ninety percent hack-blocking rate."

When he stopped talking, she slowly lowered her hand and whispered, "Ninety-eight percent."

"I owe you an apology for how I acted, for not giving you a chance to explain why you did what you did." He exhaled. "I just assumed…"

She opened her eyes and swallowed to fight the tightness in her throat. "I thought I could keep quiet and feel you out to see how I could get you to consider the program. But I did it all wrong."

"I know you want it back." He stood. "I'll trade you one thing for it."

Slowly, she got to her feet. The box was safe with Seth, but she had to know what he could still want from her that had any value to him. "What do you want?"

"Actually, it's what I don't want. I don't want you to drop out of my life. I don't care how you do it, by phone or text or email. Just keep in touch." His voice grew low and rough. "I know Tripp would like to hear from you, too, so he knows you haven't forgotten him."

His words made no sense to her. "Why would you want anything to do with me after what I did?"

He slowly shook his head. "Because you did what you did for the husband you love. You stuck with him through everything, then he was gone and you still loved him enough to try to get his work seen. I'd say you did the right thing. I was the one who messed it up."

She didn't know when she'd started crying, but as tears silently ran down her cheeks, she tried to ignore them. "I made Michael a promise. It was the only thing I could still do for him." She sucked in air on a shudder and forced herself to finish. "Michael's work was so important to him, and I just wanted to make sure it didn't go away because he had."

When Seth moved to reach out and gently gathered her into his arms, she almost collapsed against his chest. She was sobbing, now, unable to stop as he whispered, "I know, I know," over and over again.

When she had no tears left, she moved back unsteadily and dropped weakly down on the bed. She swiped at her face. "I tried, you know. I really did."

Seth crouched in front of her again and gently brushed her damp cheek with his fingertips. "I want you to know that you brought something into my life that I've never felt before, something so overwhelming I don't even understand it."

He drew his hand back and closed his eyes for a fleeting moment before he looked at her again. "When I thought of you out there alone in the storm, I knew I didn't want to be in a world without you in it." He shook his head. "I had crazy ideas of you and me and Tripp, but I understand you can't feel for me what I feel for you. That's okay, it really is, as long you're all right. As long as I know you're safe and happy. Whatever you have to do or where you have to go, I'll figure out how to live with that."

Quinn had to swallow before she could get out the words that filled her. "Seth, I can never love anyone the way I loved Michael. I can't."

His face grew taut, and he slowly stood. "I understand. You don't have to explain. Just, please, for my sake, keep in touch."

He *didn't* understand. She stood inches from him. "I need to explain," she whispered, then reached for his hands, taking them in hers and holding tightly to him. "Someone told me that real love never dies, it never goes away. I'm glad it doesn't. Loving Michael is part of who I am, what I am, but when Michael told me to keep living, I didn't know how that could work."

She hesitated. "Now I know how it works, because of you showing me that it's possible to love again. No matter how it happened, you came into my life and I slowly realized that I'm living again, because of you being there. Please, if you can, ask me to come back with you to the ranch, to be there with you, to welcome Tripp home and to let me love you both forever."

Seth was very still, then he smiled that crooked smile, and he whispered, "I need you to come home with me. I need you to be with me. I need you to welcome Tripp with me and

I need you to let me love you forever." He shrugged unsteadily. "It's simple. I love you."

She barely got out the words "I love you, too," before he had her in his arms, kissing her, and Quinn felt her new world settle into something she'd never dared to dream of. As Seth drew back, she knew she was grinning. Being happy was hard for her to contain, and she didn't try to.

Seth's smile was more hesitant. "What are you thinking?"

"That I can't wait to go home with you and see what's going to happen with us and Tripp." Her smile faltered, then she whispered, "I forgot to tell you something very important that I just realized."

"What's that?"

"Beyond loving you so very much, you're my hero."

He looked at her quizzically. "What?"

"You love me even after what I did. You rescued Tripp to give him a life he probably never thought he'd have. Then you came after me in a raging snowstorm." She framed his face with her unsteady hands. "You're my hero, and I love you so much."

EPILOGUE

A MONTH LATER, it was almost Thanksgiving and Quinn was sitting with Sarge in the great room, watching the snow falling outside. He'd been out of his room a lot more since Tripp had come home. They were listening to the sound of laughter that swept down from upstairs. Seth and Tripp were having a man-to-man talk, as the little boy had solemnly explained to her an hour ago.

Sarge was smiling. "I sure love hearing a child's laughter in this house again."

Quinn loved it, too. "It's pretty wonderful."

Tripp and Sarge had quickly formed a deep bond, and both were better for it. Sarge was more engaged in life, and Tripp seemed to feel more secure as each day passed. "You know, Maggie wished every year on the moon that the boys would find the loves of their lives." He chuckled. "Two out of three ain't bad, and I'm a grandpa, too."

She tugged at the cuffs of her white sweater and drew her legs up to sit cross-legged on the large couch. "Strange how life just turns out perfectly sometimes, isn't it?"

"It sure is." Then Sarge frowned up at the ceiling. "You know, it got real silent up there suddenly. That's usually not a good thing."

Then Seth and Tripp walked into the great room side by side. They came over to the couch, and Quinn smiled at the two of them dressed alike in white T-shirts and jeans. Tripp was wearing his hat that looked like Seth's. He hardly ever took off the hat or the Western boots that had been there when he'd finally come to the ranch to stay. "I was just getting ready to come up there and see what was going on," Quinn said.

Tripp stood close to Seth, but his blue eyes were on her. He'd had good days and bad days, but he was still settling in, getting more secure in feeling that he was actually wanted here. He wasn't as good at the small schoolhouse in Eclipse, with some separation anxiety, so Quinn was volunteering to help with his class and be close by for him. After the New Year, she'd be on staff teaching first and second grade. She knew Tripp needed her to be there.

Seth had his hand on Tripp's shoulder, and when Quinn looked at him, she saw a touch of mischief in his hazel eyes. "Tripp and I came down to ask you two very important things," Seth said to Quinn.

"What's going on?" she asked after she'd glanced at Sarge, who was smiling as if he knew something was coming, too.

"Hold on," Seth said. "First, Tripp has something important to ask you."

The little boy stood straighter. "Real important." Then he looked up at Seth. "Is it okay?"

"It's okay. I promise."

Tripp came closer to Quinn, took off his hat, set it crown-down on the couch the way Sarge had taught him, then looked at Quinn. He asked in a small uncertain voice, "Can I call you Mom?"

"Oh, Tripp," she whispered and pulled him to her. "Yes, yes, please, yes. I would love that." Seth had been *Dad* for two days and she loved that Tripp had finally asked her.

"Tripp, we have one more thing to ask… your mom."

When the little boy grabbed his hat to put back on and scooted back to Seth's side, his smile was huge. "Real important, too."

Seth cleared his throat. "We talked this over and Tripp and I both agree that this is the right time to do this, before everyone gets here for Thanksgiving."

"Come on, boy, get to it," Sarge urged good-naturedly.

Quinn stood slowly. "Now you two have my full attention."

Tripp looked up at Seth. "Go on, Dad."

Seth took a breath, reached into the breast pocket of his T-shirt, then nodded to Tripp. They both got down on one knee in front of Quinn.

"What are you two...?"

Seth was the one who spoke. "We both love you so much." His voice broke slightly on the last few words as he lifted his hand toward her and opened it palm up. The flash of diamonds sparkled in the overhead light. The ring was beautiful—three small hearts overlapping in a circle, framed by diamonds and set in gold.

"Oh, my gosh," she breathed.

"I know you said you didn't care about an

engagement ring, that as long as the three of us were together and we got married in April, that's all you needed. But you do need this."

Their commitment to each other and to Tripp was all she'd ever need. "It's beautiful."

Seth smiled at her. "The jeweler finally finished, and we want to make this official. Quinn, will you marry me…and Tripp?"

She could barely take it all in. "Yes," she breathed.

Seth and Tripp stood in unison. Seth took her left hand in his to slip the ring on her finger. Her gold band had been put away for safekeeping with her memories of Michael in the small leather box. Then she was in Seth's arms. Everything about him melded in that moment for her—the small scared boy he must've been, the angry teenager and now the man. He was offering her a life with joy that could only come from being with him and making a family with Tripp, who was jumping up and down with excitement while Sarge clapped.

"Tell her, tell her!" Tripp said.

She looked at Seth. "There's more?"

"It just gets better," Seth said. "I received a call from Burr. He said we've been cleared to petition the court to adopt Tripp. No guarantee on when it will happen, but it *is* going to happen."

She bent down to hug Tripp to her. He was tiny, but his hold on her was so tight that she almost couldn't breathe. "This is perfect," she said, kissing the top of his head, then standing, she held his small hand as she looked at Seth. "It's really going to happen?"

"Yes, it is. Oh, there's one more thing."

"What's that?" An unsteadiness grew in her when Seth gently touched the nearly invisible scar at her hairline. The strength of the love she felt for him stunned her.

Seth glanced down at Tripp. "Is it okay if I take your mom to the office for a minute?"

Tripp looked from one to the other, then nodded a bit reluctantly. "I guess."

Sarge spoke up. "How about me and you play some cards? Go Fish is always good."

As Tripp ran off to get the deck, Sarge looked at Seth. "I sure wish Maggie was here to see you so happy." His smile seemed bittersweet. "She would have loved being a grandma, too." Then Tripp was running back into the room with the cards. While the two settled to play, Seth took Quinn by her hand

and led her back to his office. Once they were inside with the door closed, Seth pulled her into his arms and just held her.

"What did you want to tell me?" she whispered against his chest.

"That Owen called to tell me that the concept of Michael's Shield is brilliant. He's excited about working with it, and it looks as if it's going to hit the market early next year."

She closed her eyes tightly. She'd kept her promise, and doing that had brought her Seth and Tripp. She moved back enough to look up at Seth. "You really are my hero. You make my wishes come true."

"How did I do that?"

"Well, that night in the hay loft I wished that I could be in your life with Tripp, and now I am. How about your wish?"

"Oh, that's a simple one. I just wanted to kiss you and have you kiss me back."

"Well, that certainly came true," she said and slipped her arms around his neck to keep him close. "I'm willing to make sure that happens every day, if you'd like."

His chuckle was rough. "A wish a day."

"Sarge told me that Maggie's wishes on the

Wishing Moon were all the same. She wanted each of you to find the love of your life."

"So, wishes do come true," he said with that smile she loved.

As he kissed her again, the door swung open unexpectedly. Seth drew back and Quinn turned to see Tripp standing in the doorway frowning at the two of them. "You're kissin' again."

Seth motioned to the boy. "Come here."

He picked Tripp up. "What's going on?" he asked his son.

Tripp looked at Quinn, then back at Seth. "You keep kissing…Mom," he said, not looking very pleased about it. "And she kisses you…a lot."

Seth smiled at the boy, then at Quinn. "When you love someone with all your heart, a kiss is a good way to show it."

Quinn nodded as she took Tripp's hand in hers. "It doesn't mean you can't love more than one person. I mean, right now, I love Seth so much, and I sure do love you a lot."

Tripp was silent, his look intense before he took off his hat, then unexpectedly leaned toward Quinn and kissed her on her cheek, then he turned to do the same thing to Seth.

When he moved back, he grinned at the two of them, put his hat back on and wiggled to get down. As Seth let him go, the boy said, "Gotta go and see Grandpa!" and with that, he was out the door.

Quinn laughed. "I have a feeling that Sarge is about to get kissed."

Seth pulled Quinn back into his arms. "I love you so much," he said. Then he told her something she already knew. "I think that every road in my life led me right here, to this moment with you. It took me a while to get here, but I'm so thankful I finally made it."

"Welcome home," she whispered and kissed him again.

* * * * *

Get 4 FREE REWARDS!

We'll send you 2 FREE Books plus 2 FREE Mystery Gifts.

Love Inspired Suspense books showcase how courage and optimism unite in stories of faith and love in the face of danger.

FREE Value Over $20

YES! Please send me 2 FREE Love Inspired Suspense novels and my 2 FREE mystery gifts (gifts are worth about $10 retail). After receiving them, if I don't wish to receive any more books, I can return the shipping statement marked "cancel." If I don't cancel, I will receive 6 brand-new novels every month and be billed just $5.24 each for the regular-print edition or $5.99 each for the larger-print edition in the U.S., or $5.74 each for the regular-print edition or $6.24 each for the larger-print edition in Canada. That's a savings of at least 13% off the cover price. It's quite a bargain! Shipping and handling is just 50¢ per book in the U.S. and $1.25 per book in Canada.* I understand that accepting the 2 free books and gifts places me under no obligation to buy anything. I can always return a shipment and cancel at any time. The free books and gifts are mine to keep no matter what I decide.

Choose one: ☐ **Love Inspired Suspense Regular-Print** (153/353 IDN GNWN) ☐ **Love Inspired Suspense Larger-Print** (107/307 IDN GNWN)

Name (please print)

Address _____ Apt. #

City _____ State/Province _____ Zip/Postal Code

Email: Please check this box ☐ if you would like to receive newsletters and promotional emails from Harlequin Enterprises ULC and its affiliates. You can unsubscribe anytime.

Mail to the Harlequin Reader Service:
IN U.S.A.: P.O. Box 1341, Buffalo, NY 14240-8531
IN CANADA: P.O. Box 603, Fort Erie, Ontario L2A 5X3

Want to try 2 free books from another series! Call 1-800-873-8635 or visit www.ReaderService.com.

---

*Terms and prices subject to change without notice. Prices do not include sales taxes, which will be charged (if applicable) based on your state or country of residence. Canadian residents will be charged applicable taxes. Offer not valid in Quebec. This offer is limited to one order per household. Books received may not be as shown. Not valid for current subscribers to Love Inspired Suspense books. All orders subject to approval. Credit or debit balances in a customer's account(s) may be offset by any other outstanding balance owed by or to the customer. Please allow 4 to 6 weeks for delivery. Offer available while quantities last.

Your Privacy—Your information is being collected by Harlequin Enterprises ULC, operating as Harlequin Reader Service. For a complete summary of the information we collect, how we use this information and to whom it is disclosed, please visit our privacy notice located at corporate.harlequin.com/privacy-notice. From time to time we may also exchange your personal information with reputable third parties. If you wish to opt out of this sharing of your personal information, please visit readerservice.com/consumerschoice or call 1-800-873-8635. **Notice to California Residents**—Under California law, you have specific rights to control and access your data. For more information on these rights and how to exercise them, visit corporate.harlequin.com/california-privacy.

LIS21R

HARLEQUIN SELECTS COLLECTION

19 FREE BOOKS IN ALL!

From Robyn Carr to RaeAnne Thayne to Linda Lael Miller and Sherryl Woods we promise (actually, GUARANTEE!) each author in the Harlequin Selects collection has seen their name on the *New York Times* or *USA TODAY* bestseller lists!

YES! Please send me the **Harlequin Selects Collection**. This collection begins with 3 FREE books and 2 FREE gifts in the first shipment. Along with my 3 free books, I'll also get 4 more books from the Harlequin Selects Collection, which I may either return and owe nothing or keep for the low price of $24.14 U.S./$28.82 CAN. each plus $2.99 U.S./$7.49 CAN. for shipping and handling per shipment*.If I decide to continue, I will get 6 or 7 more books (about once a month for 7 months) but will only need to pay for 4. That means 2 or 3 books in every shipment will be FREE! If I decide to keep the entire collection, I'll have paid for only 32 books because 19 were FREE! I understand that accepting the 3 free books and gifts places me under no obligation to buy anything. I can always return a shipment and cancel at any time. My free books and gifts are mine to keep no matter what I decide.

☐ 262 HCN 5576   ☐ 462 HCN 5576

Name (please print)

Address   Apt. #

City   State/Province   Zip/Postal Code

Mail to the Harlequin Reader Service:
IN U.S.A.: P.O. Box 1341, Buffalo, NY 14240-8531
IN CANADA: P.O. Box 603, Fort Erie, Ontario L2A 5X3

Get 4 FREE REWARDS!

We'll send you 2 FREE Books <u>plus</u> 2 FREE Mystery Gifts.

FREE
Value Over
$20

Both the **Romance** and **Suspense** collections feature compelling novels written by many of today's bestselling authors.

YES! Please send me 2 FREE novels from the Essential Romance or Essential Suspense Collection and my 2 FREE gifts (gifts are worth about $10 retail). After receiving them, if I don't wish to receive any more books, I can return the shipping statement marked "cancel." If I don't cancel, I will receive 4 brand-new novels every month and be billed just $7.24 each in the U.S. or $7.49 each in Canada. That's a savings of up to 28% off the cover price. It's quite a bargain! Shipping and handling is just 50¢ per book in the U.S. and $1.25 per book in Canada.* I understand that accepting the 2 free books and gifts places me under no obligation to buy anything. I can always return a shipment and cancel at any time. The free books and gifts are mine to keep no matter what I decide.

Choose one: ☐ **Essential Romance** ☐ **Essential Suspense**
　　　　　　　　(194/394 MDN GQ6M)　　　(191/391 MDN GQ6M)

Name (please print)

Address　　　　　　　　　　　　　　　　　　　　　　　　Apt. #

City　　　　　　　　　State/Province　　　　　　　Zip/Postal Code

Email: Please check this box ☐ if you would like to receive newsletters and promotional emails from Harlequin Enterprises ULC and its affiliates. You can unsubscribe anytime.

Mail to the **Harlequin Reader Service:**
IN U.S.A.: P.O. Box 1341, Buffalo, NY 14240-8531
IN CANADA: P.O. Box 603, Fort Erie, Ontario L2A 5X3

Want to try 2 free books from another series! Call 1-800-873-8635 or visit www.ReaderService.com.

COMING NEXT MONTH FROM

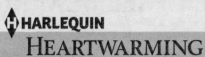

HARLEQUIN
HEARTWARMING

Available April 13, 2021

#371 HOW TO MARRY A COWBOY
Wishing Well Springs • by Cathy McDavid
When Kenna Hewitt comes home for her mother's wedding, her longtime friend Channing Pearce is determined to finally tell her how he feels. Can he win this bridesmaid's heart, or will she run away like always?

#372 THE BAD BOY'S REDEMPTION
Matchmaker at Work • by Syndi Powell
Josh Riley is running for mayor...against the woman he loves! He wants to win the election and make up for his checkered past, but winning Shelby Cuthbert's heart would be even better.

#373 THREE MAKES A FAMILY
City by the Bay Stories • by Cari Lynn Webb
For lawyer Molly McKinney, love is only a distraction. So when she needs help from former rival Drew Harrington with her custody battle, she's all business. Unfortunately, staying professional is tough when you're falling in love!

#374 A MARRIAGE OF INCONVENIENCE
Stop the Wedding! • by Amy Vastine
Evan Anderson agreed to marry his best friend strictly as a favor, but he didn't expect to fall in love with their wedding planner, Sophia Reed. Is the attraction strong enough to break a promise to a friend?

HWCNM0321